EXCALIBUR

A NIKKI DOYLE NOVEL

Paula J Longhurst

Ingram Spark in Association with Open Flame Press

Copyright © 2023 by **Paula J Longhurst**

All rights reserved. No part of this publication may be reproduced, distributed or transmitted in any form or by any means, without prior written permission.

Open Flame Press

Publisher's Note: This is a work of fiction. Names, characters, places, and incidents are a product of the author's imagination. Locales and public names are sometimes used for atmospheric purposes. Any resemblance to actual people, living or dead, or to businesses, companies, events, institutions, or locales is completely coincidental.

Book Layout © 2017 BookDesignTemplates.com

Book Title/ Author Name. -- 1st ed.
ISBN 978-0-9989258-6-8

For Chris

Also by Paula Longhurst

A Case of Espionage
A Shot of Treason
A Robust Revenge

Rollover
Thunderball
Ms. Scarlett In the Library with the Lead Piping

Writers get to create new worlds every day and the characters that inhabit them can take on lives of their own. Both Nikki and Mary have had their share of scrapes, mistakes, loves and losses but it was always up to me to know when to press the pause button on their stories and that time has come.

Thanks go to the usual team of beta readers including Jack, Linda and Anne, your comments, coffee and company always help to smooth the writing process. Bob, thanks for your editorial skills and your patience. Judy, thanks for taking me on as a newbie author seven books ago, here's one more signed copy for your shelf.

Last, but not least the customers and staff (old and new) of The King's English Bookstore in SLC, Utah.

CHAPTER 1

"Is she in?" I ask the faceless buzzer mounted on the wall outside Dr. Bradley's consulting rooms. "It's Nikki Doyle, I don't have an appointment."

Behind me the black cab that just brought me from Heathrow airport rattles away into the Friday afternoon traffic; the cabbie probably still shaking his head at the idea of being given a tip for agreeing *not* to talk to his passenger before I got into his cab.

Caroline Bradley's secretary, young Ms. Maltravers (old Maltravers retired recently) emphasizes her heavy sigh over the intercom.

"There are no more appointments available today, Mizz Doyle, and the office is closed."

Click.

Great, now I have to get all of these spinning thoughts out of my head and onto my iPhone so that I can discuss them next Tuesday at our regular appointment. I walk away from Caroline's door heading vaguely in the direction of the Albert and

Victoria tearooms. I can feel spots of rain on the shoulders of my suit. And of course I'm not carrying an umbrella.

"Nikki!"

I turn to see Caroline calling from her own doorstep with Ms. Maltravers, who has a face like a wet weekend in Grimsby, locking the door behind them.

Since I started my new job, I've upped the therapy sessions with Caroline to once a week; they have become my safety valve. A session with Caroline is like running a mental inventory with the emphasis on the stresses generated by all things work, and the decisions I make in the privacy of her office are the ones I'm likely to stick to.

Caroline comes towards me while her receptionist sweeps off in the other direction, possibly to audition for a part in the 'Scottish' play (bad luck, they say, to call it 'Macbeth'). Caroline always has a leather-bound journal on her desk where she makes notes of our sessions. She pulls the journal out of her briefcase as we settle into one of A&V's private teahouses. It's a new venture for the teashop. They took out five of the private but open booths after they surveyed their regulars and learned that noise was an issue. A new wall now bisects the room and when the covers came off there were five enclosed rooms, modeled on the private carriages of the early railways but with higher seats.

You enter from the back and the tea trays are slid through the pull-down window, straight onto a Formica table of the same height. They rent the teahouses out for £10 an hour, which is pretty reasonable. The main room is awash with people, but as soon as the waitress finishes delivering our cakes

Caroline slides the window back up and the outside racket subsides to an industrious hum.

"What is on your mind, Nikki?" Caroline asks in that direct yet gentle way of hers. "Your exact thoughts right now, no editing."

"I was actually wondering how you can make sitting look like an art form."

Caroline rarely blushes but she does so now.

"Finishing school," she says, "walking around for hours with a pile of heavy books on your head. That teaches you a lifetime of poise and balance." She makes a face. "I'm sure you didn't rush over here to compliment me on my posture." She pushes her newly short snowy hair behind her ears. I hope mine turns from honey to snow like hers has, if not, chemicals may have to enter the equation.

"I'm not quite sure where to start."

Caroline says nothing, sampling one of the cakes.

"Remember the Domino affair?"

Caroline pages back through her notes.

"Sandra Miller," she says. "Called herself Domino; associated with the gun smuggling ring your chap helped to bring down a couple of years ago. We're going over old ground. I know how guilty you felt for..." here Caroline tails off.

There was a lot of shouting done by me during our sessions back then to help me deal with said guilt. Eventually I cornered the emotion and metaphorically stuffed it into a canvas sack where it sank into the depths of my psyche. But it still surfaces, usually when I'm rubbed raw by another emotion. Then it turns into a headache of piercing intensity, one for which migraine tablets have no effect.

"You carry no responsibility for what happened to her, Nikki," Caroline is saying, "She knew what she was doing."

I silently disagree. I cannot go back and change what happened, but it was my blunder that Domino was trying to fix when Colonel Ravenwood's son laid her out with a punch so vicious it put her into a coma.

I avoid drumming my fingers on the Formica table, which would show Caroline how I really feel. I pick the edible ball bearings off the dollop of vanilla icing threatening to suffocate my fairy cake and pop one in my mouth, sinking back into the embrace of the microfiber covered seat.

Caroline's pages ruffle forward. "Parents still on their cruise?" she asks, pouring more tea. She places the empty pot on the tray, flush with the window.

"Yeah," I say, "I talked to them yesterday. They seem to be enjoying themselves."

"I must say I was surprised when your mother told me they were going on an Alaskan cruise. It is a bit of a change from their normal frugal jaunt to Europe."

"That was my doing," I say. Caroline holds her pen poised. "I sat the pair of them down and told them to drop the 'Hollywood poor' act. This new job pays more, a lot more, so I'm putting money by and dabbling a little in stocks and shares, not enough that I could lose my shirt," I say before Caroline gets the wrong idea. "I told them they should spend the money on themselves. Gav and I were supposed to fly out and join them for a couple of days before they sailed out of Seattle."

"Don't tell me, something work related came up."

"No, that blasted Volcano, the one that sounds like a clogged-up woodpecker."

"Eyjafjallajökull." Caroline wrangles the word. I don't speak Icelandic. As far as I know she's pronouncing it correctly.

"They'd been in Seattle a couple of weeks when it blew and the backlog of flights meant we arrived one day too late. Gav was really pissed off about it. He didn't really calm down until we arrived in Victoria. I didn't know why at the time."

The waitress replaces our empty teapot with a full one via the window. "And now you do?" Caroline looks up from her pages straight into my eyes. I can feel myself colouring.

"He'd planned on asking dad for, you know, my hand."

One month ago

We'd spent the last day of our lazy ten-day vacation whale watching. During whale watching you don't expect a whale, especially a *killer whale*, to get up close and personal with you by swimming underneath the rigid inflatable boat you are a passenger in. At least I didn't. Orange boat, orange waterproofs, red lifejacket; we must've looked like a happy meal encased in bubble wrap. Fortunately, the whale wasn't hungry.

Later as we were entering the calm of the harbour, Gav rubbed his eye and dislodged a contact lens. When he got down on his hands and knees in front of me to rescue it the rest of the passengers thought he'd gone down on one knee for a different reason. We managed to laugh it off but Gav, it turns out, had been thinking about getting serious for quite a while. On the wooded path back to the hotel, he pulled out a small box. Before he asked, he rubbed the lid with his thumb, like a hunter with his lucky rabbit's foot. The lid was so well worn that the gold leaf had been almost buffed away.

As I said 'yes,' my throat clenched involuntarily making me a little lightheaded.

Now

"He only wants your hand?" Caroline isn't writing anything. "What about the rest of you?"

"Very funny."

"So you're engaged?"

"Little bit," I say.

"I see no ring."

I swallow the 'no flies on you' comment I was about to make and carefully pull the thin platinum strand around my neck until the ring appears, made of the same material, a narrow band at the base becoming two intersecting strips at the top.

"Simple with a twist," Caroline inspects it.

"It's perfect, but..."

"You don't seem all that thrilled to be Gavin's fiancée." Caroline's head is bent over her journal.

"We haven't had the chance to discuss it properly, and we haven't told my parents or Paddy yet. We both had jet lag from the flight home, then Gav had to fly straight off to a security conference, and I've been shuttling between here and Holland."

"How do you think Paddy will take the news?"

"I honestly don't know." I'm still getting to know the son Gav only recently discovered he'd fathered.

"Sounds to me like you're having reservations."

"This is Gav's idea, not mine. I've seen too many relationships crash and burn once the couple gets married. It's happening too fast. I can't get the image of a thousand guests and a poufy white dress out of my head."

"You're not afraid of taking on more adult responsibilities are you Nikki?"

Trust Caroline to sum up my fears in a nutshell.

"I love him, no I adore him. But, come on, can you see us getting married in church?"

"No," Caroline says, "You're both private people. A registry office wedding in your lunch hours would be just the ticket for you."

I got so hung up on the big white wedding I didn't want, I hadn't been able to see an alternative. Caroline regards me with quiet satisfaction; then a thought creases a line between her eyebrows. "You mentioned Domino. Why?"

"I could've sworn I saw her as I was boarding the flight back from Schiphol today, two rows ahead of me."

"How do you know it wasn't her? They can work miracles with coma patients these days." Caroline, ever the voice of reason, points out.

"We were in business class and under the excuse of locating the toilets I wandered up and down the aisle. There was no sign of her. Unless she was flying the damn plane, she wasn't on board."

"Interesting, you proved to yourself she wasn't there but you still came straight here, without an appointment." Caroline bestows a gentle smile on me. "Remember how our minds work; Domino to you is guilt, pure and simple. No matter how much I attempt to convince your stubborn self to the contrary." Caroline reaches into her pocket.

"Put your wallet away, Caroline, this is on me."

CHAPTER 2

I play sardines as I ride the tube to Victoria and then the DLR to get home. Home is now in Docklands, has been for the past few months. My idea of buying the adjoining flat to Gav's and knocking the two together is working a treat. We had applied for one of the penthouses on the very top floor and didn't get it, which turned out to be a good thing because we have even more space with this arrangement.

Keying open the door, I'm greeted by shouts and gunfire, but it's just the PlayStation.

Paddy, son of Carita Malloy, is an avid 'Call of Duty' player and he crashes here a lot, even though he has his own flat near the University of London campus; he likes to be close to his rediscovered dad. Paddy and I are still working on being around each other. It's not that he doesn't like me or I him, and the kid is freakishly smart, but a year or so back, in trying to rid himself of a human cockroach, Paddy almost turned me and former DI Martha McGuiness into acid rain which didn't endear him to his dad. Normally I'm against cover-ups but Paddy would be rotting in a prison cell without the 'gas explosion' theory DI Randle came up with. Paddy knows that as long he keeps his nose clean his secret is safe and he's got a new mentor in Professor Gantry who is working very closely with his tutors at UofL. Paddy is helping the Lancaster/Malloy clan beat the odds. Long may it last.

Of course the downside of living with Paddy is the mess. I thought I was bad but to look at the place now you'd be under the impression that he only has to walk through a room and things untidy themselves. I pick up the nest of cushions on the floor and dump them in a pile on the sofa.

"Paddy!" I call, wondering if he's eaten, "I'm ordering takeout, want anything?"

The gunfight pauses.

"Nah, I'm grand thanks."

I wait for the shots to resume, they don't. Instead Paddy's lean frame appears around the doorjamb.

"Yous want me to go?"

Yous, not you. Paddy didn't have such a pronounced Irish accent last year. Gav thinks the small affectation is his way of declaring independence from us mainlanders. Since Paddy's arrival Gav says it too, another echo of his boy. Paddy's jeans are as crinkled as his shirt; his new shorter hair is like the crest of a wave poised to break on his forehead. He gets his darker hair and slightly plump lips from his mother, Carita; the rest is all Gavin.

"No, you're," pause, "you're fine Paddy." I came so close to saying 'grand' and just managed to stop myself because it sounds ridiculous in my lower home counties accent.

He drops his shoulders. "Later," he says.

The game starts up again. I call in an order for some hot and sour soup, prawn crackers and a dozen spring rolls from the Golden Panda around the corner and put the cash and a generous tip next to my keys. Then I recycle every magazine in sight until I've unearthed the smoked glass of the coffee table.

When ten minutes have passed I take the stairs down to the lobby. Tonight my timing is perfect; the delivery boy and I swap what we're carrying.

Back in the flat the smell of food rouses Paddy who demolishes all but a couple of the spring rolls and most of the prawn crackers.

While watching reruns of *The Big Bang Theory*, he sits on the floor with his back against the sofa, which vibrates whenever he finds something funny. I wrestle with translating a report that my employer commissioned from the University of Delft on suitable locations for a floating test community. I keep spacing out.

"Give it up, for now," Paddy suggests.

"I just need some coffee, that's all." I don't move from the sofa, and finally sleep wins over the report. I wake up still lying on the sofa. The lights are all out, Paddy is gone or sleeping, and a blanket covers me up to my shoulders. I wish Paddy a good night as sleep rolls over me again.

CHAPTER 3

Saturday morning

Gav calls just as I'm jogging back to the flat.

"I can't talk for long," he says, a tannoy message in the background requests that delegates assemble in the main hall. "Just wanted to say hi, and good luck."

"Hi yourself," I pant, "and good luck for what?"

"Your press conference, they announced it on the morning news. Hang on." His hand muffles the phone for a moment. "I've got to go, catch you later."

Press conference?

Topher 'Sully' Sullivan is my first official project for Excalibur, and he's proving to be a multi-million-pound loose cannon. Sully doesn't need to count money anymore, his lottery win only added to his massive fortune. He went public, giant cheque, champagne, legions of flashbulb popping paparazzi, jealous howls of protest from many quarters.

"Why would a billionaire play the lottery?" screamed the tabloids. "Why not?" was the reasoned response from Avalon's press officer, "It is a lottery after all, and Mr. Sullivan is using his winnings on a humanitarian project which will greatly benefit this country for years to come. Stay tuned and we'll explain."

Sully, we realized, was the perfect fit for Avalon's new project consultancy arm, Excalibur. Last year I became the unwitting guinea pig for the program and that translated into this job (well there were a few bumps and bodies along the way but you've met me, right?)

I hit speed dial and get Sully's weekend secretary.

"Mr. Sullivan's office."

"Hi, it's Nikki, is there a press conference today?"

"Yes," the voice at the other end replies. "We're live in five minutes. Better turn on your telly."

"Thanks," I say, leaving the stream of expletives until the line is dead.

Sully's humanitarian project is to bring floating communities to the UK. The man's a walking sound bite. His wife, CeeCee (to call her Lucy is to get a dagger in the eyes) nicknamed him 'Sully', which is kind of appropriate as he's built like a bear, just not a blue Pixar one.

At our first meeting I told him we already had floating communities; houseboats and canal boats. He hooted with laughter and said, in Dutch, he was thinking bigger, *much* bigger.

This was just the 'in' I'd been hoping for. The Dutch are the leaders in floating house design. A quick Google search, an afternoon of watching YouTube clips, and reading articles gave me a good overview of the subject.

It follows that Sully (or his project manager) is going to be spending a lot of time in Holland interacting with the Dutch and Sully's much-publicized aversion to flying rules him out.

"Give me an example," I say, responding in the same language.

"Ah, that saves me from having to ask if you speak the lingo," Sully says, with a hint of approval, "Did you grow up in Holland?"

"No, but I have an ear for language; I studied the basic romance languages at school. They don't teach Dutch of course, but I got the chance to spend several summers in Holland."

"School exchange program?" Sully asks.

"Family exchange program," I reply. I'd normally be a lot more cautious about revealing this part of my childhood, except Sully has a reputation for respecting frankness.

"My mum's younger sister, Maggs, spent three years working as a translator for the European Space Agency. My brother and I would go and visit her while my parents did their own thing. I learned Dutch using the immersion method, hanging out with the local kids on the beach."

Aunt Maggs always wore suits; even on the weekends she'd live in trousers and shirtsleeves. She wore her red hair like a 1950's starlet, used shades of lipstick mum labeled as 'garish' and one Saturday a year she flew to Gatwick just to drive to Storr Downs and invite our whole family over to stay with her for the summer. Mum and Aunt Maggs didn't see eye to eye on, well, *anything*, and after Maggs had issued the invitation mum would bring out a pot of tea and some store-bought cakes (which always struck me as odd because she can bake for England.) After one cup mum would 'go up for a nap,' leaving dad and us two kids to entertain my Aunt.

Dad would refuse her offer for himself and mum but then arrange a date for Stephen and me to fly over. As she was leaving, dad would always hug Aunt Maggs and whisper 'sorry,' and Maggs would give him a small sad smile and drive back to Gatwick.

"My Aunt Maggs rented a small beach front property out at Scheveningen, which she shared with a Jack Russell terrier called Castro and an artist named Marina."

"Hmmm," says Sully.

"Marina kept an eye on us while Maggs was at work. At the weekends the four of us would roam around Europe in Maggs' Audi convertible."

I labored under the impression that Marina was sleeping in Aunt Maggs's room so that Stephen and I could come and stay for the summer. The very last time Aunt Maggs dropped us at Schiphol for the flight home I told Stephen what I thought and he laughed until he could barely stand.

"Maggs and Marina are a couple, you idiot!"

"But they're *girls*," I blurted out.

"You sound just like mum. She'll be checking us for signs that Maggs has been corrupting us. We mustn't give her any hint that we know what she's doing.

"Look Ronnie, (Stephen never called me Nikki), Maggs and Marina are great and I want to keep spending time with them, maybe get a job over here, so don't blow it for me, promise?"

Little did I know that we'd never visit Aunt Maggs again. Stephen's tragic car accident was only a couple of months away and I was still wrestling with the fact that my mother, that beacon of peace, diplomacy, and wonderful cooking was covering up a prejudice a mile wide. It made me wonder what else she was hiding beneath that pleasant exterior.

After Stephen's funeral Aunt Maggs took a job in New York as a translator for the UN and Marina went with her. Now even if I wanted to go back, I had nowhere to stay. Last I heard Maggs and Marina had married and moved somewhere upstate.

I still know enough Dutch to get by on day trips but in anticipation of this meeting I've been polishing my conversational skills by immersing myself in all things Dutch. Among them, a Dutch retrospective (with English subtitles) at the Prince Charles theatre just off Leicester Square, a conversational program on my desktop, and one rather racy Dutch porn film which caused Gav to rename Blockbuster to Bonkbuster.

"Impressive," says Sully. "How about your written Dutch?"

"I get by."

Sully veers back onto his original track of thought.

"The Dutch used to reclaim land and protect it using their system of canals and dykes. There's new thinking afoot, young lady." (Sully calls everyone young this or that). "A new mindset; work *with* the water not *against* it."

Sully has identified several flood plains that he thinks are suitable for a test community and that are up for sale. The report I spent most of last night translating details the recommendations from the team of Dutch experts.

* * *

I go in through the garage and up the back stairs at a dead run. I forgot to ask which channel, so I flip back and forth between stations until BBC News 24 announces a live link-up with 'billionaire philanthropist, Topher Sullivan.'

Sully and CeeCee stand on the grass in front of the houses of parliament. Sully begins his preamble. It includes 'housing problems', his forecasts for how high the sea levels will rise with global warming, the predicted failure date of the Thames Flood barrier (believe me when I read the projections for flooding in the next five years it made me really glad we live three floors up), and the failure of successive governments of both stripes to do anything to address the problem.

So far, so safe, I turn the volume up and go into the kitchen to brew some coffee.

My phone plays 'I wrote the book' by Beth Ditto, my boss' personal ring tone. Beth can only be calling about one thing.

"Hi Beth."

"Are you watching the news?" Her calm voice is actually an indicator that's she hopping mad.

"Yeah, he's blathering on about his usual soapbox issues, but it's all window dressing. I just got the report back. They're recommending we go ahead and buy the land closest to the Hackney marshes."

Sully's voice announces from the other room. "I have bought a plot of land to begin tests on a future forward housing design, constructed by a Dutch company."

"What!" Beth now sounds like a talking icicle.

"I didn't know Beth, I swear. When we took our break everything was on course but no purchase is, was, pending until the results of the report."

"Furthermore," Sully continues, "I'm happy to announce that our project partner, Excalibur, has agreed to participate in the experiment. Heavy rain is forecast for the next few weeks so we will have the first structure arriving just in time for a comprehensive test."

"Nikki," Beth says, "I don't care what you do, reign him in. I'll try and cover us with the board members."

She hangs up. Sully has just completed his presentation.

"Any questions?" he asks over the flare of flashbulbs and ticking shutters. He answers a couple of environmental questions, while his phone pulses in his breast pocket. CeeCee points to the screen. Mine says 'calling Sully'. He can see it's me. Sully sketches a little wave to the camera and kills the call. Grrrr.

I turn off the TV and try calling Sully again.

"Sully, you are putting me in an impossible position," I say. "My boss just watched your press conference and she's not happy." Time to embroider a bit. "She's threatening to reassign me if I can't regain control of the project. Call me back."

And it seems he has, but not from a number I recognize.

"Hello?"

The person on the other end clears their throat.

"Hello?" I say again.

The line goes dead.

Then a text message appears; a map reference. (Sully's peace offering?) I plug the co-ordinates into Google maps and, zooming in, find myself looking at a cinema complex. I type *Showcase Cinemas Winnersh* into my search bar and as the results populate things become a lot clearer.

Winnersh is in Berkshire and *not* on the list of possible sites Sully had earmarked. However, from the look of these YouTube clips that people have posted, the cinema's car park and the surrounding area floods a lot. In fact it is difficult to find a picture where anything looks dry.

I text Sully back, 'going to check it out now.'

Since the mini went to that great scrap yard in the sky my luck with cars hasn't improved. The car I was supposed to be buying, a secondhand Fiat 500, showed up clean when I ran the basic checks on the VIN number, but the guy failed to show up with the car or the paperwork the day he'd promised to and that made me suspicious so I got Randle to run a PNC check. The car turned out to be a cut and shut, two crash damaged Fiats welded together. Randle calls my near miss the Fiat 250 squared.

For the time being I'm using Gav's old Land Rover Defender. I unhook the keys, pull out a pair of Gav's waders from the hall cupboard and with nothing else but my purse and my phone stuffed into my jacket pocket, lock up and head down to the underground car park.

The Defender starts up with the usual pong of petrol. I let all the gauges settle before easing her out onto the street, then pull over for a moment to let the GPS acquire all the satellites it needs. With that done I plug in the address and off we go.

As I start to drive away, a motorcycle, a blue BMW, is pulling up to the garage; Paddy, arriving to bash the Play station again. I recognize his blue leathers with the orange star logo on the back as he peels off his glove to put in the entry code. He disappears into the garage as I turn the corner and head for the motorway. M25, M4, off the M roads onto the A roads. To my annoyance a familiar blue BMW appears several cars back after I join the M4. Paddy doesn't need to nursemaid me and I intend to tell him that. I slow down for the first layby I come to.

He coasts in behind me, cuts the engine and dismounts, pulling his helmet off as he walks to the driver's side window.

"Grand day for a drive," he says, leaning both elbows on the just-opened window ledge. "Where are yous taking Dad's classic?"

"I'm inspecting a site, and this thing isn't a classic. It doesn't even have carpets and it's bloody uncomfortable. Go home Paddy, don't you have papers to write?"

"I'd like nothing better, but there's someone on your six," Paddy says. "I saw yous parked up as I was coming down the street and when you pulled out, the Red Audi parked about three cars back started moving. He waited until you'd turned the corner before gunning it after yous. It could've been a coincidence except Dad doesn't believe in coincidences so I turned around and followed the Audi. He's been one or two cars behind until we pulled in for this little chat we're having."

An Audi did pass me just now.

"I didn't notice him," I say, thinking that Paddy should be explaining how he managed to tail me. Then I remember the fluorescent tips of the radio aerials on this car, an easy way to keep track of the occupant. I've used it myself.

Paddy's eyes gleam. "He's got one of those Yankee baseball caps on so I couldn't catch a glimpse of his face. I think he'll be waiting a bit further up the way there. We could see what he wants?"

"He could be a reporter, it's common knowledge I work for Sully. He might be digging for dirt or getting some background, you know *actual fact checking*."

"Not acting like a reporter."

"True."

Paddy's determined to get to the bottom of this and frankly, now, so am I.

"Alright, I'm going to the Showcase cinemas just off the Winnersh roundabout." I read him the co-ordinates in case he gets lost. "Hang back and let me go in first, Ok?"

I start the Defender and pull back into traffic; my last glimpse of Paddy is him slipping the helmet over his head. The red Audi glides out of a side road and takes up station several cars behind. The Showcase roundabout, a sure sign I'm close, has traffic lights and they're red. I can see a garden centre to the left. On the green light I follow the Showcase signs, going through the roundabout, around a corner and down a gentle incline into the car park. There are plenty of cars around. All the patrons are inside enjoying the movies. I don't feel threatened with so many people and staff within yelling distance.

I circle the cars and spot a FOR SALE sign on the far end of the parking area, past the overflow car park. Crossed through, the sign now says SOLD in big red letters. I park up and take out the waders, just in case. That also gives me a good reason to be sitting on the tailgate of the Landy where I pull them on. I can't hear the purr of Paddy's BMW yet. I reach into my pocket, fingering the small pressurized can that says 'Evian' on the outside but contains a nasty dose of mace. Beth's self-defense instructor sells these by the case load. It would be stupid to go into an unknown situation armed with no defense whatsoever.

My feet are paddling inside these waders. I have to jam my toes into the front and almost tip toe across the overflow car park. The fence has a 'no trespassing' notice attached to it alongside a triangular sign showing a car being drowned by black wavy lines. Each step off-road is slow going; the path already stippled with boot prints feels like freshly chewed gum sucking at the heels of my waders.

Clumping along I can see how much and how regularly it floods around here. Everything is vibrant green. Lacy ferns crowd the sides of the path, blades of grass sprout between the fern fronds, raising them, giving the optical illusion of a two-tier path.

I squelch my way across, testing the ground before I put weight on it. I have no wish to be up to my armpits in mud.

The burble of the stream increases, and the closer I get to it, the more weeping willow boughs I have to push my way through. There is a main road less than a couple of hundred yards from here, but you'd never know it. The boughs deaden the traffic noises and form a tunnel that diffuses the midafternoon sunlight.

The makeshift path curves. I round a corner and halt in mid step, surprised because there is a house here, a two-story ruin. On the upper floor, rotten planks have come adrift from their nails and lean away from the walls. It gives the appearance of having stalled mid regeneration.

Next to it four shiny silver pilings rise out of the ground, soaring over the ruin. I'm certain I've found the test area. As it was explained to me in detail by Sully, the modular house gets lowered onto these pilings and when the water level rises the house floats, using a nifty piece of science discovered by Archimedes (the clever, bathing ancient Greek, not my old department at Avalon.) The roof collects rainwater feeding it to a filtration and storage tank inside. The panels on the roof collect energy in a super-duper secret process that mimics photosynthesis. If the house reaches a certain height, according to the computer models I have seen, the house goes 'off the grid'. If the water level rises too high or if the house is in jeopardy from debris or other threats, there is the equivalent of a hovercraft skirt around the float that can be deployed for extra stability. With the addition of an engine the house can be maneuvered like a super tanker, which the planners assure me is *exactly* how she handles.

I don't get the chance to go any further as yells and screams start coming from behind me.

It is not easy to run in these things, but I rapidly retrace my steps to find Paddy struggling with a wiry figure in a hoodie.

The kid's voice hasn't broken yet because the screams are coming from him. Paddy has both arms wrapped around his opponent's waist. He must've snuck up behind him, which means he was coming up behind me. As I reach them the figure goes limp. It's a feint. As Paddy relaxes his grip, the back of his opponent's head catches him full in the nose. The hood slips down.

"Paddy!" I yell. He goes over backwards as his leg sweeps around, bringing the woman to her knees. At the same time I'm shouting, "Don't hurt her!"

Paddy flops onto his back and the woman twists away from him. She crouches on the ground taking long panting breaths before she regains her composure. Paddy hauls himself to his feet, wipes drops of blood from his nose, and stands over her like an Alsatian waiting for the attack command.

In the struggle her hair has fallen across her face. As she pushes it back, I pinch the flap of skin between my thumb and forefinger until it hurts. Good. I am not losing my mind. I did see Domino on the plane. Because she's sitting, winded, on the ground right in front of me.

"Domino!"

I push past Paddy, and help her to her feet. The three of us must look a right odd little trio. Domino has her arm around my waist as I plod along in my giant boots, her jeans and hoodie and slender frame giving her the look of a tired teenager. Paddy hangs back several steps, treating us like we're a pair of radioactive isotopes.

Domino's weight gradually lifts and, close to the end of the path, she's walking unaided. I go straight over to the Defender, unlock it and have Paddy open the tailgate so that Domino can sit on it. Her struggle with him means her jeans and the sleeves of her hoodie are mud smeared. And her face is shockingly pale. "God I could use a drink," she says, her voice gaining strength.

"I don't get it," Paddy says. "She was following yous, sneaking up that path."

"I wasn't sneaking," Domino shoots back, pointing at her muddied trainers, "I was just making sure I didn't end up in a bog. There were so many paths I wasn't sure which way Nikki went."

"Who is she?" Paddy asks me.

"She's an old friend," I say, which causes him to shake his head.

"*My* mates don't tail me down to secluded parts of the Berkshire boonies."

What am I supposed to say to that? "She's been away," I say.

"*She* is right here," Domino points out, "and *she* could still use that drink."

"Paddy, Domino, Domino, Paddy," I say. "Paddy, you'd better bring your bike in here. Domino and I will be fine."

"It's yous funeral."

CHAPTER 4

We sit in silence for a few moments, side by side on the tailgate. Domino is a lot paler than I remember and she has lost the healthy country girl look. She has more of a chiseled athletic build now.

"I guess I'm going first, then," she says. "I wanted to see you."

I suddenly twig the parade of hang up phone calls the last few days including this morning's. They were her.

"How long have you been back?" I ask.

"In England? Just a few weeks. I came back from the coma several months after I went in."

"I *did* see you on the plane the other day," I say.

"Guilty as charged." Domino tosses her hair, shorter than I remember, banging off her shoulders. "I saw you chatting with the stewardess and then my request to ride in the jump seat got approved and I didn't want our first meeting to be a rushed 'hiya' on the aisle of a commuter jet."

"How did you swing the jump seat?" I ask, intrigued.

"Pilot friends."

"Are you still with..?"

"If you mean Simon, he's out of the picture."

I admit I heave a sigh of relief at that news. The thought of Simon, my ex-boss, hovering in the background like one of those predator drones isn't a pleasant one.

"Domino, I am..."

She cuts me off tugging down the sleeves of her top, an unconscious movement that covers up the patchwork of punctured veins that vine her arms.

"Nikki, no one made me do what I did." Domino reaches across and takes my hand. "It was a conscious decision. I wanted to help. I'm still dealing with the consequences. It's hard to talk about it because to do that is to relive it." She shudders.

"I know a great therapist," I say and she looks at me, suddenly wary. "A few years back I got caught up in a bank robbery, shooters, masked men, the lot."

"That sounds exciting."

"They killed a man, a security guard right in front of us. I had nightmares for weeks afterwards, and Simon ordered me into therapy."

Paddy rides up, giving me an odd look, especially as I squeeze Domino's hand.

She pulls herself together.

"Who is your little watchdog?"

"Paddy Malloy, he's Gav Lancaster's son."

"Lancaster?" Domino's eyes widen, "That's the chap you were seeing, the one who worked with my brother, the guy we all thought was dead."

"Yeah, he's as much to blame for what happened to you as I am."

"His son," Domino repeats. "Seems we both have a lot to talk about."

Paddy stands with his hands on his hips in front of Domino.

"If yous are such good friends, why tail Nikki all the way down here?"

"I didn't know she'd be coming all the way down here." Domino does her thing, giving Paddy a quirky little smile that he can't help returning, "Why *are* you down here?" she asks, looking my way.

"Let's get that drink and I'll tell you."

The other two wait while I hop around, exchanging the waders for trainers and we walk up past Domino's red Audi and across to a pub called The George. The place is packed with wedding guests.

"You can go and sit in the garden," the landlady offers over the din. "They've got a coach coming to take them up to the smoke, a wedding isn't a wedding without some London clubbing is it?"

I'm reaching for my wallet when Domino produces a twenty with the dexterity of a Vegas magician. The landlady takes Domino's money, putting the two wines and a coke for Paddy on a tray. Domino pockets her change and Paddy leads the way outside. As soon as we enter the beer garden Domino looks at me and I know what she's thinking, 'We can't talk here'. I thought we could find a quiet corner. The only table free is close to the fence.

Paddy snags it, totally oblivious to the multiple female stares directed at his face and his bum. Domino and I get some looks too, that kind of up, down, dismissive look perfected by women the world over. Domino may seem frail, but she can deflect those kinds of looks in her sleep. I just ignore them.

The noise is relentless, every conversation vying for attention. Everything is on offer, dirty jokes, private work secrets, kid woes. The group of women who gave Paddy the most attention discuss their (absent) friend's Friday night fling with a bus driver, all flavours of laughter are available, including forced, raucous, and belly.

Paddy drinks in silence.

Domino leans over, "It doesn't change does it?"

I shake my head and try the wine, light and sharp on my tongue.

"Why are you down here?" Domino asks.

While I answer, telling her about the new gig and the test site, she openly flirts with Paddy. I should be annoyed with that but I'm not, as it shows me that she didn't lose her personality to the coma.

For his part, each time Paddy starts to flirt back, he catches himself and fights against his hard-wired impulses by yawning with his mouth wide open. The yawns throw Domino off her game. I sympathize, he used to do this to me (the yawning, not the flirting) before we got used to being around each other. It seems rude but it's just him showing how uneasy he's feeling. At least that's what he told Gav when Gav had a word with him about it.

Domino looks away from Paddy's display of healthy tonsils and asks me "Which poor sod gets to babysit that house?"

"One of Sully's minions, I suppose."

Privately I'm wondering if Domino's mental armour is strong enough to cope with what she's been through, or will she, in moments of inattention, forever see Connor Ravenwood's fist flying towards her face.

Paddy finishes his coke and stands up. "I have a paper to write. I'll see yous back at home." He walks off, shaking his head and muttering to himself.

"Cozy domestic bliss?" Domino asks, with a wicked grin.

"Sometimes," I say. "He's pretty much self-sufficient. His dad is away at a conference so he's being extra vigilant."

"I guess he doesn't want you close to any more gas explosions," Domino's voice is innocent but her eyes spark with mischief. "I read the papers you know and the foreign press were much more aggressive than the UK lot, if you can believe it."

"Foreign press?" I'm startled by the notion that that was anything but a domestic story.

"It was all over the Italian rags, that bloke Ogilvy was linked with the mob. They insinuated that it was a mob hit."

My mind goes back to the three men banging on Ogilvy's front door, while I strain to stay focused on Domino's words.

"The Italian press swarmed the site. They reported that a couple of witnesses saw two cars, a big blue Daimler and a small red mini close to the house, before the place blew sky high. My employer knew I'd been to that area before so she sent me down to check the story."

"You're a researcher?"

"I'm an event planner, and whatever else she needs me to be; a Jill of all trades if you will.

"Later, I walked into the local pub and who do I see but Zach, that bloke you and Simon were showing around the plot of land when we first met, although he seems to be going by James these days. I chatted up a cute guy I'd seen at the site, he was only too happy to fill me in. That's when I confirmed the mini was yours. I had to go back to Europe for the multiple launch parties we had planned. But as soon as I could, I came back over here."

While Domino has been explaining herself, a couple walks past our table. They'd been having a private chat at the wooden walkway that leads to an observation point.

"Come with me," I say, picking up my glass and moving towards the walkway. "We can talk more easily out here."

She joins me and leans on the railing. According to the plaque attached, the walkway was opened two years ago. The planks feel solid underfoot. The lumber is all treated to be water repellant, and the pilings, like those of our soon to be test house, are sunk deep into the bedrock under the clay/mud layer.

From the car park the belch of diesel and black smoke announces the arrival of the wedding party's coach. A light breeze springs up and couples start to move inside.

"It must seem strange to you that I turned up like this. To be honest, I didn't know how much you knew about…"

The wind rustles the leaves, gently seeming to shush her.

"I didn't want to just drop back in like nothing happened. For all I knew you thought I was dead or close to it. The few people I have reconnected with up until now have either fainted or yelled at me, you did neither."

I hold up my pinched, seriously bruised hand.

"Oh, ouch," she says.

It actually looks more painful than it is but I'm not going to let on about that. "Last time I saw you, Simon was carrying you to hospital. He spirited you out of the country not long after."

Domino unconsciously tugs at her sleeves again. "He put me in a very expensive Swiss clinic."

I let out a soft whistle, wondering how far to push. "He paid for the clinic and then you dumped him?"

"No, it's more complicated than that." Domino refuses to go into too much detail. "That's a conversation for another day."

What did she do to pay off her stay in an expensive Swiss clinic I wonder.

"I know you're probably thinking it. Don't worry; I didn't go back to the dark side,' Domino says.

"As I mentioned I have a legitimate job now. We're doing a massive launch party next week, the invites went out yesterday."

Sully, is always sticking me on the guest lists of benefits and movie premieres and charity shindigs. I could paper a room with those things. "I'll have to check and see if I got one. What's it for?" I ask.

"You won't have one of these, this launch is very exclusive. It's for the new Mary Snowfire book."

I nearly spit out my wine.

"You work for *the* Mary Snowfire?"

"Turns out she's a friend of the family. She bumped into me in Switzerland and she offered me this job. She's the one who paid for my clinic stay."

I decide not to ask if Snowfire volunteered payment or if Domino used blackmail.

Everyone was raving about Mary Snowfire when she self-published last year. I had other things on my mind at the time, like James Farmer and the Cluedo project. Mind you I didn't start reading Harry Potter until the first movie came out and now I've read all seven. Seems I'm always late to the party.

On a recent trip to Holland I'd picked up Snowfire's *The Dubai Debutante's Last Will and Testament* in the airport bookstore and wished the flight were longer because the heroine was kick-ass with buckets of snark and her put downs were killer, in some cases literally. That climactic finale on the helipad at the top of the Burj al Arab hotel left me reeling long after I turned the last page.

Snowfire scored a publishing deal on the back of *Dubai Deb*, and her second book (title unknown, but rumoured to be some kind of tech thriller) was put in the starting gate faster than a bargain hunter in the January sales.

"What's the next book called?"

"I could tell you, but then I'd have to kill you," Domino says, a brief flash of amusement on her face. "You're a fan?" she says, "wasn't expecting that."

"Domino, my normal reading is reports and textbooks, *Dubai Deb* was a pleasurable change. I felt like I'd been to Dubai after reading that book."

"I'll talk to Mary, maybe we can get you on as a plus one." Domino checks a text flashing on her phone.

"Oh lord, I have to go."

We make our way out of the pub and pause at her car, parked in the main car park. "I'm still working my way through the thing with Simon," Domino says. "Apparently I have a lot of unresolved issues that I've blocked, which makes me sound like a drain. Once I'm unblocked, we'll talk, and I mean chapter and verse, Nikki. You still haven't told me how you ended up with a teenager."

"Chapter and verse, I promise."

Domino hugs me and I can feel her shoulder blades through the fabric of the hoodie.

I wave her off and go to collect the Defender. I plug the charging cable into the cigarette lighter and dig in my jacket pocket for my phone. It isn't there. I curse softly and fluently. It must've dropped out of my pocket, but not at the pub, I would've heard it fall. A fruitless half an hour later, I've retraced my steps back to the test site and still no phone. I'm Kryptonite to iPhones. I've had them stolen, destroyed, bricked; Apple is making a bundle off me. I'm on first name terms with Midge at the Apple store in Covent Garden. He suggested I back my vital data up every week to the cloud so it's not a total disaster. I check the tailgate is closed and turn the Defender back towards town.

CHAPTER 5

Tuesday morning: Sullivan Inc HQ

I punch Sully in the face, enjoying the look of pained surprise; my knee comes up, connecting with his ample stomach. As he doubles over I skip back a couple of steps, his forehead hits the floor with a satisfying 'thud'.

Shame it's all in my head.

CeeCee flounces out of the office, rare for her. She normally floats serenely. Very new age is our CeeCee, all herbal tea and yoga. The reason she's pissed off, and I'm mentally attacking Sully is because the poor sod who is going to be staying in the amphi house is me. Clearly CeeCee wanted it to be her.

"You're doing it, right?" says Sully.

Dragged back from my reverie, I blink.

"Oh come on young Nikki, it'll be character building."

"Then why don't you do it?"

"Things to do, people to see, deals to broker, not enough hours in the day."

"Sully, I work *with* you, not *for* you. Sometimes I think you forget the controlling interest Excalibur has in this partnership." I say, attempting to assert a semblance of authority.

"So you'll do it then?" he says after a few moments.

At this point I exercise my right to remain silent and walk out of Sully's office.

CeeCee is on the phone, her back to me, her normally soft voice rasping a little.

"Yes, we'll have to reschedule," she's saying. "I know it's inconvenient for you, there's only so much I can do from this end. Perhaps you'd prefer to whinge to Sully, I can put you through right now."

She waits, impatient fingers thrumming a tattoo on her leather upholstered desk as the person on the other end of the call vents their anger or frustration. She holds the silence at this end for a few more beats.

"Got it out of your system?" she finally asks. "That's better, I knew you'd see things my way in the end."

Another reply from the other end, then…

"What?" CeeCee clamps the phone so hard against her ear she'll crack the screen if she's not careful, "Yes, I'm sure he will understand."

Who will understand? I wonder, clearing my throat as if I've just come out of Sully's office. I don't want CeeCee to think I'm eavesdropping on her.

She swivels her chair around and I point to myself and then at the outer door to see if she wants the conversation to remain private. In reply she uses her foot to push the wheeled chair on the other side of her desk towards me.

"Why don't you ring me from somewhere quieter next time, your office for instance? CeeCee asks her caller, as I plant my behind on the chair. "We'll stick to the original delivery date then, shall we?" Her finger taps the back of the phone, "Hello?" She unwelds the handset from her ear, looks at the display, and mutters a rude word under her breath.

She places the phone, none too gently, down on the blotter, the only open area on the desk; the rest of the workspace is taken up by piles of papers for the three different companies she has a stake in, and so many cosmetics samples that the little bottles seem to be an invading force. I invariably leave the building with CeeCee pressing some of them into my hands, which is a problem, as then I keep having to buy the full sizes. This holistic stuff doesn't come cheap.

"How rude! He hung up on me."

"Partners can be a pain," I say. CeeCee narrows her eyes at me.

"Sully?" I say.

"Yeah," she says, sighing the word. "Sully."

"Look, if you want to babysit a floating house in a rain storm, I'm only too happy to let you persuade him otherwise."

Her bad mood drops away and it's like the sun coming out. She almost falls off her chair laughing. "Nikki," she says, between guffaws and giggles, "You make it sound so enticing. But seriously, you know once he's made up his mind about something there's no turning him around.

"Here," she says, dumping yet another bottle in my palm. "New formulation, really good for the décolletage," she pokes her chest out. "No crepe here. You need to moisturize more; oh your skin's still smooth now but…"

"What's the main ingredient?" I ask, not wanting a repeat of the green tea perfume incident where I smelt like an Assam plantation even after multiple showers.

"It's a blend. All natural oils, and none of them make you smell like a Hawaiian Tropic commercial," CeeCee promises.

I take a careful sniff; it is pleasant, almost buttery. I re-cap the bottle and drop it into my pocket.

Sully's HQ is about a brisk quarter of an hour walk from Dr. Bradley's offices and my regular appointment isn't for another half hour. The weather is typical April, almost May; sunlight that doesn't warm and a wind which doesn't bother going around. For my birthday last year my friend, costume designer Cass Blake, presented me with a kid leather duster in a lush dark green, made to measure. Gav swears he wasn't the one who handed over my measurements. The hem swings below my knees flicked about by the wind. I button the coat, turning to watch a pavement race between two Styrofoam cups and an empty coke can and that's when I see him. The winner bumps up against his fluorescent trainer. He kicks the can into the road and stands there, openly staring.

A kid, roughly Paddy's age, maybe a titch younger. I saw him hanging around Sully's offices earlier. He has tech start-up written all over him but less 'cube monkey' and more 'about to sell to Microsoft for millions'. The messenger bag casually strung across his body has a logo on the strap, the dark blue skinny jeans have no visible creases, the sweater over his striped shirt looks soft enough to be cashmere, his mousey hair is artfully tousled and isn't moving an inch in this wind.

"Can I help you?" I call. "Are you lost?"

His lips curve up but there's no humour there. He has that hungry entitled look that kids who come from money have. Whichever private school he's AWOL from should try muzzling him, and there's something odd about his geek glasses. I don't have time for this. I take out my newly replaced phone (How Midge from the Apple store wishes he got paid on commission!) and snap a photo of the stranger. Then I pick up the pace, using some of the surveillance techniques Gav taught me to check if I've shaken him off. Arriving at Dr. Bradley's door a couple of minutes before my appointment, I buzz twice and get a huffy, "Who is it?"

"Nikki Doyle, here for my ten o'clock."

The door clicks open, I shut it firmly behind me. At the top of the stairs stands young Ms. Maltravers, hands on hips, sneer on lips.

"Cutting it close aren't you? I was about to mark you down as a no show."

"I had to shake off a tail," I say, enjoying her open-mouthed expression.

"A tail?" Caroline's voice enquires. "Another brush with the security services, Nikki? I've told you they can be hazardous to your health."

Maltravers nearly swallows her tongue.

"No just some bloke. He followed me from Sully's. I didn't like the look of him."

"Describe him," Caroline says, leading me into her office.

"I can do better than that." I call up the picture on my phone and hand it to her. She studies it.

"I'd recognize that one if I saw him again," she says, her fingers zooming the photo in. "Look he was filming you!"

I go round to her side of the desk. Looking over her shoulder. I can see that the odd bump on the side of geek boy's glasses is a lipstick-sized camera. And he's vain; he's wearing tinted moisturizer making his face a slightly different colour from the rest of him.

"I'll show the picture to Gav and have him look into it."

Whilst I'm in the middle of telling Caroline about Sully's loose cannon impression young Ms. Maltravers flounces into the office, dumping a pot of tea and two mugs down on the table with a china-cracking thud. "For heavens sake Maltravers," Caroline says, "knock first. You know some of my sessions are delicate."

"Pardon me, Doctor," the new Maltravers replies, with barely a hint of remorse as she withdraws.

Caroline inspects both mugs before pouring anything into them. There's no milk. She gets up; I think to fetch the milk. Instead, she locks the office door.

"As I was saying," Caroline continues, "It seems to me that your Mr. Sullivan isn't keeping you appraised of his business decisions."

"He's not. Ideas just pop into his head. Having lunch with him is a nightmare because he is constantly having ideas and he'll write on anything, menus, cloth napkins, tablecloths, his sleeve.

"I read him the riot act this morning. There's a clause in the contract that he thinks isn't legally binding but we can, and Beth *will*, take this project out of his hands if she feels our reputation is at stake."

"Maybe you should suggest that to her."

"No, because then I'd lose my first ever assignment with Excalibur. I can handle him. I should've known he'd want me to be the guinea pig. I'm not one of his people. His wife, CeeCee, even volunteered to do it, she was quite miffed when he said no."

"When will this start?"

"Soon. His forecasts say rain and lots of it starting Wednesday afternoon. The barge carrying the house arrived at Portsmouth harbor yesterday morning. People are working on the cavity wall as we speak, and then it'll go on a truck heading for the site. They'll crane it into position."

"His weather does seem to be spot on."

"That's down to CeeCee. Long before she became Mrs. Sullivan she was 'the weatherbabe' on 'Dave', that TV channel for guys. She's a qualified meteorologist."

"How useful." Caroline raises the cup to her lips, remembers the lack of milk, and sets it back down again. "Apart from that, anything else we need to address. No more phantom Domino sightings?"

I want to say *'she's no phantom, she's back, she's reformed.'* I stop myself because I'm projecting my ideas onto her, especially the reformed part.

Caroline only has my secondhand account of Dominque La Fleur (to use her full pseudonym) and viewed that way some of Domino's actions were pretty calculating. You might even say cold-blooded. Two years ago Caroline tried to convince me that Domino's fate was a direct result of the criminal company she kept. As I mentioned before, there was a lot of shouting from my side of the desk whenever the subject was raised. I don't want to start that up again.

"No," I lie.

"Good, I was thinking we might need another hour." Caroline says, a little archly, for her.

The session ends with me suggesting that she buy a mini fridge for her office and keep it stocked with milk.

Leaving, I feel a little silly doing it, but I let my gaze track up and down the empty street.

Halfway up the steps to the Albert Hall, I hear Gav's voice and there he is standing at the top. As I reach him he picks me up and swings me around. "Hello gorgeous," he says, pulling me close.

"How did you find me?"

"It's Tuesday," he replies. "Therapy day."

I don't bother asking how he knows that. Maybe now is the time for a serious chat. "Look, I've been thinking, about the wedding." I watch a cloud scud across the sun and a similar one cross his face.

"Cold feet, Nik?"

We sit down on the steps.

"No." I try and put my thoughts into some kind of order. "First of all, we can't start planning anything until we've told my parents and Paddy."

"Planning?" Gav gives me the 'I'm going for a root canal but I can handle it' look. "A full on white wedding it is then," he says.

"Stop it," I say. "You know I don't want that. What's the point of chucking a load of money around just to show everyone how much we love each other? Let's just do it on the quiet."

"Vegas at the end of the month suit you?"

"End of the month suits me, not sure about Vegas."

His fingers meet at the nape of my neck. Unclasping the necklace, he lifts it clear, drops the ring into his palm, the necklace slides into his pocket.

"We'll talk to Paddy, soon as this seminar is done. I don't think it'll be any shock to him." Gav slides the ring back onto my finger. "Matt's comment was 'what took you so bloody long, you idiot'."

"I've always liked Matt," I say, grinning.

The new phone rings in my pocket. I haven't even tried to reset my complicated system of ring tones so I'm playing phone roulette. At least they let me keep my number this time.

"Hello?"

"Nikki? Domino. Listen I've got you in for the book launch tonight."

"You have? That's great!"

"I'll pick you up around six; it's black tie, mobiles off, cameras are forbidden, open bar."

"My kind of party."

"If you want a laugh, head over to the O2. Me and the boyfriend are leading the press a merry little dance. I'm sure we'll be on the lunchtime news."

"I wish I could," I say. "I'm looking forward to tonight though."

"I guess you have plans for tonight." Gav says.

"Are you done with the seminar?"

"No, we just had an unexpected break. One of the instructors had to deal with a personal issue and they've cancelled this morning's session. We reconvene after lunch." He checks his watch, "I'd better be getting back."

I stand when he does.

"You and Paddy getting along?"

"He's dropped in on me a couple of times, no drama."

"Good."

Gav's kiss makes my toes tingle all the way down into the tube.

CHAPTER 6

I give up my seat to a tired looking lady my mum's age and strap-hang all the way to Victoria. The DLR is busier. I take the front carriage, nodding to the DLR employee opposite. These trains are driverless so you can sit right at the front and just tune out as the familiar scenery of Docklands rises before you. The flat is a convenient few minutes' walk away from the station. Avalon's headquarters a quick quarter of a mile the other way.

I tap out, and while there's no queue at the machine, I refill the thirsty Oyster card, with the added bonus of letting the station concourse empty. A quick nod to the doorman of our building and I'm off to the third floor. I key open the door of the flat and flip the lights on. Paddy's been in. A cereal-encrusted dish sits on top of a magazine with the University of London logo in the corner. Another reason I'm glad we live three floors up; if we were on the ground floor I might walk in and find Paddy's BMW in the front room in all its oily glory. The glossy 'zine format strikes me as a bit old-fashioned. The topics range from an article on student gambling, tips on moving from halls into a flat share situation, "Adderall: Study Hall

Miracle Or Brain Cell Killer?", "Party ON, Party Hotspots in the Capital," and "Your Major sucks, now what: Tips on Changing Courses mid stream." The cover shows a UofL student with lab coat and protective glasses swishing something around in a beaker. I drop it back on the table.

Pulling up iTunes I set it to 'shuffle' while I hang up my coat, put my suit on the to-be-dry-cleaned pile, and take a shower. Post shower I take the dark crimson dress I bought during the latest fashion week out of my wardrobe. Full war paint tonight, but I won't put the dress on yet as I don't want to spill anything down myself. Even water could cause a stain on the taffeta silk. I'm at the age where I can still walk around in my skimpies and not have to avoid the mirror. I put out the crimson clutch I snapped up at Portobello market, place my phone on top with my driver's license, keys and four twenties in case I have to get a taxi back. The dress will stay hung up by the door until 5:30. Domino's not picking me up until 6:00. I've got plenty of time.

The buzzer goes.

"Hello?"

"Nikki, I've got a car and driver down here for you," says the doorman.

Crap, she's early.

"I'll be right down." My hand reaches for the dress. I slip it over my head and seat the arms, then realize that without Gav's help I can only get the zip halfway up. "Damn!"

"Come on, Nikki." Domino's voice comes over the intercom, sounding amused.

"I'll be there in a minute," I tell her, checking my teeth for lipstick.

I take the lift and from three to ground, using a combination of the mirrored wall and almost dislocating my shoulder, I get the zip done up. The camera is pointing at me the whole time. One day I'm sure my antics will end up on YouTube. The doorman has a smirk on his face as I exit the lift and, with as much dignity as I can summon up wearing three-inch heels, strut out to the car with Domino.

The driver sees us coming, runs around and sweeps the rear door open. I follow Domino in, planting my bum on the seat, keeping my knees together as I swivel inside, the door slams shut and we're off.

"Mary is really excited about tonight," Domino says as I try not to stare at her arms, which do not have a trace of scaring on them.

"I have a great makeup artist. The clinic recommended her. She's the Cinderella of scars, makes them disappear for the night."

Her eyes zoom straight to the ring.

"This chapter and verse conversation we are going to have is getting more interesting by the minute," she says.

"Are we actually going to see Mary tonight?" I ask.

Just this afternoon the press trotted out their ideas of who Mary really is and the group of paparazzi outside the venue will be thicker than an Atlantic fog bank.

"Oh she'll be dropping in," Domino says with a grin. "Are you on Facebook or Twitter?"

"Not really," I say, "I have a Facebook profile, courtesy of Avalon but I hardly ever use it."

"We're really into social media. A single tweet can send a crowd of people wherever we want them and sometimes we can hang out with them."

"Mary actually does that? The whole hide-in-plain-sight thing?"

"Of course. I think she gets a kick out of the mystique that surrounds her."

The car turns towards the Tower of London. For a couple of seconds I speculate, can you rent the Tower?

"This isn't the venue," Domino says, reading my thoughts again. "We're just picking up my boyfriend and checking to see if my ruse is working."

Again with the boyfriend.

"Anyone I know?"

"I did meet him in Storr Downs..."

She leaves the sentence hanging.

"Won't be a tick, hold us here," she says to the driver as she slips on a well-cut long coat that hides her party dress. I crane my neck to follow her. She crosses directly to a group of about ten men and women, checks the time and hands over some shiny looking tickets. A flash of movement catches my eye and I see the first of the paparazzi lurking behind a pillar further down, snapping pictures. More paps converge on the group, who are doing a great job of ignoring them. Domino slips away, presumably to fetch her boyfriend, but she returns alone.

"Didn't you forget someone?"

"Oh, he'll be along in a minute."

"I take it the ruse is working?"

Domino smiles and rubs her hands together, "As long as our people get onto the ferry without the press getting too close it should work."

"I like the golden tickets."

"That was my idea, something shiny to distract the magpie paparazzi."

"You're sending them where?"

"Down to Greenwich. A friend of Mary's is having a very hush hush engagement party. Our decoys had a meet and greet with Mary this morning and they're on the guest list for the Greenwich party. So they get a double scoop. If the press try and find out whose party it is, they'll be told that the event is private and security will keep them locked out."

"And they'll draw the obvious conclusion that they've found the Snowfire event."

"You catch on quick. I've always liked that about you," Domino says with a wink. "Ah, here he comes."

"Stark?" My mouth drops open.

Domino seems pleased with the effect her revelation is having. Stark looks more like a businessman on his way home from a raft of meetings than the forensics genius whose unorthodox methods range from abseiling off a church tower (almost impaling himself on a metal spike in the process), to a clever device that located normally invisible blood evidence in broad daylight. He's carrying a smart briefcase, which probably contains sandwiches or some climbing rope or maybe both.

"Surprise!" Domino grins, hops out of the car and gives Stark a passionate kiss. I watch through the smoked glass, eventually having to avert my eyes, not because seeing Stark kiss Domino is uncomfortable, but because public displays of affection always feel a bit cringe to me.

When he follows Domino into the back, it's clear that he wasn't in on this.

"Nikki?"

"Stark, meet your plus one."

"But you're my plus one Mina, no offense Nikki."

I indicate that none is taken.

"It's perfect d'you see?" Domino says. "You two can catch up, while I check the final arrangements and then the night is ours." She pushes a button and a bottle of champagne rises from the console along with glasses. Domino expertly twists off the metal and pops the cork; she dishes out the champagne.

"To a wonderful night!" she toasts, and we toast her back.

London's streets have a party atmosphere, pavements heaving with pub and club goers, painted brown by the sodium lights. I sip my champagne. Just peeking above the buildings behind us is the top of the millennium wheel, and then we make a left turn.

"No way!" I say, as the car crawls forward. Looming in front of us is Battersea power station. I came here as a kid, on a heavily regulated school trip, before the health and safety Nazis closed the place down.

Not much information went into my ten year old brain, but I remember it was like being inside a Cathedral, one savaged by some prehistoric big cat that left deep groves in the walls of the place. The four giant white chimneys sprout from each corner of the building. This place *can* be rented, there is a very exclusive nightclub called the Boiler Room deep inside the turbine hall. I know this because a client was looking at hiring the venue for a birthday party a few years ago but the dates she wanted clashed with some kind of company product launch so we never moved forward.

Domino gets out of the car with Stark and me trailing in her wake. We walk into the mouth of a long white tent tunnel. Domino whisks us past security just inside the entrance. With her around we're being treated like VIPs but both Stark and I have to sign in as our invites and driver's licenses are carefully scrutinized.

Stark drops back a little and out of Domino's earshot says, "I can't help feeling I'm walking down to inspect a crime scene. Mina's put so much effort into making this go with a bang, I'd never say that to her."

That's the second time he's called her Mina.

And just like that we're inside. Calling it a tent would be like calling a Rottweiler a handbag dog. Steel ribs, a hybrid of plexiglass and fabric, big enough to have sofas and love seats lining the walls, a massive bar and DJ booth set up in the middle. Dotting the floor are small circular tables at the perfect height to lean against. In the pictures I've seen of this place there is a transparent wall at one end. Tonight that is absent. Instead, in front of the missing wall sits a large dais, a book cover projected onto the bricks behind it.

I COULD TELL YOU BUT THEN I'D HAVE TO KILL YOU.

When I see what the title is I start laughing. When I asked Domino the title of Mary's new book she'd actually told me.

Stark wanders off to check out the sound system.

Domino raises her glass and we have more champagne.

"I have to ask, before the bubbles go straight to my brain, Mina?"

"Mina St Clare. I was always going to change my name," Domino says, "I didn't want to be Sandy anymore. Mino isn't exactly sexy. It makes me think of fish."

"Domina?" I suggest.

"No, it's much too easy to stick 'trix' on the end."

"Domina-trix, oops, yes that wouldn't work. Mina it is."

The invitation was very specific about mobile phones; they stay powered off and out of sight, no exceptions. We walk past several signs reminding guests of that fact. Domino, I mean Mina waves at the guy in the DJ booth and he waves back.

The volume of the music starts to climb, a thudding bass beat that makes the bubbles in my champagne hop around.

"Rats," Domino/Mina says, consulting a small jeweled wristwatch, "I have to go and meet Mary. I'll catch up to you later."

For a fraction of a second I think about following her, but turn and walk in the opposite direction. The floor is starting to fill. Holding my purse in one hand I avoid more champagne, going for the sparkling pear instead. The first one of these parties I attended I felt so out of my depth I literally hugged the wall. Now, I cast my smile around the room like a fishing net and land Sully's wife CeeCee. She steams across the room, her usual floaty, gypsy look abandoned in favour of a sea foam green corseted creation.

"Nikki!" She hails me, her weathergirl smile warming the room. "What a fabulous surprise." CeeCee plants two smackers on both my cheeks, no air kisses for our CeeCee. She reminds me of Patsy from *Ab Fab*, minus the Stoli-Bolli. "See them," she points at a group over in the corner, "Indiegogoers. Miss Mary raffled off the chance to be here and this lot are the lucky investors. God look at their tiny, minuscule clutches. My iPhone is bigger than that!"

"We're all carrying invitations," I say, "but theirs must be folded over and over. Imagine the strain on the plastic or metal evening bag clasps. It's like carrying around a paper hand grenade."

CeeCee gives a full-bodied laugh that draws quite a few glances our way.

"And where did you get that?" CeeCee's staring at my hand. "Are you engaged?"

"Yep."

"Congratulations Nikki! Sully'll never notice, unless you want him to know. Speaking of Sully, he'll be here in a mo," CeeCee says as she grabs another drink from the tray of a passing waiter. "He had to check on Justin."

"Justin?"

CeeCee's face darkens.

"Sully's nephew, trouble with a capital T that one." CeeCee's face stays in her 'overcast, good chance of showers' mode. "The only thing Sully and I disagreed on, was adopting that little toad." She might've said 'turd.' "As far as I'm concerned Sully shouldn't have to be responsible for his sister marrying an idiot. Sully keeps on sending Justin to boarding schools and he keeps getting kicked out of them.

"So this time we decided to send him as far away as possible. He always wanted to study in America and there's no doubt he does have some of the Sullivan talent. Sully always says that Justin can work the same magic with pixels as Picasso did with paint."

CeeCee slurs her words a little and I'm thinking that the champagne she's drinking isn't her first one of the night.

As someone used to dealing with the press she's friendly, but guarded about her private life. For instance I didn't know Sully *had* a nephew until a few moments ago. I like CeeCee and I don't want to mess up our friendship with personal bombshells; except the way she's drowning her sorrows she may not remember that she told me anything.

"Where did you send him?" I ask, giving her the perfect chance to pack the conversation away. She doesn't take it.

"We got Justin into a residential graphic design program at Arizona State University and after almost a year he seemed to have settled down, happy, 'being one of the gods of the digital universe' as he so humbly puts it."

"Why did they kick him out?"

"Gross misuse of school property, whatever that means. El Principale stuck him on the first flight back from the States a couple of weeks back and only called us an hour before the plane was due to land. We've got Justin grounded until we work out what he did and what to do with him. Sully's got a contact at the U of L."

"That's where Paddy is."

"What's he studying again?"

"Chemistry and Economics," I say, raising my voice over the gentle flop-flop sound of a distant helicopter.

"Putting Justin anywhere near a Bunsen burner would be a terrible idea."

"Oh come on," I say, "What's he going to do, burn the place down?"

"Justin was a very disturbed little boy," CeeCee says. "The things he did." A shudder runs through her and she moves away from me; before I can ask her any more questions, which, as Gav would tell her is the worst thing she could've done.

When a client baits a verbal hook, gets me to bite and then doesn't reel me in, I'll assume that they have something to hide. I will then quietly ferret out that something because, in my experience, lottery winners are not always angels.

Justin goes in my 'Problem?' file for now.

CHAPTER 7

That helicopter is getting closer.

It's London; we get helicopters crisscrossing the capital all the time. But this one is bigger, the wing beats deeper; like the difference between a fly and a bumblebee. Soon we're all massed at the open end of the building, looking up. It's a warm night for a change and I'm reminded of the studies that show that one person looking up will be joined by others because they think there is something worth seeing. The helicopter hovers directly overhead now. A rope snakes down, a black clad figure attached to it.

"Ooohh," a woman behind me who sounds like Janet Street Porter, (actually it might be Mizz Street Porter) gasps, "It's like the milk tray ad." Whatever that is. Mum would know. I make a mental note to ask her.

A cargo net containing a large crate follows the figure out. As the net lowers, out of the corner of my eye, I catch the slightest movement at the edge of the roofline. The space around the stand clears because; well it would be like standing under a baby grand if that rope snapped...

"Did you see that?" I cup my hand to direct my words into CeeCee's ear. Even from its high hover the Westland is drowning out any chance of casual conversation.

"See what?"

"Up there on the roof?"

Just as the crate settles and its escort unclips the net, the chopper lifts up and away as more ropes rain down. That confuses me for a minute until I realize that these new commandos were on the roof waiting to come in, carefully cued.

Dry ice obscures the scene for a moment. "Ladies and Gentlemen, honoured guests, welcome," a woman's voice, overlaid with a slight electronic buzz hushes the crowd. "I am Mary Snowfire, thank you for coming tonight!" As the artificial smoke clears, Mary is revealed as one of the commandos, her jumpsuit clings to every curve and unlike her male counterparts her zip is low enough to flash some cleavage. She takes a crowbar that was either on the stand or attached to the crate and levers the lid off.

"Please, step up and take the book nearest you. They are all personalized. Mingle, talk to your fellow guests and find out who has your book. Who knows, it could be the start of a fruitful friendship. Enjoy the party!

"Oh, one last thing, please give a generous round of applause for our Indiegogo backers. Without you and millions of others like you, I wouldn't be standing here. You are truly wonderful people. Come up to the front, please!"

The group CeeCee pointed out earlier walks up to the makeshift stage, some beetroot red, others enjoying their moment of fame. Snowfire hugs each of them and poses for a group photograph. Stray blonde hairs peek out from her knit cap; her green eyes sparkle from behind a mask that obscures her cheekbones. The group is the first to take books from the box.

We all file up to take our turn; CeeCee joins a newly arrived Sully. The PA system announces that those who want to dance the night away should head over to the dance floor where DJ Lucky will be on the decks.

In the hubbub people introduce themselves, using the name written in their book. I lose track of Mary. She was with a group of the SAS types and they swallow her up. Clever girl, skipping the meet and greet, and she is a clever girl, because I know who Mary Snowfire is now.

I don't know why I didn't tip to it before. It all makes sense, Dubai, the spy stuff that seemed so familiar, the death, the heroine's fate, because 90 percent of it is true.

One of the five star reviews I read said it had the whiff of authenticity about it. If they only knew. Mary Snowfire is Mina!

Confirming my 'brilliant' deduction Mary vanishes through a door on the left and moments later Mina emerges. I mentally add quick-change artiste to her skills. I don't want to challenge Mina in front of all these people. I'll keep her secret. I want her to trust me.

Stark goes over to Mina carrying a book, presumably his copy. He sets the book and his drink down on the nearest table and they head for the dance floor. Stark is quite the mover as he twirls Mina across the floor. Other partygoers crowd around to watch.

Mina and Stark run off the dance floor, laughing and out of breath. Stark goes off to get us some more drinks. Mina stretches like a cat.

"Who is the blonde in the sea foam bodice?"

"CeeCee Sullivan. Why?"

"She's familiar, I've seen her somewhere, is she on TV?"

"She was, but not for years now."

"It'll come to me." Mina gnaws the pad of her thumb. "Got it!" she snaps her fingers. "She's the dead spit of some reality show boss I saw in the States, on the web, although the character is a complete bitch. She's married to this mouse of a husband, you never see him, only the back of his head. Mary watches that show religiously. I kind of watch it, but that cow makes enough of an impression to grab my attention. It's like a real life version of The Office. Remind me to send you the subscriber link."

"I'll have to check it out," I say. I don't intend to. I'm just being polite to the hostess. The DJ changes the subject for me. "These mixes are great." I tell Mina.

"I went clubbing in Amsterdam and there he was. I hopped on his website, downloaded the latest mix and once Mary listened to it she jumped on the phone and called him herself.

"Mary gave him a list of her favourite artists and soundtracks and he's working within that. When are you going to Holland next?"

The abrupt switch doesn't throw me.

"Not for a few weeks, until this test is over and done."

"Shame. Mary has me over there researching for her next book. I was thinking dinner and a night at the Casino in Scheveningen.

"Any hints as to what it's about?"

"A shady tree and a lovely lady called Tiffany." Domino rhymes in a singsong slightly slurred voice. I wonder if she just gave me the next title.

"Oooohhh, Dead Maus, I love this one." Mina makes a bee-line for the dance floor to dance to 'Sophie Needs a Ladder'. I used the app on my phone to find out what this was when I heard it on Radio 1 last week. As far as I can tell none of the words in the title are in the lyrics but it is so catchy.

Stark comes back to the table expertly cupping three champagne flutes to his chest and sets them down. "I'm a lager man myself," he shouts across to me. Raising his glass, "When in Rome."

I notice him straining to see where Mina is. I point her out.

"Don't want her exerting herself too much." Stark comes around to my side of the table, so he doesn't have to yell. "She still tires easily, as I'm sure you know."

I simply smile and rub the base of my glass with my fingertip and let him talk.

"I was fascinated by Mina the first time I saw her," Stark says, still keeping a watchful eye on her. "It was the day after Thomas Ogilvy got blown up. You and Martha were still in hospital and I was poking around at the site, trying to get a handle on what kind of explosives sent that creep Ogilvy to meet his maker. There were a pack of foreign reporters yelling questions from the other side of the police cordon we'd had to set up, and there she was, wandering in the rubble."

I don't ask how she got past the police cordon. Mina has her ways.

Stark continues, "It was so hot that my protective suit was stuck to my back and my eyes were pricking from all the sweat that kept running into them. Mina looked cool as a cucumber, even with her sleeves rolled down to her wrists. Every now and then she would unclip the water bottle from her belt and soak the blue bandana loosely knotted around her neck. Of course I thought she was attached to some other part of the investigation and my job was to pinpoint the epicenter of the explosion. Even so, I kept finding excuses to look in her direction."

"Did you find it? The epicenter I mean?" I keep the question casual because if he did, he might have taken samples of the explosive and the 'keep Paddy out of jail' club might be getting another member.

"I never got the chance," Stark says. "Internal affairs showed up at that point and hauled me off the site. The only thing I succeeded in getting that day was an indefinite suspension, pending the outcome of their inquiry."

"I'm sorry you got suspended." I place my hand on his arm. "How did Mina hear about it? Did she see you get booted from the site?"

"No, she took off because she thought she'd been rumbled. She caught up to me later in the pub. I'd decided to celebrate my suspension by getting royally drunk. The landlord put me over in a corner and kept the drinks coming. I was well into my fifth pint when Mina came over. She sat talking to me for hours, plied me with coffee, and got me sober. She even smuggled me into her rented room at the Swan overnight.

"The next morning we went for a long, long walk, up onto the South Downs and we talked a lot more. Long story short she offered me a consulting job with the mysterious Mary Snowfire, to 'tide me over' as she put it.

"Mina and I were slowly getting to know one another and then one night, I get a text. Something along the lines of 'can't sleep can I come over?' of course I said 'yes'. Our first encounter was more like a game of Battleship, because she wouldn't come out of the bathroom until I'd turned all the lights out so I couldn't exactly see which parts of her I had hold of. I could feel the scarring on her arms and jumped to the conclusion that she'd recently kicked a drug habit.

"It continued like that. Mina would text me, we'd spend the night together and when I woke up, sometimes in the early hours, she'd be gone."

"Late night booty calls," I toast him, "Go Stark!"

He flushes, "I still couldn't shake the feeling that she didn't want to be seen with me in public."

"You're not exactly a troll you know." I point out.

"Then one night I told Mina that she was driving me crazy. I didn't just want to *feel* her. I wanted to *see* her. She grabbed her clothes and ran out of the door. I really thought I'd blown it. She came back a couple of hours later, sat down on the living room floor with me and rolled up her sleeves. I saw that I'd been wrong; these weren't a former junkie's train tracks at all."

"I'm not familiar with a junkie's anatomy."

"If you look at an addict's arms, they look like a tube map with a main line of big needle marks, like major stations on the Jubilee line. Mina told me that the IV's they put in her at that fancy clinic kept blowing her veins, and the scarring was in fist-like clumps from where the blood pooled under the skin."

"Ew."

"Anyway, she sat there and told me everything; about the coma, the movement therapy while she was unconscious, the control freak boyfriend. Then her gradual recovery, running up and down those Swiss hillsides to boost her stamina and increase her muscle mass. How sometimes she had to be carried down piggyback style by her physiotherapist because her muscles had given out."

This is more than she's told me so far, but then I'm not sleeping with her.

"She never talks about what put her in a coma," Stark says, his eyes won't meet mine, "But having some experience of your track record I suspect that you are mixed up in there somewhere."

"When we met, Mina was a location scout for a film project. She tried to steal the land that my client, James Farmer, ended up buying."

"How did she get hurt?"

"She got mixed up in, well something bad."

"You were there?"

"Not when it happened. She saved a lot of people's lives, including mine."

"Nikki, I've heard of people living charmed lives but never met one."

"You still haven't," I say, "My job puts me in tricky situations sometimes. I have to do my best to keep control. I don't always succeed. I make assumptions, mistakes. Sometimes I get in over my head and sometimes people I care about get hurt. I've never chosen my friends on the basis that they might or might not get me into trouble."

"There is no fate but what we make."

"Tennyson?"

"John Connor, T2 Judgment Day," Stark says, "actually I'm paraphrasing, the less catchy version is 'there's no fate but what we make for ourselves.'"

Mina skips up to us, eyes shining, looking much more like her old self.

"What have you two got your heads together over?"

"We were swapping pop culture references," Stark says. "C'mon ladies show me your moves."

The party starts to wind down around one or two in the morning. As Mina's car takes her and Stark home I have just enough smarts left to operate the call button on the lift, get into the apartment and face plant onto the bed.

CHAPTER 8

Wednesday
Normal service will be resumed shortly.
***
Thursday morning

The promised rain rolled in early, for London. The further away from the city we get the more it eases off. Gav navigates the first wave of commuters. His seminar wrapped up last night and this morning he presented me with a freshly constructed bacon sarnie and the offer of being my personal chauffeur. I prefer that kind of wake-up call.

The journey down is devoid of crashes, speeding police vehicles or lane closures and we get to the outskirts of Winnersh around half past nine. Gav parks the Landy in the same spot as I did less than a week ago. A few changes have taken place, for a start the muddy path has been covered by wooden boards and the warning signs have been augmented by a combination padlock and rolls of barbed wire along the tops of the fences. We're parked next to a dark green van with Eco Builders stenciled down the side.

"Well this sucks," Gav says, hefting his army issue rucksack onto both shoulders. It contains two sets of spare clean clothes, waterproofs, my laptop and assorted cables, Mary's new book, my wash kit and a large fluffy towel. "I just get back and off you go."

"It's only for a week," I counter, "*yous* and Paddy can lay waste to virtual armies every night."

Gavin snorts with laughter, "Do I use it that much?"

"When you're around Paddy you do."

"That reminds me, you said you two got on alright?"

"Yes."

"I wonder what's up with him. He called me as I was getting back to the flat, wants to have a man-to-man chat."

"Search me," I say.

I carry the waders and follow Gavin along the duckboards.

"Gav, there *is* something you should know. Domino's back."

He stops dead and I have to do some fancy footwork to not smack into him.

"I know how you feel about her, but she's got a legitimate job she's changed her name to Mina St Clare, she's…"

"Don't say 'reformed'." Gav's voice is controlled; the spark of anger is there tamped down. Now I have to do some verbal fancy footwork to keep him from exploding. Gav worked with and liked Mina's brother, Sebastian, and he lays the blame for his death squarely at the door of the now deceased Connor Ravenwood's camp. Because Mina was working for him at the time, Gav thinks Mina got Sebastian killed.

"You know I'm a good judge of character, right?"

"Usually," he concedes through gritted teeth. We've reached the corner and as we round it a little chap, wearing a waterproof jacket miles too big for him, stands shifting his weight from one leg to the other.

"Hello?" he calls out before stifling a sneeze as he closes the gap between us.

"Look I don't want us to fall out over this," I say to Gav. "Just give her a chance, could you? If you two don't get on I'm not going to force the issue. She and I will continue to be friends whatever you say."

"Thanks for clearing that up," he says just as the walking waterproof joins us.

"I'm Philip from Eco Builders. Can I see some ID please?" I hand over my license and for good measure the photo ID that gets me in and out of Sully's offices. As he completes his inspection of both IDs the first fat splash of rain smacks the back of my hand.

"Is Harry around?" I ask as another raindrop slaps Philip's cheek. Sully told me to ask for Harry Eco, he described him as a 'long drink of water.' Philip is more of a shot glass. Philip locks eyes with Gavin over my shoulder.

"Miss Doyle, er," he fumbles in his trouser pocket and produces a frayed leather wallet, "I'm Philip Eco, Harry's brother." His driver's license confirms this.

"I'm out of business cards at the moment. Here, have one of Harry's." He reaches into the waterproof, which, now I'm closer, shows the initials H.E embroidered onto the breast pocket. "Harry won't be joining us today, I'm afraid. He's gone on a much-needed break. I don't make a habit of helping myself to my brother's things, especially clothes, they don't really fit me." He laughs and waits to see if Gav and I join in. From inside the waterproof he produces a shiny case and proffers a card.

My business cards are just that, cards. Harry Eco's is a small rectangle of transparent plastic with his name, a digitized photo of him looking business-like and his contact details, all 3D printed into the plastic. His face is thinner than his brother's, graying hair and some serious octagonal seventies bifocals. I have card envy.

Philip turns to lead the way towards the amphibious house.

"Harry's on holiday but the last thing he did before leaving was monitor the insulation process. We're very hands on here at Eco."

"Glad to hear it." Behind me Gav shrugs the rucksack from his shoulders and lets it drop about a foot to the ground. Luckily my laptop isn't on the bottom.

"I'm heading back," he says, "before this gets too bad."

The rain is falling faster now.

"Don't you want to see the house?"

"Nah," he pulls his hood up and hunches his shoulders. "Stay in touch and try not to get washed away." I give him a quick peck on the cheek and then he's marching back towards the Landy. I half drag, half carry the rucksack along the boards and get my first glimpse of the amphi house. A trench surrounds it. I know from the briefings with the team at Delft that the thick concrete pad is what makes it float, displacing water. Green canvas covers the inflatable skirts but other than that it looks like a normal house, excepting the flagpoles at each corner.

Phillip Eco unlocks the front door and ushers me inside, talking the whole time.

"Our company is hoping to get a bid in to build the next five at least. Mrs. Sullivan and her husband are very big on environmental issues. We already have a design on the drawing board. We call it the Eco house."

"Why didn't you build this one?"

"The time scale was impossible to meet." He rubs his nose and I can't help thinking of a hamster.

"I have a couple of questions."

"Of course, of course, can you sign the papers while we talk?" Eco produces a stack of printed sheets.

"I hope these are recycled," I joke, taking the proffered pen.

"Of course," Eco says, deadly serious.

"While I'm signing my life away, I have a security question."

"I'll answer it if I can."

"Barbed wire and padlocks won't stop a curious passer-by from coming onto the site. They can climb right under the fence."

"Our workers installed sheets of plexi around the whole site, that should funnel the flood water where we want it and keep people out."

"Where's the nearest supermarket?"

"You won't need that yet. Mrs. Sullivan made sure we provisioned the house for you. No cooker, but you have a kettle and a microwave." We've reached the kitchen. "Plates and cups are in here, cutlery there. Power, water, etcetera all hooked up, table in the dining room, sofa bed. The upstairs is pretty empty I'm afraid."

"No curtains?"

"Bathroom has blinds you can pull but you aren't exactly overlooked here are you?"

I finish signing, watching Eco stuff the papers into a plastic folder; the folder goes into a pocket inside his waterproof.

"Oh, almost forgot," he says, opening a cupboard. "The monitoring equipment is all up and running. The Sullivan's can keep a weather eye on everything going on down here," he sniggers at his pun. When I don't join in he points to the green light pulsing softly. "We're working on the traffic light principle."

I don't need the lecture and I want to have a nose around without this little Eco dogging my every move.

"I know," I interrupt him, "Green is dry, amber is 6 to 10 inches of precip, red is 10 and above. Before the house goes off grid a warning hooter starts going off."

"I suppose I'll leave you to it then. Call if you have any structural issues. These Dutch builders…" he leaves the sentence unfinished.

"Are the best in the world," I say to the empty house.

Damn I forgot to ask him about Wi-Fi. I fill the kettle and whilst it is boiling, riffle through the cupboards. All the goods come from Sainsburys according to the receipt caught inside one of the boxes. CeeCee loves Yorkshire tea, which requires more milk than my usual PG Tips. I haul the rucksack into the front room and perch myself and the laptop on the sofa bed. Not only is there Wi-Fi, it is a good strong signal. I wonder if one of the pylons doubles as an antenna.

CHAPTER 9

The rain comes down in sheets. I dig into my stash of clothes and slide the thick fisherman's jumper (Gav's) over my head, balance the laptop on my thighs and start looking through my email. Nothing important, a few policy emails from Beth, some for the junk folder and one from Mina.

Her cheery style comes through, even electronically.

Nik, here's the link I promised you. Settle in, and don't have anything hot in your hands.

Mina

Probably, I think to myself because I'll want to throw it at the screen. I should at least look at the link.

Before I do, I check the sensors, still green. I click on the link. I was expecting YouTube but this is a separate channel. A disclaimer begins rolling up the screen.

Welcome to Finger on the Pulse. I am Finger, your webmaster. Watch at your own risk, if you are easily offended, have a problem with crude language or have no sense of humour log off now. The first hit is free, watch until your eyes glaze over but after that the subscriber link will bug you to distraction.

Since I don't have a problem with any of that, I click 'play'.

By the time an insistent beeping brings me back, it's dark outside and hours have gone by. Finger (whoever he/she is) is a genius!, a stand-up comic's sense of timing, political acumen and a wicked, bordering on malicious sense of humour. If Robot Chicken and Spitting Image had relations, Finger on the Pulse would be the result. Each webcast is up to twenty minutes long. There are only two people. She faces the camera. All you see of him is the back of his head. I can see why Domino thought the actress and CeeCee look alike. Facially they do, but this woman has a giant mole to the left of her nose and blue/black shiny hair. Her dialogue, delivered in a New York accent thick enough to slice is so near the knuckle that I can't help wincing whilst I'm laughing my socks off.

These are bang up to date. Her monologue about US congress and sexual congress is one of the funniest things I've heard. At the bottom of the screen is the number of subscribers, it is in the tens of thousands and keeps ticking up. As the actors say their lines, how she manages to keep a straight face I don't know. Nothing is safe: British politics, the upcoming London Olympics (where she's looking into becoming Canadian in 2012), America's freedom spreaders, gay marriage, Wimbledon, guns, Taylor Swift, Star Wars, Strictly, and strangely '2001, A Space Odyssey'. You name it Finger spoofs it, complete with matching backgrounds and costumes for his (or her) pair of digital actors. The current one has the woman as a contestant on QI (he's on the team but facing the wall) but the beeping meant I had to pause it.

The sudden silence followed by another round of beeping makes it sound all the more urgent. The light is pulsing from green to orange. I nip outside. The puddles of water have formed glimmer like portals to other worlds in the moonlight, a new moon, I notice. The ruin next door stinks of damp and mould. Once inside again, I check all of the walls for signs of any water coming in and it all seems airtight.

My stomach roars. When it comes to choosing between 'Finger on the Pulse' or food, I'm not daft. A quick call to Gav as the microwave heats up some Sainsbury's baked beans and I search for the toaster.

"Evening Nik," he says, he sounds normal so I'm hoping that this morning's spat has passed. "How's life on Sullivan's ark?"

"I hate to say it but Sully was right on the money with this site, I'm not over ten inches yet but if the precip keeps up, tomorrow we could be."

"Well don't float away," he says, just as the final cupboard opened yields a toaster. "I had that chat with Paddy."

"Everything OK?"

"Some kid, one of the freshers offered him the chance to put his chemistry skills to some very dodgy uses. Paddy smacked the kid in the mouth, which I don't feel brilliant about. Paddy told me that he'd told the kid I was with the drugs squad. He wanted to make sure that I'd back him up if the kid went to his parents."

"Way to go, Paddy!" I say.

"Don't encourage him! He's a student not an enforcer."

"But you're proud of him. Right?" Silence. "Gav?"

"Yeah, but don't tell him I said that, I'm supposed to be pissed off that he gave the kid a fat lip."

"Noted."

"By the way I'm still deciding what to do about Domino. I haven't forgotten. And you sprang it on me when you knew I couldn't blow my top."

"I did."

"Minx."

"I am."

"Night Nik, dream of me."

With a stomach placated by beans on toast, I go back to the laptop. It is hibernating, I wake it up and click on the continue button. A message pops up.

You've had your free shot, if you want access to all of my shows from the beginning click on the link below and hand over ten measly quid. Yes just ten quid gets you this channel 24 hours a day <u>forever</u> if you choose to rot your eyeballs. Otherwise all my content is available on demand (one advert every two minutes). If you don't want to fork over your bank account details, you can pay via PayPal or even iTunes.

Several rough calculations he's making about ten pounds every five to ten minutes.

I'm ashamed to say I clicked the link. Several hours later when my eyeballs feel like they have fur on them I blink my way through the last five minutes of the ghost of Maggie Thatcher giving Boris Johnson advice on how to be the wackiest mayor of London ever and log off.

The sofa bed is easy to pull out. I close the cupboard door so the beeps are muted and wrap a blanket around me. I have no intention of getting into jammies because this is an experiment and if I have to evacuate this place I'll be doing it in warm clothing. The waders are within grabbing distance. The lack of curtains means the full moon is streaming in through the windows.

I do dream, but not of Gav. I'm standing on a windswept beach, seagulls mewing and wheeling above my head. I plod slowly along, seaspray settling on my lips. Ahead of me is a massive lighthouse. I turn my steps towards it. As I approach, instead of shining out to sea, the light pivots down. At every step, every turn the light flashes right into my eyes. I'm struggling with the lighthouse door.

And then I'm awake and there is something flashing in my eyes, a torch? Who would be in here? I locked the door when I came back inside, didn't I? Assuring myself that I did, I curl my fingers around the phone, select the camera and, jack-knifing upright, take a picture of an empty window frame. The flash glares against the glass. No one is there, my only companion, the moon, which is totally in the wrong direction to be shining in my eyes. Suddenly it hits me, something was reflecting from the air vent.

"Sully, you bastard," I mutter to myself, "You don't trust me to do this on my own, you have to watch what's going on. And watching me sleep is creepy!"

Sully has cameras everywhere at his HQ. He even has the things at his house. I guess I shouldn't be surprised.

A couple of problems present themselves. First off it's O dark, god knows what time in the morning and my co-ordination isn't the best when half asleep. Second, the vent is too high up to reach without a ladder. I settle for returning to the sofa bed and turning my back to the camera. I will document and deal with this after a decent breakfast and plenty of black coffee tomorrow morning.

CHAPTER 10

Friday

My phone comes out of night mode at 7 o'clock and wakes me with the 'bong' of incoming email. I have momentary traveler's amnesia. I haven't worked out my location or the fact that I'm not in a hotel, and I forgot to set the heating going. Even with the insulation the Eco Company put in, I'm freezing. I cloak myself in the blanket and set about waking myself up. Multi-tasking, I check the sensors at the same time as cleaning my teeth (which I couldn't be bothered to do last night). The light is now solid amber. I take my coffee and open the front door, prop my back against the lintel and survey the mini flood. As I sip the scalding strong liquid I remember that I was supposed to be finding a ladder from somewhere, for...?

The caffeine suddenly links the synapses and I remember Sully and his Orwellian house surveillance. I stick a couple of ice cubes in the coffee to cool it, swallow the lot, and go hunting for a ladder. The upstairs is echo-y and empty and while I don't find a ladder there is a Kik-Step in the kitchen cupboard, which propped up against the wall means I can photograph the camera. I snap two shots just to be certain I've got it. Still standing on the Kik-Step I check my handiwork; I don't want to send a picture of my thumb. I was expecting a single lens; instead there is a pair, large and octagonal. I instinctively back away from the wall and take the express elevator to the carpet, landing on my coccyx.

"Fire, police or ambulance?" the voice enquires after I've dialed 999.

"Police, there's a dead guy in my wall."

"I'm sorry did you say 'a dead guy in your wall?'

"I did."

"I'm not going to put you through because these University first year's pranks are getting out of hand." Click.

"Are we floating yet?" Sully's first question after he picked up.

"No, not floating,"

"Why did you call then?"

"Harry Eco, he's here, dead, in the wall. He looks just like his business card, except dead."

"Nikki, you're not making sense."

I fumble with the phone, send the photo I just took,

"Bloody hell! Don't call the police, have you called the police?"

"No," he doesn't need to know that I tried.

"Good, I'm on my way. Don't do anything until I get there."

I take my coffee and leave the amphi house, Harry doesn't need the company.

My new phone in it's bright orange case so that I 'won't lose this one' (the apple store guy's little joke) speedials Gav. His sleepy face appears on my screen because my fingers shook when I dialed.

"Morning Nik, did you have sweet dreams?"

"More like nightmares," It all comes out in a rush, not really in the right order.

"Slow down," if he says 'deep breaths' I may scream, but actually, a couple of deep breaths do help. I send him the same pic I sent Sully.

"I'm on my way. Call the police." My screen goes blank.

Now it's just a question of who gets here first. Some more of those deep breaths and I go back inside, put the kettle on and brew mum's cure-all, tea. Whilst I'm waiting for the kettle to boil I take out the phone and study Harry Eco's face.

Fingers of foam reach around from the back of Harry's head, covering his ears and his forehead, crawling up his chin, but they hardened before they reached his mouth. His head is at a slight angle, the glasses pushed forward, floating just above the tip of his nose. Something about the position is familiar but I can't for the life of me work out why.

I don't know how long I stood there before I heard feet pounding across the wooden boards. Gav appears through the still open front door. He must've broken the sound barrier to get here before Sully, and just before the police who once on the scene, send me and Gav packing.

It certainly isn't the first time I've been inside an ambulance, the one in the Winnersh Cinema car park is fully equipped with the usual complement of medical gear, including the space blanket I'm currently wrapped in. Across the way several police cars, a mobile incident room, a fire engine and Paddy's bike, which explains Gav's speedy appearance. Sully's limo occupies several spaces and the man himself is yelling at everyone. He tried to yell at me but Gavin stepped between us and Sully wisely backed off.

But everything falls silent when they bring Harry's body down the path. In between Sully's bouts of yelling we could hear chainsaws extracting Harry from his foamy tomb and as the firemen lay him down, I spot a bit of metal jutting out of the lowest end of the foam.

"That explains how Harry got up to the vent, he'd clambered up a ladder." I keep my voice soft so only Gav can hear me.

"Why didn't he call for help?" Sully wants to know, kneeling beside Harry's cocoon, "I don't know about you but if I was suddenly up to my chest in foam I'd be yelling for help at the top of my lungs."

"I'll head back to town with Gav," I say. That's if you've finished shouting at me."

"He pauses. "I was shouting wasn't I?"

"Yes Sully, shouting at everybody."

"CeeCee's always warning me about my blood pressure," he clamps both hands over his eyes, "Now I have to go back and tell her one of her closest friends is dead." He looks down at Harry again, "He looks so, peaceful."

I'd disagree with that, more like mildly pissed off at something.

"Maybe," Sully continues, "he just stopped breathing, snuffed it at the top of the ladder, maybe his heart gave out."

"Maybe," I suggest, "we should wait for the coroner's report."

CHAPTER 11

We hit the outskirts of London right at rush hour and crawl home. The flat is a Paddy free zone. I sit through several hours of evening news, on several different channels. So far the story hasn't broken, or if it has the Berkshire media outlets are the only ones covering it. I have no doubts it will break because linking Eco to Sully will turn it into a media firestorm. I call up the photo of Harry Eco and sit staring at it until a well-placed cushion bats me on the side of the head.

"I got us a table at Verdi's, c'mon."

Verdi's is a little Italian eatery just off the theatre district. The owner is Joe Green, who is married to Roberta Green, the lottery winner, which is how I know about this place. Roberta and Joe had a fish and chip place in Milton Keynes when Roberta scooped their windfall.

I hooked them up with our in-house estate agent. He found them the restaurant and the house next door. The Greens are that rare breed; a married couple that seem like they were born married. But they do not dress alike. Joe wears denim when he's not in his chef's whites. Roberta wears scrubs in the kitchen (tonight's are turquoise), her ash blonde hair Alice-banded off her face. Roberta keeps a wardrobe of Diane von Furstenberg wrap dresses to wear when she's off duty.

The Greens run the kitchen, out front is Vincenzo who is about as Italian as me. By day he studies tomography and anesthesiology and at night he's front of house and waiter for the Greens. He is also their nephew and Roberta pays his tuition. Verdi's is three courses, salad, a pasta dish and dessert. After that the kitchen closes for the night. It takes the Greens half an hour to clean the kitchen with the help of two giant dishwashers (machines not men). Then Roberta has a couple of girls come in to sanitize while she and Joe come and sit with their guests.

Pudding, if you have room, is fruit pie of the day with gelato from the freezer just outside the kitchen. Fetch it yourself, and paper plates to save on washing up. If you don't leave before ten Joe brings out the wine and lock-ins can go until the early hours. All the Greens ask for their hospitality is a phone reservation and a £25 per person donation to Dr. Barnados, their chosen charity. I celebrated my birthday here last year and now that we're back in London full time, we're in here every other week.

Everything is fine through the effusive hugs from Vinnie, the Caprese salad, the lasagna, and then…

"Happy birthday to you, Happy birthday to you, Happy birthday dear Naomi, Happy birthday to you!"

Roberta wheels out a cake ablaze with candles. The other two couples, Naomi amongst them, stand and clap until, with several big breaths, she blows out the candles. Gav and I clap, and

Roberta brings over two slabs of chocolate cake. As she places them in front of us, her eyes zero in on my hand. She claps her hands together.

"You sneaky devils! Joe-y, Vinnie, champagne!"

Joe pokes his head out of the kitchen, Vinnie from the desk, and we end up in a sort of group hug. With Roberta demanding we get a picture of the event. Champagne flows, the other four diners are dragged into the proceedings. Roberta grabs my phone after I've unlocked it and starts snapping away like a seasoned paparazzo. Joe leans in between us.

"You'd better be eloping or Roberta will become your wedding planner, she loves that sort of thing."

"We're eloping," we say together.

Roberta is skimming back through her shots, narrating as she goes.

"Ooh that's a good one of Vinnie, he's standing up straight for a change."

"He's very photogenic," I agree.

"Pah!" Roberta fumes, "You should see him on the phone." She gestures, "Look at him now." We turn and I can see what she means. Vinnie has the receiver cradled between his shoulder and his cheekbone while he writes a booking into the reservations ledger that occupies most of the desk. "How is that comfortable I ask you? He's supposed to be studying for a medical degree not how to be a contortionist."

"Love." A word from Joe puts her back on track.

"What sort of ceremony are you having?"

"We're off to Vegas," Gav looks at me and smiles. "No drama."

"Roberta!" Joe good-naturedly swats his wife's arm. "Time we had that toast, don't you think?"

We leave just before lock-in, with Roberta promising to make us a wedding cake and me promising to send her the good picture of Vinnie.

"We have to tell Paddy," I plead with Gav. "Roberta's likely to tell half of London."

"Next time he's here we'll talk to him," Gav promises.

Hours later I'm curled up on my side, Gav's head on my pillow, his arms loosely wound around me, my nose pressed against his chest, when I have a 3 a.m. moment. You've had one. We all have. Someone asks you a question and you can't remember the answer so your subconscious gets to work on it while you're asleep, and bingo! At 3 a.m. or thereabouts it churns out the answer. I wriggle a bit and Gav moves his arm enough for me to roll free. I pad into the kitchen, the display on the microwave flashes 3:05. I scroll back past the photos Roberta took until I get to Harry's death mask. Putting the phone to my ear my reflection in the microwave matches the angle of Harry's head in the picture I took. Itch, scratched. I go back to bed.

CHAPTER 12

Monday

I eat my cornflakes looking out over Docklands. Today calls for a suit. Sully is descending on Eco builders this morning and wants me along. I've texted Sully's driver to pick me up from Black Cat in Soho where Mina and I have arranged an early morning coffee. Gav's already gone. I send him a good morning text, grab my duster and head for the DLR.

"Hello?"

"Nik, it's me, I'm going to have to cancel. Mary wants me to fly to Antwerp this morning, more research."

"Shady trees and lovely ladies?" I mangle her quote from the other night.

"Yes, sorry Nik. Rain check?"

"You're buying," I tell her.

No sooner have I hung up than I get another call.

"What's all this about Soho?" Sully's voice booms down the phone. "Coffee schmoffee, my driver's on his way to your flat. We'll leave from our house with a decent breakfast inside us."

I manage to intercept Sully's driver before he rings the bell. I stifle a yawn, hop in the back and off we go. Sully and CeeCee live in Hampstead in one of those big fortified houses with a very long driveway. The car drops me at the side entrance. It is unlocked and goes straight through to the kitchen, which is rustic and bathed in sunlight, an entire copper pan showroom is hanging up on the walls. CeeCee and Sully sit facing one another at a long wooden table. She's pushing her eggs around the plate; he has the full English including black pudding. CeeCee pats the empty seat beside her; a green jumper hangs over the back. I take my coat off and drape it across the chair. Cook piles my plate high with bacon, eggs sunny side down, sausage, tomatoes, fried potato, fried bread. I wave off the black pudding.

"Shall I put some out for Master Justin?" cook asks.

Sully snorts, "I've banged on the lazy sod's door twice now, and still he doesn't come. It'll just get cold."

He's demolishing the rest of his plate load. To save time and a massive case of indigestion, I construct a full English sandwich with the fried bread slices. Cook puts out a mug of coffee. I barely get two sips in when Sully announces we should be off.

CeeCee rounds on him. "Let the poor girl finish before you go galloping off."

Skillful makeup disguises her red-rimmed eyes from a distance, but I'm sitting right next to her. And her voice wavers. "Please give Mr. Eco our condolences," she says to me. "Poor Harry, what a tragedy."

"Did you know him well?" I ask.

"CeeCee negotiated with Harry's company. She suggested him for this project," Sully interjects, giving me just enough time to finish my sandwich.

"Harry was a lovely man," CeeCee says, "He always got things done with minimum fuss and maximum results. We'll miss him."

"Time waits for no man eh, I'll get my briefcase and see you at the car." Behind CeeCee's back he makes a gesture to me of a hug.

"I'm sorry CeeCee." I get the message and give her a quick one. The fierceness of the hug I get in return is surprising.

"Thanks Nikki."

I put on my coat.

"Time to get that lazy boy out of bed." CeeCee takes a mug and tips in the dregs of the liquid from the glass coffee pot, grounds and all.

"Did Sully get around to talking to the U of L about Justin?" I ask. CeeCee does such a fast about-face that if the mug she's carrying were full, she'd be wearing the coffee.

"What's he got to do with anything?" She doesn't quite snap at me. Let's just say her delivery is crisp.

"Doesn't Justin want to go to U of L?"

"Whatever gave you that idea?" CeeCee scoffs.

"You did, at the book launch, the other night?" I say.

"I did?" CeeCee blinks, "I don't remember much about that night. What else did I say?"

"I dunno," I decide to go with mutual ignorance.

"I wasn't dancing on any tables this time was I?"

"Not that I saw," I say, which is true. I switch subjects as I move towards the door, "If you want to get the boy out of his pit, why waste perfectly good caffeine? Try a bucket of water."

During car journeys with Sully he doesn't talk, and he never makes or takes phone calls. He has all manner of papers with him that he reads and then annotates reports. I don't have anything with me so I press my face against the window and think.

Harry Eco, I'm pretty sure, was the victim of a perfect storm of bad luck. I rerun the scenario in my head. He's on the phone, thinking he has bags of time before the workers show up, only this morning they're early. This is where things start to get a bit ropey. Even if they released the foam without him hearing them, he'd see it pooling around his ankles. He'd still have time to get out. But he didn't even try.

The car goes over a bump and my forehead slaps the glass, sending thoughts spinning every which way. Behind me the rustle of papers as Sully marshals them into his briefcase. It only seems like moments ago that we pulled away from Sully's, but now we're cruising up to the closed gates of Eco Builders. Sully wants his driver to honk the horn. I stop that by getting out and unlatching the gate. We drive to the visitor's area and park.

The offices of Eco Builders are in low-slung brick buildings with solar panels covering every inch of roof space.

Sully pushes into the office with me close behind him. There are three desks. The middle one has a mumsy older lady, her clothes muted, her glasses dangling from a cord around her neck, Mascara forms a bridge across her nose and the lower half of her face is obscured by her hand.

She grips the stems of her glasses and in a movement that on a normal day would turn her into Eco's cool, efficient, if not especially glamorous secretary, dons the frames.

"Mr. Sullivan," her voice drags, she clears her throat. "Mr. Eco is with the workers, he, he…" Another effort, "Coffee for all, I will get coffee." She scuttles out of the room. A loud wail floats out of the kitchenette.

"Funny old stick." Sully says, shaking his head.

"Philip broke the news to her first. She's in shock you, you, inconsiderate…" I really, really want to say 'moron' but settle for "…man."

"Oh," the light dawns in Sully's eyes, "Oh, stupid of me, stupid. I expected the police to keep Harry on 'holiday' a little longer."

"Don't go blabbing about where he was found. My guess is that the workers will know he's dead but not where or how and you might tip the lady over the edge."

Philip Eco comes in accompanied by another man dressed in the builder's uniform of coveralls and hard-hat. Eco's black suit makes him seem taller. His sparse hair lifted by the wind is still deciding which way to fall as he closes the door behind him. He crosses to shake our hands and the other man puts chairs out for us, indicates we sit, and leaves the room without a word. Philip sits behind his desk. His brother's death has aged him, the lines run deeper in his face, his ferret eyes are dull.

I excuse myself to the kitchen and find the woman standing, looking at a kettle that is never going to boil because it hasn't been plugged in. I distract her long enough to fix that and between us we prepare coffee and a plate of wafer biscuits. Time after time she almost gets herself under control. I take the tray and give her the biscuits.

She manages to keep them on the plate before taking her seat once again. I go back and get an extra cup for her. She needs tea, not coffee. I make it as milky and sweet as I dare and when I hand it to her, her eyes clear briefly. She sips in silence.

During this time Sully has been doing most of the talking. I let him continue but in a lull towards the end I ask Philip about the status of the other houses.

"The second unit is prepped, ready to go. The other three units will be arriving shortly. I know it will be hard to get everything finished but our lives go on and we will do it for Harry."

"And we will give you all the support you need," Sully promises. "CeeCee and I are very sorry for your loss."

"Thank you." Philip rises from his chair and with more handshakes we're back outside.

Sully doesn't comment about my knowledge of the extra houses. He tends to store up slights or disobedience and sling them out during arguments. Once inside the car Sully pours himself a stiff one. "Glad CeeCee talked me out of pulling the plug."

"You were going to cancel the contract?"

"I should have," he swallows the liquor. "The negative publicity attached to this is risky. It could blow back onto my company. And yet..."

"And yet?" I query.

"And yet CeeCee managed to wrap me around her little finger."

I've no wish to know how she did that.

"She's a board member, she promised me they'd get over it."

"Let's hope she's right."

CHAPTER 13

One week later, Tuesday

My dad watches the old westerns, and there's always a scene where one of the cowboys says 'it's quiet, too quiet,' and right now it is. Sully and CeeCee have thrown themselves behind Eco Builders. Harry Eco's death is being treated as an unfortunate industrial accident. We can't move on with the tests until the police have completed their investigation. Justin, the problem child, decided that a couple of weeks in Magalluf were in order and CeeCee was only too happy to drive him over to Stansted for the charter flight.

Gav and I have invited Paddy over for dinner tonight. We're going to tell him we're engaged. I kept my regular appointment with Dr. Bradley, she didn't ask about Mina and I didn't tell.

Right this minute I'm sitting at the spare desk in CeeCee's office staring at a postcard from my parents, well mainly my dad.

Your Mum has had a small fall. The on-board medical staff were great. She has to wear a sling for the next couple of weeks. We are on lazy sight- seeing trips for the moment. We miss you,

Love Dad. (and Mum)

My computer dings. The Google alert I set up for mentions of Harry Eco has found an article from BerkshirePost.com.

The coroner investigating the cause of death of 43-year-old Harold Eco, a builder from Greenham in Essex has ruled the death 'accidental'. Local police were convinced that Eco was murdered before being interred in the wall of his own experimental house. However, the cause of death is listed as asphyxia. Eco choked on a square of Nicotine gum and friends and family confirmed that he was trying to give up smoking.

The investigating officer was present at the hearing and commented that his team were 'still processing some recently gathered forensic evidence and looking for information on a package of cubic zirconia found in the vicinity of Eco's body' but would be releasing the body to Mr. Eco's family for burial. 'If no one comes forward the stones will go to the family as well.'

"Hey CeeCee, Sully, I'm forwarding you an article."

The office door is ajar and I can picture Sully reading the report out to CeeCee who will be perched on the front of his desk, her bracelets clinking as she drinks her rooibos. When he gets to the cause of death, CeeCee comments sadly, "I always told him smoking would be the death of him."

No, I think, quitting was the death of him.

CeeCee sweeps out of Sully's office, "Thank you, Nikki, I notice there wasn't a sniff of the Sullivan name in that article. Was that your doing?"

"Beth's probably, she has much better press contacts than me."

"I'd like to buy her lunch, she's spared Harry's family a lot of unnecessary pain. The police had some crazy theory that he was a drug courier which I told them was ridiculous. The only thing Harry ever brought back from his European travels was Belgian chocolate because he knows – knew – I loved it."

She casts around the office for a change of subject and spots the postcard on my desk.

"Ooh, who's in Juneau?" she asks, looking at the picture, but not flipping the card over.

"My mum and dad, they're on a cruise."

"And they're sending you postcards, how sweet."

"Postcard," I correct her. "Any word from Magalluf?"

"Huh?"

"Justin?"

"Oh, the problem child. Nothing since I let him out of the car at Stansted so I can only assume he got to Majorca. Believe me, no news is good news on that front.

"Sully will only worry about him if he overdraws his bank account. He takes the 'out of sight out of mind' approach. So, I'm off to lunch. Want me to bring you anything?" she asks.

"No thanks, CeeCee."

"It's not healthy you know, eating lunch at your desk."

"I'll go for a walk, later and I'll see if Beth's free for lunch in the next couple of weeks."

"Humph," CeeCee sails out of the office, her boots tapping away down the corridor.

I pick up the report I was working on and stare straight through it for a few minutes.

CeeCee's lack of enthusiasm for Sully's flesh and blood bothers me and it sets me thinking again about those things she told me at the book launch party when, I realize, alcohol really had loosened her tongue.

The question I wanted to ask CeeCee at the party was how come the sister was allowed to dump Justin on them so easily and why doesn't she want anything to do with him now?

I put down the report, pull up Wikipedia and type in 'Christopher Sullivan' because I can't go walking into Sully's office and ask him his sister's name out of the blue; he'd be bound to mention my request to CeeCee, whether he gave me the name or not. I want to keep Sully sweet. I also want to head off any potential bombshells so; technically, it is my duty to check this out.

I always take the information on Wikipedia with a pinch of salt but Alison Sullivan has her own wiki entry. Clicking on it takes me to a stub.

Allie Sullivan younger sister of billionaire Christopher "Sully" Sullivan married Trevor Reagan (against her family's wishes) in a private service at Peckham registry office on June 1st of 1989. The marriage produced one son, Justin. In 1999 the family was caught up in the Montroc tragedy.

Montroc is a clickable link; I position the mouse over it.

"Nikki?"

Sully's voice comes from directly in front of me. My head jerks up. The mouse flies out of my hand and arcs towards the floor, narrowly missing the rubbish bin.

When CeeCee first alluded to Sully's stealth capabilities she joked that he could be 'quieter than a church mouse wearing hush puppies,' when he wanted to be. I know big men can be light on their feet, but not that light so I thought she was kidding. Clearly not.

"Jesus, Sully!" I kill my screen, in case he decides to come around and see what I was doing; all the while blushing furiously, hoping I can carry it off as anger. "You nearly sent me to the moon without a rocket!"

"Not my fault you're so jumpy, young Nikki." Sully pats down the air in front of him, then beckons me into his office.

I scribble *Montroc 1999* on a Post-it note and stick it into my pocket before following him in. Sully remains standing and even though he offers me a seat I don't take it.

"I'd like you to do a job for me," he says, "Hush, hush, totally off the books." He spreads out a series of photos across his desk. "This is Max Clausen, of Clausen Technik. He was Harry's silent partner in the business and in his shoes I'd be rushing over here to persuade the other major shareholder, CeeCee, to sell him her shares.

"He's been trying to gain a controlling interest in Harry's company for years," says Sully.

"Why?"

"Because, between you and me, despite being a sneaky little kraut; Max and the late Harry have always had this kind of business voodoo. When Harry started his company a lead was what you walked a dog with. Without our financial backing he'd never have got Eco Builders off the ground. Now LEED certification is exploding worldwide and Max isn't satisfied with just invading Europe. He wants to get his krauty little paws into the UK market."

"Krauty? Is that even a word? And did you just say invade?"

"Slip of the tongue," Sully says, dismissively. "Believe me, the moment he learned Harry was dead; he'll have been working out how long he could decently wait before approaching CeeCee.

"And you want me to follow CeeCee?"

Sully nods. "Call it a favor. I'll set up a credit card for you, anything you need on the job, charge it."

"You think he might be after more than just her shares?"

"That is exactly what I think."

"Can I keep these?" I ask.

"No," Sully says. Before he gathers them up I snap a photo of the clearest head shot, where Clausen is looking straight into the camera's lens, giving the unnerving impression that he's glaring at me.

CeeCee returns a bit later but doesn't leave the office for the rest of the day so *Operation Follow CeeCee* will start in earnest tomorrow.

5:00 p.m.

Gav will be by to pick me up soon. Paddy thinks we've invited him to have a meal at our place. Instead we've reserved a table at his favourite Argentinian steak house for tonight, where we'll finally get to tell him our news. Right on cue reception calls to say they've sent Gav up. When he walks in, I know that dinner's off. Gav has oil smudges on his face and up one arm. His khaki shirt has matching stains and reeks of two stroke oil.

"Some idiot ran into Paddy's motorbike while he was in classes," Gav says. "He came out to find a bent and twisted mess. After he called me I helped him truck it over to the repair place on the other side of town. Poor kid is gutted. He loves that bike."

Sully and CeeCee make the appropriate noises of concern, and offers of help.

"We'll take care of it," I say from the door.

"Can the repair boys fix it?" I ask Gav as we wait for the lift.

Gav shrugs his shoulders, "When I left them they were working on trying to untwist the frame. My insurance guy is on his way over to assess the damage. At the very least I think it'll need a new frame and a partial engine rebuild which is far more than the insurance company would have to pay to write the thing off."

"That means he's not going to get the full cost back," I groan. "He can't replace the BMW like for like, he'll have to go for something second hand.

"Did anyone see it happen?"

"No, the University doesn't have security cameras covering that area and of course the git who hit him didn't leave a note."

I reach for my phone. "Better cancel our dinner reservation; he's not going to want to eat after this."

"Um, it's already cancelled." Gav shuffles his feet, "I told Paddy why we wanted to treat him to his favourite restaurant."

"You did what?"

He wards off my words with his hands, "I know you wanted us both to be there when we told him, but he knows now and he's okay with it."

"Oh, well, that makes it so much better!"

"Whoa, Nik, don't be pissed off at me, be pissed off with the muppet who ran over Paddy's bike."

We've reached the Landy and Gav unlocks his side, gets in and pushes my door open, "Come on, let's go and see the patient."

"And what can I do when we get there?" I ask, still not getting in and forcing Gav to crane his neck to at look me. "Can I draw on my extensive knowledge of metallurgy and motorbike frame construction?"

"Oh, sarcasm, just what we need," Gav shoots back.

"Gav, how well do you know me?"

"I know you as well as I know myself."

"No, you just think you know me."

"Nik, I see you pretty much every day. Oh I get it." Gav snaps his fingers. "Paddy left that copy of FHM open in the flat. You read the same article that I did."

"Huh?"

"You know the one, 'Does my bum look big in this?' & 'What colour are my eyes?' 'The basics of how to speak girlfriend: a crash course for blokes' "

"All right genius, what colour *are* my eyes?"

"They're blueish grey, you're a size ten and you have that little bull's-eye birthmark on your,"

"Oi! Tell the world why don't you!" I manage to cut him off before he tells everyone within earshot where that birthmark is located.

"If you know me as well as you think you do, you'd let me go home and cogitate in a bubble bath, instead of insisting I go and sit in a drafty motorcycle E.R. where the only way I can help is to offer Paddy hugs he's too embarrassed to accept and make pots of tea."

"Well when you put it that way," Gav says, offended.

"I do." I reply, "In fact let me put it another way. Is my presence crucial to getting Paddy's bike fixed?"

Gavin shakes his head. "Then go and be with your son," I palm him, "I can walk back from here, it's only a couple of miles."

"Alone?"

"Are you saying I can't handle myself?"

"No ma'am."

"Then get going soldier."

CHAPTER 14

The following morning:

It took me several hours to walk back to the flat last night. I just followed the Thames and ignored my aching feet. By the time I arrived in the Docklands area, I wasn't angry, just tired.

This morning there is no sign of Gav or Paddy and I'm sitting at the breakfast bar eating my cornflakes while sifting through the day's first batch of emails. Both feet are soaking in a bowl of Epsom salts solution and I've got the window open to let in some fresh air.

Nikki,

I have to give my weekly report to the board this afternoon. Is there any movement in the police investigation of Mr. Eco's death?

Do you want to look at other projects or stick with this one? I should stress that it is the board members who are getting antsy about this project being stalled, not me.

My personal view is that we have an obligation to see this through to the end whatever that turns out to be.

However, I will support any decision you make.

Beth

I flex my fingers and reply.

Beth, they're ruling it accidental, barring any other disasters I think you can tell the board we're back on track.

BTW CeeCee Sullivan would like to take you to lunch. Let me know when you're free.

Nikki

I hit 'send'. The breeze rustles my hastily scribbled Post-It note from yesterday against the laptop. I retrace my steps from Sully's Wikipedia entry to his sister's and this time I click on the Montroc link. The information, stark in black and white, sends my memory rocketing back to February of 1999. The evening the newsreader's somber face intoned the terrible news.

"Good evening, our main story tonight is of a tragedy unfolding in the French Alps. We are receiving reports that an avalanche has partially buried a little village deep in the Chamonix Valley."

That town was Montroc, and a small group of skiers from my home village of Storr Downs were killed in the slide. We all knew them; the entire village was in mourning for weeks. The press kept calling it 'The Chamonix Avalanche' or 'The Impossible Avalanche' because it occurred in a supposedly 'safe zone'.

Allie Sullivan and her husband are listed among the dead. A blurry photo of Allie with her husband and a kid that comes up to her hip is posted; along with pictures of several of the other victims, including the Storr Downs' trio of Effie, the banker's daughter, Paul, son of the pub landlord and Andy the headmaster's boy. They're all laughing. Paul's dad took the picture at Gatwick before they boarded the plane.

It strikes me that I still can't see what Allie Sullivan looked like. I search for photos of her and get a slew of Allie Sullivans; blondes, brunettes, redheads; they come in all shapes and shades. I'll get nowhere fast this way.

I stare out of the window, past my own family photo, which makes me think of another route to try. Justin might be able to tell me.

A search of the University of Arizona's website yields multiple entries. Every time I click on them it asks for his University ID and password.

My frustration grows as I mouse over the final link. It opens.

Before Justin's downfall he was featured in the online campus magazine. Justin in the studio, painstakingly sticking small white motion capture markers on a fellow student. Justin in his dorm room, fingers blurred over his keyboard. No pictures of his parents to be seen. But one small mystery is solved. Justin is the kid who followed me the other day. Okay, he looked a bit more intense, but so would I if I'd just been kicked out of Uni.

From CeeCee's description I was expecting someone more demonic looking. Next time I'm at their house I may have to drop in on him. According to the article he was 'excelling in his chosen field' and that old chestnut, 'a model student'. It seems his downfall was swift. Less than a month after that photo shoot, he was sent home. The photos show Justin reveling in his work, a smile that gives him dimples, nothing seems fake, or he could just be a really good actor.

The ping of an incoming email makes me check my watch. Crap! I've been sitting here for over half an hour. The email is from Sully.

Niki amphi house has bee repaired You are off the hook one of Philips people will conduct our next test

Sully PS CeeCee is lunching out today

Is she now? Sully's appalling punctuation shows he one finger typed this email himself, rather than have his secretary see it. I tidy the kitchen, leave the window open about an inch, encase my feet in flat boots the same colour as my duster, lock the front door, and trot down the stairs to join the flow of human traffic walking towards the DLR station at Canary Wharf.

A text pops up from Mina as I'm standing on the platform.

I'll be back in UK tomorrow. We're going to have a girl's movie night Friday into Saturday. There will be ice cream and plenty of booze. Join us if you can, love M

The message is followed by an accept/reject new contact message. Accepting gives me a Wandsworth address and phone number. I set up a reminder, in case I'm free. The train pulls in just as I'm finishing.

* * *

After a morning of paper shuffling, deleting emails and signing off on a series of updated safety procedures that Philip Eco is putting into place, midday finally crawls around.

"Join me for lunch, Nikki?" CeeCee asks, taking a mirror from her bag and checking her makeup. It's an invitation she's made loads of times before.

"Yes," I say, "I'd like that."

Sully wants me to tail CeeCee and I am well versed in surveillance (it says so on my CV) but it is more CCTV monitoring than what Gav's spook friends would call 'trade craft'. According to Gav, what I do have is 'more front than a welsh dresser' and 'a gold medal in the art of blagging.' Why follow CeeCee when I can just go with her? Once she is over her surprise, CeeCee seems almost relieved that she isn't going to be alone for lunch.

We go downstairs to the car, CeeCee chattering the whole way. She puts on her midnight purple chinchilla coat; it swirls around her ankles as the car draws up. I keep my duster on; CeeCee always has the inside of the car set to 'fridge'. As we're being dropped off in Knightsbridge, CeeCee takes the driver aside and makes a quiet suggestion.

"Valet the car, would you? It reeks of Sully's cigars."

I can't smell a thing but she does have a very sensitive nose.

"Right away Mrs. Sullivan," the driver says, "Right away."

The lunch venue is a restaurant called *Cinquante*, off the main drag of expensive Knightsbridge shops that each comes with its own personal security guard. The entrance is via a black shiny door that you would expect to have a number 10 on it. In keeping with the posh sounding name the number is a 50. The uniformed doorman has a little gizmo in his hand with a button. When pushed, it slides the door to the side, allowing the diners to walk into a steel walled foyer.

"Welcome back to Cinquante, Madam. May we take your coats?"

CeeCee allows the Maître D' to remove her coat, a gesture so familiar that I can see she's been here plenty of times in the past.

My own coat is whisked off my shoulders and the pair are handed over to the coat check girl whose uniform is beautifully tailored and several sizes too big for her petite figure.

CeeCee whispers to the M'aitre D, "If you're going to keep her, that uniform needs to be taken in; poor little thing looks like she's been at the dressing up box."

He puts a hand on the small of the girl's back for a second, which seems a bit too familiar for a boss and employee. "She is here doing work experience, madam. We handpick some of the St Paul's girls every year. Give them a taste of the real world."

I manage not to react, but the girl does. Behind the backs of the adults she casts her eyes heavenwards, mouth open in a silent uttering of the time honoured moan of teenagers everywhere, "Gaaaawwddd."

I send out a silent signal of agreement, *real world my ass*. Whatever is in store for this St Paul's graduate it won't involve wearing any kind of uniform or getting any dirt under those perfectly manicured fingernails.

The Maître D', un-phased, checks his reservation book.

"Your party has arrived Madame and is waiting for you. Please follow me."

He escorts us to the door of a lift; selects the floor, pushes the button, steps out and the doors close.

"I didn't know this was a business lunch," I say. "You should have said something."

"This isn't a business lunch, just catching up with an old friend," CeeCee says. "And I'm glad of your company."

CeeCee dabs at her upper lip where a tiny film of sweat has appeared.

The doors open and even though we went down; the illusion is that we are still above ground. 'Windows' provide ambient light and show people walking past outside.

"Isn't it wonderful?" CeeCee says, "My friend Max installed cameras that look onto the street above and LED panels that use one of his gadgets to project the images onto the walls so that the basement feels more like a pavement café. And there is oodles more room down here." She's babbling a bit, a sign that she is a little nervous.

Another penguin clad Maître D' greets us, giving CeeCee a peck on each cheek.

"So nice to see you again, madam. Right this way, ladies."

"So if Front of House is upstairs, what is he, Bottom of House?" I whisper to CeeCee.

"I prefer Second Front of House," the Maître D' answers my question. "Bottom sounds rather vulgar."

CeeCee covers a smile and I take my foot out of my mouth.

Our table is as far away from the chef's doors and the bathroom as you can get. Sitting with his back to the wall is Max Clausen, in the flesh.

Clausen jumps to his feet as CeeCee and I thread our way through the lunchtime diners. Sully's private detective's pictures didn't show how tall Clausen is. His eyes are that same piercing blue but the photo must've been taken with a zoom lens; it washed away the lines on his face, which softened his appearance. His suit is clearly handmade. Polished shoes click together at the heels as he plants a kiss on CeeCee's cheeks. Smooth, blinding white shirt, silk tie; the tiepin draws my eye, a single lightning bolt. He smiles and draws CeeCee into a hug.

"CeeCee, Liebling! It is good to see you again." He gives a violent shake of the head. "Even under such a circumstance."

"Max." CeeCee continues the hug, then gathers herself and steps back. "Max Clausen, this is Nikki Doyle, she's consulting with us on our floating house project."

I like that she didn't clarify my exact role, 'consultant' covers a multitude of sins.

"A pleasure," Max reaches for my hand, I think to shake it; instead he lifts it to his lips and plants a dry kiss on the back of it. "Please call me Max. Sit down ladies. CeeCee," he indicates that she take the chair closest to the wall on his side of the table, the last place I would choose to sit. In my head I can hear Gav's voice saying that that is a terrible position to be in, hemmed in by Max *and* the wall; thinking to myself that I've been hanging around Gav too long when I start to look at a meal out not for the quality of the food but in terms of where it's safe to sit! I take the seat facing Max.

Max and CeeCee do talk about business and he makes no attempt to make a play for her or her shares (well not with his hands, they're either sketching shapes in the air or gesturing with knife or fork), and he does his best to include me in their conversation.

He orders oysters, but only for himself. CeeCee and I opt for the Ahi Tuna salad, which is delicious. Max dispatches the oysters clinically. Between forkfuls, CeeCee brings him up to date with company matters.

CeeCee's bag starts purring like an oversized cat; her phone must be set to silent. She excuses herself, Max jumps to his feet, and she heads towards the ladies to 'fix my face,' and presumably answer her phone as well. I'm left with Max.

"You and CeeCee go back a long way?" I ask, as he sits back down, fully expecting him to fall silent if I don't attempt to keep the conversation going.

Max uses his napkin to wipe oyster juice off his lips. "We met at school, I was one of CeeCee's fan club at the BSN."

"BSN?"

"Forgive me, a lot of my associates went to the BSN. It is the British School in the Netherlands. Mein Vater, my father was attached to the German Embassy and CeeCee's worked for Royal Dutch Shell, (he pronounces it 'Schell')."

"It may be different now. Back in our day, if your parents worked for ESA, Oil, Embassy or were über rich, their children attended the BSN."

"Did you follow your father into the diplomatic corps?" I ask, causing Max to snort with laughter and nearly recycle his oyster.

CeeCee returns as Max gets himself under control. She seems a little unsteady and has removed the silk scarf covering her throat.

"Are you alright?" I ask her.

"I always forget how warm they keep it in here," she says, picking up the desert menu and fanning herself with it.

"Your Nikki thinks I might be a diplomat," Max snickers as he gets up to usher her back into her seat.

"You have your father's diplomatic skills," CeeCee counters, placing her napkin back on her lap. "Max is a technocrat, Nikki. He runs Clausen Technik; his company has many arms."

"We are like an octopus, yes." Max laughs at his own joke. He zeroes in on CeeCee's now exposed emerald pendant and reaches toward it. "Green fire, authentic, exquisite."

"Sully bought it for me."

"Ah, the big winner of CeeCee's fan club."

"Oh don't start that again." CeeCee bats his fingers away. "There was no fan club, just four lonely souls who didn't quite fit the school's profile."

"You, me, Harry and. . ." Max stops with another oyster halfway to his mouth. "Yasser?"

CeeCee's eyes widen. Max puts the oyster back down on his plate with a 'clack'. I swivel around in my chair. Striding across from the lift is a white robed figure, not that uncommon in Knightsbridge. He's wearing gigantic aviators and his robes billow like a sail, brushing against hair, knocking several water glasses to the floor and in one case removing a pair of spectacles from their wearer. Max gets up, not in the snappy way he greeted us, more of a reluctant rise.

The majority of the Knightsbridge crowd are hyper rich. As the driver was letting us out earlier, a total of five Rolls Royce cruised past us, one of them gold plated. Foreign money doesn't just talk around here, it takes a megaphone and yells 'look at me, see how much money I have, look at me, look at me, look at me.'

In the burnoose wearer's wake the second front of house guy is picking up all the objects the billowing robes have knocked to the floor, smoothing flared tempers and giving the gentleman back his specs, his blonde companion wiping them on her napkin before carefully seating them back on his face.

"I didn't invite him, I swear to you." Max mutters to CeeCee.

"Well don't look at me," she says.

"Your highness." What I thought was a dig at Max is actually directed at the newcomer.

The man reaches our table, he pays no attention to the second front of house chap behind him, dismissing him with a curt 'leave us'.

He removes the sunglasses. His face is distinctly bovine in shape. Eyes that seem to be trying to reach the cover of his ears are the colour of dates. They slide right over me before coming to rest on CeeCee. It bugs me; being ignored is a fact of life in a big city like London, but it's a long time since I've been made to feel totally invisible.

* * *

Back when I first moved up to London, I shared a bedsit with a psychology student named John Smith, his real name. John and I had no chemistry whatsoever. I answered his flat share ad in TimeOut. Between his grants and my barmaid's job, plus tips, we could just about cover the rent.

About a month after we moved in, Smith told me he'd seen the landlord with a Pakistani chap. Within days we knew the reason for his visit. The flat underneath us was being used to run a mini cab business. The landlord took their money as well as ours and turned a blind eye to everything including fire regulations and business licenses. In the evening drivers would clog up the stairwell on their way up to the roof to pray to whichever way Mecca faced. Despite this, we settled into an uneasy truce. I became adept at sliding down the banister feet first to get past them (hard to ignore flying feet) and locking the front door when I got home so that they didn't just wander into our flat on their way to or from the roof and stink up the bathroom.

One of the mini cab drivers kept stealing our post. When the idiot stole my credit card statement, causing me to miss a payment, I started staking out the lobby and caught the guy in the act of opening my bank statement. I grabbed him by the ear and hauled him in front of his boss to complain.

My threats to call the police and report the guy didn't even register with his boss. Because I was a woman, he wouldn't speak to me or even acknowledge me. He and the driver simply shut the door in my face.

I reported the company. The police and immigration raided the block. Most of their drivers, including my thief ended up being deported. For my trouble I got kicked out by the landlord for losing him his most lucrative tenant. My boss at the time, Declan, took pity on me and let me live above his pub in Kilburn for about a year. It was cramped but at least I had a roof over my head and I saved a bundle on busses and the tube; enough in fact to put down a deposit on the south London apartment on Redfern street.

That chapter of my life is one my parents have no idea about. I was determined not to come running home from the big city with my tail between my legs at the first hurdle I encountered.

* * *

Sitting in the restaurant I try and channel my anger and fail to come up with anything productive that doesn't involve actual bodily harm to 'Yasser'.

His high and mightiness makes no attempt to apologize for gate crashing lunch; instead he grabs Max by the arm. Max allows himself to be pulled into the corner and the man he calls 'Yasser' begins yammering at him, but not before he sweeps a glance around the restaurant. The two men are standing almost nose-to-nose.

"Who's the charm school reject?" I ask CeeCee.

"Shhsh!" CeeCee says, "He'll hear you."

"Tough to hear me when he couldn't even see me."

"He can be a little abrupt, he only notices those who are worth something to him."

"If you're trying to make me feel better, please stop."

"It's just the truth. He only sees me because we went to school together. And to answer your question he is His very Royal Highness Abdul Hammid bin sidiq bin Abu Simbel."

"That's an Egyptian temple," I point out.

"Oh I can never pronounce his full name. His nickname at school was Yasser, because of that checked keffiyeh thing he wears on his head.

"His father was the UAE Ambassador, Yasser went to BSN. His father thinks that ruined him, I think his father ruined him.

At school Yasser was the slightly awkward kid who bought friends with his father's money. Now he's the rich kid desperate to gain his father's approval. He's never done a day's work in his life.

"At school Max used to come up with ways to part him from his allowance. He has shares in Max's company and mine and Harry's. In a way Max is still messing with him."

I study the man she calls 'Yasser'. It's weird that I can stare at him without his even noticing me.

Suddenly it gets heated. Yasser grabs Max's suit lapels and attempts to treat the German like a tablecloth. He seems to be very upset with some bloke called Kevin as he yells his name several times.

Max, who also seems familiar with the mysterious Kevin, breaks Yasser's grip in one fluid motion. Yasser's robed arms fly apart, leaving his chest wide open. Max punctuates the one-sided fight by ramming the heel of his hand into the Arab's sternum and Yasser adds a broken chair to his list of misdemeanors as he lands on it.

All the while Max's mouth is still moving. Whatever he is saying to his fallen opponent definitely isn't in German.

Now the place is in uproar, they all want to stop the fight; only it never escalates past Max shoving Yasser to the floor. CeeCee's phone starts ringing, she must've unsilenced it. I don't have to look over to know it's hers because only a former weathergirl would have 'It's raining men' by the Weather Girls as her ring tone. It rings again, but I'm still watching Max dusting himself off. He leans down, about to help Yasser up, pulling him up by the robe, when someone behind me tries and fails with the tablecloth trick. I turn around to see what happened. Our table is cleared and there's no sign of CeeCee.

Max, dropping Yasser, dives under the table. I pull both chairs back on my side and with the help of the bespectacled customer we haul the table back. CeeCee is lying on her side in a heap of crockery. Max starts yelling for an ambulance.

CHAPTER 15

An hour later nearing the Sullivan Residence:

"How is she doing?" Gav asks.

We've already caught up on Paddy and I've had an apology from Gav for acting, 'like an arse' last night.

"I don't know," I say bracing myself as the mini cab Max commandeered and stuffed me into lurches across three lanes of slow moving traffic, narrowly missing a cyclist, "They loaded her into the ambulance and commandant Max sent me out here to get some of CeeCee's clothes. She got chili sauce all over herself when she collapsed."

"Want me to send someone to pick you up?"

"No, thanks," I say, "I'll call you later."

I hang up and rap on the privacy screen; the cabbie slides it open.

"Here is fine." I take some cash out of my purse and he pulls over on Hampstead high street. I give him a twenty, plus a five quid tip for not killing us both on the way over here. Once the cab has clattered away, I stroll along the high street toward millionaire's row; very conscious of the battery of security cameras I'm currently being recorded by.

Before posting me through the door of the mini cab, Max handed me CeeCee's keys and a paper from his wallet, which has the code for the Sullivans' security system. A curious development. Back when I lived in a building sans doorman only Gav and my across the hall neighbour Declan (the same Declan I used to work for) had my alarm code. Why would CeeCee give Max her entry code? Maybe Sully's right to be suspicious of Max.

No time to think about that now, my job is to get CeeCee some fresh clothes while Max's is to get in touch with Sully. Yasser vanished long before they put CeeCee into the ambulance. From the back he looked like a manta ray heading back to the Sea Life Centre.

The code for the gate is eight digits long. I count to myself to make sure I got the number of zeros right, key in the final two numbers and push the button that enters the code and hopefully opens the gate. As with the 'things always take longer when you want them to happen' law, a snail could move faster than those yawning gates.

"Nik!"

My concentration was so focused on getting the code right that I failed to notice a newer model black cab stationed roughly five feet away outside the gate. At the wheel, former Captain Matt Black, Gav's close friend at Ravenwood, who still looks like an off-duty soldier even when he's trying to dress like a cabbie.

"The boss said you needed a helping hand. Congrats on the engagement by the way." Matt is pretty average looking, until he flashes that cheeky grin. The boys at Ravenwood are always teasing him about whitening his teeth; he swears he doesn't.

Matt drives the cab past me and through the open gates, cutting off any more discussion. The house is still a long walk away. I move between the gates, which seem to be closing a lot quicker than they opened.

"Hop in," Matt says, "I'm going your way." I get in the back and lean through the privacy screen. "Like it?" Matt asks, "It's electric, we can follow anyone in central London because we blend in."

We cruise up to the house; Matt turns the engine off and gets out at the same time as I do. A keen observer would notice that he walks with a slight trace of limp, a result of being shot in the leg during the same operation that put Mina in the hospital.

"That'll be fifty quid," Matt jokes.

"You want a limp in the other leg?" I fire back, grinning. "Besides I can't afford that, I'm saving up for a wedding."

"Just for that I'm not coming in with you." Matt banters back. "I'll wait for the police to roll up, outside the gate. You got your ID on you?"

I hand him my driver's license and the Sullivan Inc ID. "You really think someone is going to call the police on us?" I ask. "I wasn't exactly sneaking around."

"Oh trust me," Matt says, "this is Hampstead, more nosey parkers per square yard here than anywhere else in London. They'll come. I'll make sure you get in OK and then I'll take a quick run down the drive. I'll call you if we have a serious problem."

He waits until I've unlocked the front door. The keypad is just inside. I punch in the number. The rapid beeping stops and I give Matt the thumbs up. He jogs back towards the gates. I've been in this house many times but usually just the kitchen and sometimes Sully's office. There's been no reason for me to ever be upstairs.

At the top of the stairs is a long landing, with doors at each end and one door mid way along. I start at the door closest to me, which turns out not to be CeeCee and Sully's room. There's more electrical equipment in here than the local branch of Curry's and the walls are painted black. Justin's room, I presume. What is it with teenagers and black? I mean I get the goth thing, I still have some of the pictures of my own goth phase, but I never painted my whole room like the inside of a coalscuttle.

Reaching inside the door I flip on the light switch. Two massive spotlights shine down on the desk. This is the point where I should leave. Clearly this isn't the room I'm looking for, and yet.. I slip off my shoes and in my bare feet cross to the desk. Justin's iPhone is wedged, screen up, between the arrow keys and the del, end, and page down trio on the keyboard. Surely he'd need that in Majorca, unless he has two phones, which in this family isn't beyond the realms of possibility. I mean Justin's mouse is shaped like a Porsche 911.

I turn to leave and my thigh bumps against the arm of Justin's office chair, the other arm of the chair strikes the slide-out part of the desk jolting the mouse and with a buzz and a hum the screen light pulses from red to green and Justin's screensaver appears; a selfie of Justin and a girl. She has hair blacker than a raven's wing, dancing eyes and a caramel skin tone that no amount of tanning could ever produce; definitely not a local girl. At a guess I'd say she's from Brazil or Argentina.

With her right cheek squashed against his left, she is blowing a "mwah" kiss at the camera. The words 'Earl's Diner' and a picture of a giant hamburger hover over her left shoulder. I've seen enough and I plunge the room back into darkness.

The Sullivans' bedroom turns out to be at the far end of the landing. I keep my shoes in my hand, letting my feet sink into the thick, soft carpet.

"Brrrr." The bedroom is freezing. Sully or more likely CeeCee must have some Celtic blood in their veins. Which reminds me, in all the confusion of loading CeeCee into the ambulance our coats are still hanging up at the coat check in Knightsbridge.

I pick out a dress from one of CeeCee's walk in wardrobes, which is full of long coats, and some flat shoes in case she doesn't want to wear her heels. I'm shivering as I close the bedroom door behind me. It's at least two maybe three degrees warmer out here on the landing. I don't hang about. I trot downstairs with the clothes over my arm, push the reset button on the security system and lock the door behind me.

No sign of Matt, but he left the cab unlocked. I put the clothes on the back seat and spend a couple of minutes getting the hang of the bigger pedals and giant steering wheel before pressing the button that starts the motor. I turn the cab around and cruise down towards the main gate. Out front, the scene is chaotic. Two police cars, lights pulsing, angled in front of the gate, five uniformed officers standing close to the bars. Matt, his arms folded looking like he has all the time in the world, standing inside just out of grabbing distance. As I approach he wheels around and walks up to the driver's side window.

"I'm waiting for them to rustle up an officer in charge," he says. "They've made it plain that we're not going anywhere until a higher rank has cleared it."

"You know the gate opens inwards, right?" I whisper to Matt.

"*I* know that." His eyes twinkle for a second.

"Gav tells me that you're the diplomat, Nikki. Do your thing."

In reply I put the taxi in 'park' and slide out of the cab. On the kerb a small group of maids and chauffeurs has gathered.

Approaching the gate I call out, "Hello boys, you know you're kind of blowing our cover. My driver's shown you our IDs. Mrs. Sullivan suffered an accident, earlier on today. She sent me over here for some fresh clothes, which I am happy to show you. The longer we stand out here the more chance there is that one of the rubberneckers over there will call the press."

"Let 'em," says the oldest, "Our orders are to block these gates. You two might have the balls to try and bluff us, those IDs could be fake."

"You can search the cab," I offer.

"Why don't we escort them back to the hospital?" one of the younger coppers asks.

"We're trying to minimize publicity not start a parade," I counter.

"Sorry Miss Doyle, if that's your real name, that gate is staying shut for the time being." Matt ruins the older copper's speech by pressing the button on the gate, I step back and several people amongst the onlookers titter with laughter as it opens away from them. I try and reason with the officers before Matt ends up getting the pair of us arrested.

"Two of you in the back of the cab with me? You can see where we're going. Or you can arrest us, and Sully will have to waste time sending legal to extract us. Your choice."

I'm gambling here, they could just arrest us out of spite because we made them look like idiots; hopefully they're better than that.

CHAPTER 16

CeeCee was brought by ambulance to the private wing of the Royal Brompton hospital. We arrive there at the same time as Sully, a white-faced Sully, whose first action when I get out of the cab is to paw CeeCee's spare clothes out of my hands.

"C'mon we need to get these to CeeCee so that I can take her home."

"You go on ahead," I say and he runs inside. Alone for a moment I give Matt a small salute and he returns it, turning the cab around, presumably driving his police passengers back to their car.

I go inside and the first person I come across is Max. He's staring at the curtained off area. We can both hear Sully talking softly to CeeCee as he helps her on with her street clothes.

"Do we know why she fainted?" I ask.

"Stood up too quick, lack of oxygen caused her to faint? Mein liebling is lucky those chairs are so well padded. The doctor says she should rest up for a couple of days to ensure the full recovery."

He steps closer than I'd like.

"We have some unfinished business to discuss."

I have no idea what he's talking about and the sound of Sully pulling the curtains back gives me the opportunity to step away from Max. Sully, pushing a dazed looking CeeCee in a wheelchair, looks like he might use the chair to run Max down. Max gets that impression too.

"I will be in touch," he says, before marching away down the corridor. I have never been more relieved to see someone walk away. And I'm still not sure why.

Sully loads CeeCee into the car, which has been valeted inside and out as she requested. He closes the door and then rounds on me.

"Where the hell were you?" he snaps. "Why didn't you call me as soon as this happened?"

"We couldn't get hold of you, the receptionist said you went running out of the door like a scalded cat. Max was supposed to call you while I got the clothes from your house."

"My nephew, Justin. He's dead."

I feel a small twinge of sympathy. Justin was a name I'd barely put a face to and Sully doesn't seem all that cut up at losing him.

"I'm sorry for your loss. What happened to him?"

"I know he's dead, I know the police are investigating and that's all I know."

The words trip out of Sully's mouth like a well-rehearsed line in a play and his eyes are locked on the passenger cabin of his chauffeur driven Mercedes.

I'm already mentally running logistics; Sully's focus is on CeeCee not on funeral arrangements.

"Do you want me to fly out to Majorca for you? If you can organize the paperwork I could leave first thing in the morning."

"What are you talking about?"

"Someone needs to go to Majorca, collect Justin's body and bring it back here for burial."

"He's not in Majorca, where the hell did you get that idea?"

"From CeeCee, she told me several weeks ago that he wanted to party in Palma. She bought him an airline ticket and took him to Stansted and made sure he caught the flight."

Ever heard the expression, 'never speak ill of the dead'? Sully hasn't. He doesn't just speak ill of the dead he curses his nephew up, down and sideways.

"That bloody trickster! They always overbook those charter flights," he says, more to himself than me, his mouth mired in a frown. "It wouldn't be unusual to be asking for volunteers to take a later flight and get compensation vouchers. He could sell those. Why did he do it, why?"

For the first time, a single salty tear pools in the corner of his eye, but he blinks it away before it has the chance to escape. If I'm reading Sully right, Justin may have done away with himself.

"Sully?"

"Go home Nikki, nothing else for you to do here."

"But.."

"Go home Nikki."

CHAPTER 17

"You cooked," Gav says, sniffing the air as he stands in the doorway of our flat.

"Yeah."

I've made mum's hybrid spaghetti: pasta, cream, bacon, lots of bacon, and mince, with added garlic and tinned tomatoes; a mash-up of carbonara and Bolognese that I've helped my mum with cooking so many times that I could seriously make it in my sleep.

"Hell of a day, eh?" Gav says, wrapping his arms around me.

"Thanks for sending Matt. Thing's might've gotten a bit sticky otherwise."

"Hmmm, I think you're slowing down," he teases. "You've not been in trouble for at least a week."

"Hold that thought," I snuggle against him, "It's not Friday yet."

The timer goes off in the kitchen, and I push him towards the table, "Anything I can do?" he asks.

"Light the candles, and pour us both a drink."

We sit down and for a little while there are just the sounds of two hungry people eating.

"That's one of the things I love about you," Gav says. "You don't just eat one lettuce leaf and a pea and call it a meal."

"And that's why I don't blow away during a gale."

"Seconds?"

"Yes, please," I say, letting Gav ladle more pasta onto my plate.

I clear the table, load the plates and saucepans into a hungry dishwasher, and turn it on. "I wish there was a pause button we could push sometimes," I say.

"You'll be wanting a fast forward and rewind next," Gav jokes. "Alright," he says, "consider the pause button pushed." We sink onto the sofa and I clink my glass against his. "Tonight we aren't our jobs, we're just us.

"Look, Nikki before we fly to Vegas we should go and see a lawyer."

"You want a prenup?"

"No, but we should update our wills."

"I've never made a will." I pause, "You've made a will?"

"Of course," Gav replies.

"That's morbid."

"It's practical," he says. "Most of the chaps in my unit made wills. We were serving in Northern Ireland; death was always in the back of your mind. We lost a lot of good men and if something happened to them they knew their families were provided for."

"Can we talk about something else? Talking about death, it's like tempting fate."

"I'm not planning on going anywhere at the moment, Nikki."

"I thought I'd lost you once," I slug back the wine. "Can we please change the subject?"

"Ok," Gav stays silent for a moment, "I've blocked off the last week of May does that work for you?"

Oh, I walked right into that one, the wedding; our fast approaching wedding.

"Sure."

I decide to just ask. If you don't ask, you don't get. "Can you talk to Mr. Evans about borrowing the Ravenwood jet? I mean the only direct flights are charters full of boozy stags and hens."

"I can ask. Several of the guys want to come to the ceremony, they want to make a weekend of it."

"What happened to 'just the two of us?'" I put down my wineglass and turn to face him. "And the big party for all our friends we were going to throw when we got home?"

"We can do both," Gav says, "If people want to come to Vegas under their own steam, let 'em. I'm sure when I tell them that it's not some country house bash, the cost of the plane ticket will convince them to come to the party and not the wedding."

"That's fair," I say, "except *we* don't know where we're getting married yet."

"Let's fire up the laptop." Gav does his best Gene Hunt impression. "We can start at one end of the strip and work down." Gav mock groans, "God we'll be here all night."

"No," I say, "we can narrow down what we want by saying what we don't want."

"No Elvis impersonators, no drive-through," Gav says.

"Somewhere close to Vegas but not on the strip, and definitely not the Little Chapel O' Love," I say. Feeding our search into Vegas Weddings.com, the site kicks back a multitude of web pages, so many that we can't read the tabs.

"You're right we are going to be here all night."

"We need to narrow it down." Gav takes control of the laptop, "I'm going to kill every other tab."

Still too many. He repeats the process until we have ten tabs. Among them, still not fully readable, are Red R, Green, Lake, Area5, Valle, Zoo We, Drive, Shark, and two which when clicked on are just adverts for more wedding sites.

"Divide and conquer," Gav says. "You lose three, I lose three. You go first."

"You know this could all go horribly wrong?"

"Choose, or be tickled."

"I choose 'Green', 'Area5' which must be Area51 and 'Shark'."

"And I'm getting rid of 'Valley', 'Zoo We' and 'Drive'."

Gav hands me the mouse. I use his thigh as my mouse pad.

"This is great. Our Russian roulette wedding edition has given us the Red Rock hotel. It's far enough off the strip but they don't do wedding packages just for two."

"Click on my pick," Gav says. Up pops a destination-wedding site.

"How about staying at the Red Rock and going off-site for the ceremony?" Gav suggests. "Get a limo from the Red Rock out to Lake Mead overlook or one of these other venues, Valley of Fire, Spring Mountain. I don't really fancy getting hitched in front of the Las Vegas sign, which is the last option. They provide the minister and the photographer and they do evening weddings so we won't melt."

"You know," I say, "That sounds fantastic." I mean it.

"You got a dress yet?"

"I have one in mind and I'm not wearing white."

"So it's red then is it?" I chuck a cushion at him. He snatches it out of the air and lobs it back.

"Shouldn't you be more concerned with your wedding suit?"

"How about this, you book the hotel and the ceremony. I'll sort out the marriage license and organize our flights. We each take care of our wedding kit."

"Okay, what about the rings?"

"They're in the safe," Gav says, "Want to see?"

I follow him into our bedroom where he lifts up the cluster of carpet tiles covering the floor safe and unlocks it. He holds out two boxes, his and hers, both rings are platinum. His is a simple band; mine has a swoop that fits the pattern of my engagement ring.

He puts them back into the safe and we go to bed.

CHAPTER 18

"**B**loody hell," Gavin runs into the bedroom scarfing a cereal bar, because even though I went shopping for milk yesterday I came back with everything but. "These things taste like those carpet tiles."

He takes another bite, and dumps the rest in the bin in the corner.

"Days like this should come with a government health warning." He groans, slipping a tie around his neck as I search for my wristwatch which is caught somewhere in the funnel of twisted sheets.

"Excuse me." I button, unbutton and re-button my shirt; "You said you'd set the alarm for six."

Gavin's face lights up with a wolfish grin. "What can I say? I was distracted by a leggy blonde." He pulls on his suit jacket. "Wish me luck, I might just make my client meeting."

There's a brief collision between us during which his kiss leaves crumbs on my cheek and then he's gone.

I make myself a cup of tea, my stomach growls but stops when I pick up the next cereal bar in the packet and threaten to unwrap it. With the volume turned up on the TV, I listen to the news while I'm putting the bedroom back together; closing drawers, changing sheets, I pick our clothes up off the floor. All clothes and sheets go in the washing machine.

After telling viewers about a planned demonstration in Central London, set to take place this weekend, the newsreader drops a bombshell.

"A double tragedy for captain of industry Christopher Sullivan. Yesterday his nephew, Justin Sullivan, was found dead in what the police are calling 'suspicious circumstances' and Lucy, Sullivan's wife of nearly twenty-five years and a business mogul in her own right, suffered a mild stroke after an incident at a Knightsbridge restaurant yesterday afternoon. She has since left the hospital and is reported to be recovering under the care of Sullivan's personal physician at the couple's Hampstead home."

I turn down the volume and call Sully.

"I'm not going in today," he says. "CeeCee needs me and the place is swarming with detectives scouring Justin's room. They're bagging and tagging everything."

"It's what they do when a death happens under suspicious circumstances." I flash back to my visit to Justin's room, the day before. Did I touch anything? I don't think so and even if I did they're not going to dust his room for prints. That wasn't where he died.

"I never told you his death was suspicious!"

"It's all over the news, and the police won't just be collecting evidence. I've had experience with this type of investigation and you and CeeCee and anyone else Justin knew well will be answering a lot of probing questions in the next few days."

"Bloody marvelous!" Sully sounds rattled, "Even dead the kid's still causing me problems."

"That's a pretty cold blooded thing to say." I can feel my hackles rising when I should be advising Sully to act a little more grief stricken.

"You're not the one who walked into a police investigation. I had to identify him." Sully's tidal anger and probably his blood pressure are rising again, "Then they stuck the pair of us in separate rooms and questioned us for hours on end."

"You should've let the office know where you were going. Called CeeCee even."

"I did call her!" he bites off the end of the sentence, "She wasn't picking up, for obvious reasons." His sarcasm is thick enough to have a cherry on top of it.

"Okay, I deserved that." I attempt to calm him down; at the same time wondering who else was with him when the police used their divide and conquer approach.

"It wasn't the police who called you was it?"

"Philip called me, those new safety procedures you and he put into place are the only reason they discovered Justin's body. Philip was with the team checking the next house before they foamed it. Philip's men came across the body and he went through the pockets, found Justin's wallet and credit cards.

"First thing I knew about it was Philip calling me in a panic asking if I knew a Justin Sullivan.

"One of his workers must've called the police. I was already enroute, and Philip didn't know to warn me."

I keep to myself the suspicion that Philip covered himself by calling the cops and Sully.

"CeeCee doesn't know about Justin yet. She can't even get out of bed let alone walk across the room. Doc is with her now. He says she's too fragile to hear more bad news.

"You can go into the office today if you want but the project is stalled, again, until further notice."

The phone 'beep beep beeps' in case I didn't realize our conversation was over.

I go back to the news. They're doing a medical segment, in light of Sully's story. Information about strokes and how to spot the symptoms. I would normally tune out information like this because, let's face it, heart attacks and strokes and brittle bone disease are for older men and menopausal women. I am neither. The fact that CeeCee may have had a stroke in front of me and I didn't even know it makes me pay attention this time.

Their medical correspondent explains to me how wrong I am about what a stroke is. My assumption has always been that it is some kind of mental short circuit, like my toaster when it blew a fuse last summer, but it's not. Stroke is caused by a blood clot forming somewhere else in the body and traveling into the brain, starving brain cells of vital oxygen. A small clot and you might not even know you're down a couple of neurons, but a big clot can strike you down like a bolt from the blue.

"Mini strokes can affect motor functions, causing the patient to lose their balance," continues the medical correspondent.

Your mother's had a small fall.

Dad's words just pop into my head. Another symptom of stroke is migraines and mum told me she was having really bad ones during the couple of days before they went on their cruise. She blamed the long flight from Heathrow to Seattle. I dial Dad's mobile,

"Hello Petal."

Dad sounds fine, he sounds normal.

They've been back from Seattle a couple of days now and the jet lag should have worn off.

"Hey Dad, I was just thinking about you and mum. Everything okay?"

"Yes Petal, we're fine, we're both fine." Dad's running out of his daily conversational allowance. "How are you?"

"Um, I'm fine."

I'm into extra time. Dad's totally out of anything else to say; he'll be thanking me for calling any second now.

"How's mum's wrist?"

"Healing well."

"Can I talk to her?"

"No, she's at home, I'm at the newsagents," Dad says with devastating logic.

"Good, well, I guess I'll let you go. Love you Dad, give mum a hug for me."

"I will. Bye Petal."

"Bye dad."

Sometimes, I tell myself, *a fall is just a fall.*

I intend to enjoy my bonus day off, with one little errand to run first. I have the doorman call me a cab to take me back to Knightsbridge.

***

Cinquante seems to be popular for brunch; my cab sits at the front of the queue at a red light so I have a clear view of the drop-offs and pick-ups going on outside the restaurant.

"You want me to wait for you luvvie?" asks the cab driver.

"No, thanks." I give him a twenty, "I don't need any change."

It takes all of two minutes for the front of house guy to remember me from yesterday and lead me over to the coat check booth. He gives the ticket to the girl behind the desk (not the girl from yesterday) and she scuttles off into the forest of coats.

"I do hope Madam is feeling better, we've sent over some flowers."

"That's very thoughtful. I'm sure CeeCee will appreciate that," I say. The girl returns with CeeCee's coat swathed in a layer of thin rustling plastic. She hands it to him, whispers in the Maître's ear.

"What do you mean you can't find it?" he hisses back, "Green leather duster, it was right in front of Madam's coat!"

"I'll look again sir, but I swear it's not there." She rushes back behind her counter, again returning empty handed.

The Maître, pushes past her, goes into the back and he too comes back without my coat.

"I don't understand how this could've happened," he says, "Your coat is not where the girl left it."

"They were hung up together, my coat was *in front* of CeeCee's."

"Then we still have it and rest assured we will find it." He takes my business card. "This sort of thing simply doesn't happen at Cinquante!"

Shouting at him won't get my duster back any faster. So instead I suggest that the restaurant pays for a cab back to Sullivan Inc's HQ so that I don't have to tote CeeCee's coat around with me all day. I could take it to the Sullivan house except I don't want to get under Sully's feet. Maître is only too happy to oblige.

"I can arrange a taxi," he says, "on our account."

He walks me out to the cab, "My sincerest apologies," he says and he looks mortified enough to mean it.

I sling CeeCee's coat over my arm and get into the taxi. The cabbie slices through London traffic, using some very creative short cuts, pulling up outside Sullivan Inc. just after 11:30 a.m.

Every employee is supposed to come in the front door and sign in. Going in through the delivery entrance means I can flash my pass at the loading dock manager along with the promise of a round of fresh coffees next time I visit. With a wink and his blessing I nip up to the shared office; use my keys to gain access and hang the coat on the circular rack in the corner of CeeCee's office, slotting it in between her black mink and the pink cashmere. By 11:40 I'm strolling towards Covent Garden.

Before Beth and I moved to Excalibur, we worked out of Archimedes' offices just off Covent Garden and there's a pavement café in the piazza, close to the covered market area, that does brilliant coffee. Their specialty is a chocolate espresso, small intense and very, *very* rich. And I fancy one. Before I take a seat I have a good long around. I don't mind running into my old colleague and mentor Fred, or Beth's husband Tony but I do not want to run into Simon.

All I see are tourists, wearing waterproof jackets in various combos of red, yellow, and blue. Sorry green, not your year.

Two people do catch my eye though. Young guy, black T-shirt, blue jeans, buzzed hair. Under my gaze everyone else keeps moving. He stops stock-still. This would be normal, if we were all playing a game of 'statues'.

What he gets for stopping like that is an angry business-woman who just rammed her cardboard tray of coffees into his back. As she continues to rant at him, I see the second person; I blink to see if the face changes, if I've superimposed her face onto another body, that happens sometimes, but not this time. Sitting at the café behind me is the Aztec looking girl I last saw blowing kisses from the screensaver on Justin's computer.

I claim an empty table. The waiter comes over, takes my order. I force myself not to turn around and stare. Instead I study the girl's reflection in the glass, the blue-black hair flows to her shoulders like water. She wears a biker jacket, her shoulders hunch and her hands clamp around an espresso cup.

I take my eyes off her as the waiter approaches with a tray of coffees. As he doles them out to the various tables I wonder if he really knows who gets what or if we just take what we're given. There is only one espresso cup left on the tray, mine, I think, and then, not mine. The cup arcs sideways, a chocolate rainbow hangs in the air for a split second before decorating another empty table. The tray slices downward banging into the legs of a metal chair with a conversation silencing 'clang!' The cause of all of this? The girl I was watching a few moments ago has shoved her way past the waiter and barreled to a stop at my table.

"Tell them to stop following me!" she yells, "I don't *wan* their blood money. You tell them that!"

I just watched my chocolate fly away. I let the pout that wants to come out, out. I used to be good at this stuff. I mostly have it under control now. But growing up I had my wild child moments and my share of catfights. I'd go in full throttle. That's what I do this time.

"What the hell did you do that for?" I yell, pushing my chair away, coming up fast, getting in her face. "Are you nuts or something?"

"Just tell them!"

"Tell who?" I'm really not sure what she's on about, but I try a trick that Caroline taught me. With an effort I pause, take a couple of deep breaths and in a lower voice keep my words slow and calm.

"I don't know who you think I am but if you think someone is following you, you should go to the police."

"But why are you here?"

"My day off, I used to work around here, this place used to be my local."

"I don' believe you!"

"I don't know you," I shrug. "And I'm not following you around. I'm just trying to enjoy a quiet cup of coffee. So sit down and stop making a scene or leave me alone."

She digs a hand into her pocket and everything goes into slow motion. Whatever she pulls out, I can be under the table in seconds. Her hand returns with a wad of cash. She tosses some of it on the table along with some other pocket scraps, including a mascara-smeared tissue. Then she turns and bolts, almost knocking the poor waiter over again before running towards the market. I want to go running after her. Instead I ask for a replacement drink, while I ponder what just happened.

My main question being, up until now Aztec girl and I have never met. She didn't just pick me at random and we only have one factor in common, Justin. Justin, who had a camera attached to those geek glasses when I confronted him the other day. So I guess Caroline Bradley was right, he was filming me while he trailed along behind me. At the time Justin was supposedly grounded at the Sullivan house while they worked out where to send him next. That sparks another connection. Sully having me follow his wife. Was he having Justin follow me? Was he having someone else follow his nephew's girlfriend?

Is Sully dangerous?

Now there's a daft question, or is it? He has a business reputation for being ruthless, and always getting his own way.

I have never been on the receiving end of his full temper, but I know he has one. And the more I think about it, the more guilt I feel for getting in Aztec girl's face like that.

"Hello, there." A familiar voice interrupts my thoughts.

"Paddy!" I stand up and give him a warm hug. It's the first time I've seen him since his bike was trashed and Gavin told him our news. "Sit down, you want a coffee?"

"That would be grand, thanks."

I cast around for a waiter, mine has gone off shift but there's one loitering in the café's doorway and he's studiously ignoring me.

"Oi," Paddy calls out to him, when that fails he sticks both fingers in his mouth and whistles. The waiter approaches us with all the enthusiasm of a soldier on latrine duty.

"My man, I'm thirsty," Paddy says, "and I'm a big tipper." After taking Paddy's order the waiter fairly runs back inside the café.

"I never got to say, congratulations." Paddy snags a handful of the little sugar biscuits that came with my replacement espresso and munches on them. "Yous are great together."

"Thanks Paddy. Look I'm sorry your dad broke the news to you like that; he thought he was helping," Paddy shrugs. "You haven't been around to the flat since. Any news on the bike?"

"Written off, they're sending me a cheque. The garage guy is letting me borrow one of his older bikes. It's a Triumph and a beaut. Who knows, I may end up buying it.

"But that's not the reason I haven't been around. I've been busy with finals and stuff." Paddy breaks off as his coffee and more of the sickly little sugar bombs are placed in front of him. "Don't worry I'll be getting play station thumb again soon."

"Great," I look him up and down. "You're wearing a suit," I say, watching him adjust his tie. "Interview?"

He shakes his head.

"Okay, I give up, the only other things I can think of are a wedding or a court appearance, and you're too smart for either of those."

Paddy looks away for a second and then back at me, "Promise yous won't tell dad?"

"I can't tell him what I don't know, if you tell me and it's sufficiently heinous I'll have to tell him. As long as you haven't killed anybody or blown anything up I think your secret's safe with me."

"There's this girl, her name is Alexandra, Alexandra Cooper. She's in my chemistry class, she's brilliant, she's pretty and she wouldn't even look at the likes of me."

"Pad, you've got great genes, a twinkle in your eye, that Colin Farrell accent, and you're no doofus. She'd be an idiot *not* to look at you."

"She's in the University of London's choral arts program and runs a student choir that I joined several months back. Me mam, Carita, she used to be a backup singer for a U2 tribute band. I'd get roped into her hobby to sing the bass parts if the normal guy went on one of his benders, so I knew I had the pipes for it. Tuesday night is practice night and I'm one of only five guys in the choir."

"I won't tell your dad," I say, "You have nothing to be ashamed of. You're in a choir, not a member of One Direction."

"Yeah, but dad's this tough guy ex-soldier. He went straight from school into the army. He's going to think I'm turning into a wimp."

"Erm, that's not exactly true. He didn't choose the army, more like it chose him."

"It did?"

I meant to say that to myself; Nikki, meet slippery slope.

"Look, he's not singing in a choir, you are. It doesn't matter what I think or what he thinks, you do what makes you happy right now. I wish I'd known that when I was your age, call it my gift to you. For the record, *I'm* proud of you."

"Yous haven't heard me sing." He gives me a knowing look that comes straight out of Gavin's playbook, "and yous didn't answer my question."

"Ask your dad. All I will say is that if he hadn't gone into the army you and I wouldn't be sitting here now."

"I'll ask him," Paddy checks his watch. "Jay-sus, I have to go." He gulps down the remains of his coffee. "Alex has the choir entered into a competition and so far we've made it to the second round, which starts in twenty minutes!"

"Good luck," I give him another hug. "Gav won't hear about your extra choral activities from me."

"Extra choral, that sounds dirty." He smoothes down the creases on his trousers.

"Grow up!" I tell him, laughing. He gives me a smart salute and vanishes into the café to pay.

CHAPTER 19

I take my time going through more emails on my phone as I finish the chocolate espresso. The patrons at the tables around me have changed at least twice by now. I slide a tip under my saucer, using a napkin to dump Aztec girl's blackened tissue onto the thick dregs left at the bottom of my cup. As I do so a small purple stub falls onto the table. I twist it in my fingers; it's a dry-cleaning ticket.

I flatten the stub out, and place it into my wallet, typing the address of the Quick Clean franchise into the contacts list on my phone. Google maps shows me that it's around half a mile from the café I'm sitting in to the dry cleaners. I'm toying with the idea of going there when an incoming call kills the map and makes the table vibrate.

"Hi Gav."

"Nikki, good news is I made my meeting and we signed up the client."

"That's great," I gather up my things and wander away from the table. "What's the bad news?"

"Matt's girlie in Brighton just Dear John'd him by text."

"The cow." I say. In truth I've never met her but I like Matt and he's always the one making the effort to travel down South most weekends to see her; she's never once come up to see him.

"He's making plans to go out and drown his sorrows after work. I want to make sure he doesn't do anything stupid. D'you mind if I crash at his?"

"Go," I say. "I might catch a movie, later." That triggers a thought, vague plans, something about Mina and I catching a movie?

"Thanks Nik. Bye."

As I hang up several messages pop up on my screen.

Google Calendar:

Reminder: Flight to Vegas for Wedding @ 29th May 2012. All day. (Nikki&Gav)) more details *

Reminder: Wedding in Vegas 31 May 2012 All day (Nikki(me)) more details *

One week until the wedding? How did that happen?

Reminder: M&D back from Seattle, All day (Nikki(me)) more details *

The final reminder

Reminder: movie marathon w/ Mina in Wandsworth 7:00p.m. drinks starting at 5:00 p.m.

(Nikki(me)) more details *

I hit snooze on that one and dial the phone number that came attached to the Wandsworth address. From the look of the code it seems to be a landline rather than a mobile.

It rings four or five times, then the rather breathy sounding lady from BT answers and starts suggesting that I "Press one to leave a message." As soon as I try to do that she tells me the recipient's mailbox is full and with more than a hint of glee in those well-bred tones, follows this up by cutting me off.

Rather than try and forge a way through the crowds watching the street performers, and knowing that this is a hot spot for pick pockets, I go the same way as Aztec girl, into the covered marketplace. A mobile phone starts ringing close by and people around me start checking their pockets.

"I think your phone's ringing," says the extremely tall woman standing right next to me. I pull the phone out of my front jeans pocket; the screen says 'unknown caller' which is why I didn't recognize the 'Marimba' ring tone.

"Sorry," I direct the apology to anyone who wants to take it, slipping out of the flow of people and into the shuttered doorway of a small shop that has a 'To let' sign in the window.

"Hello?"

"I got a call from your number a few moments ago, didn't get to it in time, who is this?"

The voice isn't Mina's, it has a slight Scots burr.

"I'm Nikki Doyle, Mina gave me this number."

The voice warms up instantly,

"Nikki, does this mean you can join our little gathering tonight?"

"Yes, it turns out that I can."

"Oh that's wonderful, this is going to be fun. I've heard a lot about you."

"I didn't know Mina had a roommate," I say, "Sorry, I have no idea who I'm talking to."

She laughs,

"I should hope not. Are you coming by car or train?"

"Train."

"Good," she interrupts me again, "The nearest station to us is Wandsworth Common. Call when you get to the station and I'll have Mina pick you up. Come any time after four, and we can chat before the movies. I'm so looking forward to meeting you." And she hangs up, leaving me scratching my head.

And now to call Mum at home and make plans to go and see them next weekend. They are the last ones to know what Gav and I have been up to but they don't know that. The other night Gav suggested we drive down and spend the weekend in Storr Downs with Mum and Dad and take them out to dinner to celebrate our engagement. Mum picks up on the first ring,

"Hello dear," it's not the words that put me on alert it's the over perky way she says them. Either mum's had a double shot espresso from the bakery this morning or something's wrong.

"Hi Mum. Everything okay?"

"Everything is fine."

"Are you around next weekend?"

"Yes dear."

"Good, can Gav and I come down? We've got something to tell you."

"OOOOOOHHHHHHH."

"Mum?"

"Ohhhh, Paul!" she yells. From somewhere overhead an ominous rumble; it could be dozens of tennis balls bumping down the stairs, or dad at a dead run. "He's making an honest woman of you, isn't he?"

"Suzi!" Dad's voice, shot through with panic, "What's the matter, darling? Did you fall again?"

She drowns out the end of his sentence.

"No, no Paul," Mum says, "Our Nikki's getting married." She backtracks for a second, "That is what you were going to tell me isn't it?"

"Mum!" I'm a little, okay a lot, miffed that we didn't get to tell them in person. You can't re-create a moment like that. "Yes, Gav and I are getting married, but we wanted to surprise you."

"I told you," she trills at Dad, "I've seen the way he looks at her. Didn't I say it was only a matter of time?"

Dad's still breathing hard, from his charge down the stairs,

"I think you've rather ruined the surprise, Suzi."

"Nonsense! So darling, when's the wedding?" Mum prattles on to herself, "Next summer? I love a summer wedding, me. I'll have to buy a hat and your father'll need a new suit."

"I am here you know." Dad now sounds more peeved than panicked.

"Er, we're having a big party when we get back."

"Back from where?" That forced, jolly hockey sticks enthusiasm is gone. The flatness of her voice worries me. "You're not making any sense, love."

"We're flying. To Vegas. Next. Friday." Only my mum could reduce me from a confident adult to a bumbling William Shatner impersonator.

"I see."

"You could come. If you want to."

The phone flashes up 10% power left. I forgot to charge it this morning and the charging cable is on the breakfast bar.

"Mum, my phone's dying, I'll email you the details."

"Congrats, Petal!" Dad calls before the line goes dead.

That is so not the way I wanted this to go. I should've guessed that Mum would work out our news. Normally she would hoard that knowledge, keep it secret, then pretend to be surprised when I flashed my engagement ring. What I didn't expect was her blabbing like that to dad. Oh well, the damage is done. If I dwell on how I could've made a better job of it, I'll be driving myself straight to Doctor Bradley's.

I power the phone off to save the battery. This particular model's phone battery has a habit of plummeting to zero in minutes.

For the next couple of hours I blend in with all the other suits, clicking away on their laptops, with the help of a waitress called Emma and copious coffees. An email to Ravenwood's travel department confirms the flight arrival times, then online bookings for the Lake Mead overlook ceremony, which has one evening slot open (7:00 p.m.) and the Red Rock hotel. Deposits and confirmations from both. I don't need to buy a new dress and I can do my own hair and makeup. My watch says half past three. Emma runs my card through her little portable payment machine and I give her a generous cash tip. Mid-way through powering up the phone runs out of juice, so I have to retrieve my contacts from the computer. Emma offers her pen to write the Wandsworth phone number down on the back of my receipt.

I run some quick calculations in my head. I'll have to go through Victoria station at some point and I feel like a walk.

Flocks of visitors walk away from the Covent Garden area; matching their leisurely pace in less than a mile I reach the Thames Embankment. Without the crutch of my iPhone, I have to ask a passerby which way to turn to get to Westminster Pier. He points to the right, so not quite a conversation. The tide is turning on the Thames, sunlight glances off the wavelets as they flow past me.

The main entrance to Westminster tube is just across the street from the houses of Parliament; on the other side of a very busy junction. There are numerous other entrances though, and one of them is guarded by the massive blackened statue of the warrior queen Boadicea, her horse drawn chariot charging hard towards the palace of Westminster.

It's no coincidence that Westminster Station is one of the cleanest and most modern tube stations in London, nothing but the best for our 'honourable' members. Plenty of steel and glass and security, it looks more like a spaceship than a tube station.

Once I've used my Oyster card to get onto the platform for the circle line, I plant my back firmly against the wall next to the Westminster sign and wait for the train to Victoria. That's another of Gav's maxims, if your back's against the wall that's one less angle to worry about. The tube train arrives on time, we board, one and a bit songs have leaked from the headphones of the hoodie slumped in the seat next to me by the time we reach Victoria. In Victoria train station I check the boards to find the correct platform and spend a very uncomfortable standing journey, jammed up against a pair of French tourists who really could do with a stick of le deodorant.

"The next station is Wandsworth Common, please exit through the doors on your left." As usual the train driver sounds like he's speaking through a pair of old socks.

Once off the train I follow the exit signs, which take me over a bridge and out of the station. Graffiti tags decorate the payphone outside the station and there are tool marks around the base where some budding criminal has attempted to lever open the coin collector. The black receiver feels heavy in my hand and smells of cigarettes but more important it gives off a dial tone. I reach into my pocket, no coins.

My laptop bag yields multiple receipts, a packet of chewing gum and a screen cleaner but nothing else. The ticket office only opens from six in the morning till early afternoon, according to the notices posted on the wall. There's just me, a ticket machine, and a bloke in an anorak leaning against the fence who appears to have fallen asleep standing up. I take out a tenner and feed it into the ticket machine, in the hopes that it will give me change. It spits the note back at me when I hit 'cancel'. I curse myself for my dependency on my phone. Pre mobile I used to carry a roll of fifty pence pieces in my bag, useful for parking meters, pay phones, bus tickets, vending machines, beggars. An article on Wikipedia states that a roll of coins inside a sock makes a very effective cosh. So far I haven't had to try the last one.

"'Scuse me Miss." The anorak is looking my way, his fingers interlaced with the metal of the chain link fence, "I think I can help. You need change and I'd like to get onto the platform without being accused of trespassing by the transport police."

"Buy me a platform ticket, and you'll have plenty of change." He turns and unzips his shabby anorak, flashing an old Nikon camera that dangles on a strap around his neck. "It's what they gave me when I retired. I don't want some spotty 'oik, knifing me for it. I only use it when I'm on railway property." He zips the coat back up again.

I turn back to the machine, and not only is there a platform ticket option, it's only twenty pence. I slip the note back into the machine and this time it gives me all the change I need and the platform ticket. I walk over to the guy, see the weather beaten skin, and the Waitrose plastic bag lurking by his ankle and the puff of white hair under his flat cap. He doesn't smell like a homeless person. The Waitrose bag has another cloth one inside it, with a shirtsleeve poking out. I can see matches and a tin of Heinz baked beans, several yellow boxes with Kodak film written down the side. I decide not to mention what I've seen.

"Here," I give him the ticket and all but a pound of the change. "All that train spotting will give you an appetite."

"Thank you," he says, and moves into the station, carrying his life with him. I watch him go. Then turn back to the payphone.

I feed the pound coin in and start dialing, keeping both ends of the receiver away from my ears and mouth.

"Mina? it's Nikki, I'm at Wandsworth Common Station. Do I just cut across the common to get to you?"

"Can you see the common?"

"I can see grass and trees."

"You've come out at the front of the station, wait right there, I'll be round to pick you up."

I replace the receiver and rub my hand on my skirt. There's only one road she can come up and, due to the half empty bike corral taking up most of the pavement, no benches to sit on. I wander up and down on the grass, checking every driver that pulls up. Mina roars up in a gleaming teal colored Fiat 500 less than five minutes later.

"Hop in!" she calls, using her foot to swing the passenger door wide. She waits until I've buckled my seat belt, then performs a breakneck three-point turn and rockets back up the road. I'm sure this part of Wandsworth is very nice, it flashed past too fast for me to see any of it.

Mina keeps up a constant commentary mainly about her time in Holland. She slices her way through traffic, sliding the Fiat into gaps that don't look big enough for it to fit.

"Where's your flat?" I ask.

"It's a house and we're here," she says, bumping the Fiat over the kerb and onto a tiled area, which might have once been a walled front garden.

"Like it?" she asks, pointing at the beautiful red brick, bow-fronted three story Victorian. "Mary bought it last year."

"She bought you a house?"

"No, silly, it's hers. She bought it under her real name. It's funny, the press are so keen to find out who she is and she's had a number of them in her living room when she has garden parties." Mina steps back and looks up at the second floor. "Blinds are closed, she's still working."

"She's *here*?"

"Of course she's here."

Mina unlocks the front door.

"I thought *you* were Mary Snowfire."

"Oh, that's hilarious." When she finally stops laughing, she says, "I can't even keep a diary. You thought I was Mary?"

"Yes I did, you two were never in the room at the same time, you're the same height."

"Sort of a Clark Kent/Superman thing?" Mina smiles. The smile turns sly.

"You want to meet her? Because she wants to meet you."

CHAPTER 20

"Why would she want to meet me?" I ask, following Mina into a light airy and massive room panelled in blues and greens. A giant TV, inset into the wall, rough sanded wooden floors, throw rugs, sofas lining the back wall. Mina sinks onto one and pats the seat beside her.

"Nik, something you should know about Mary, we didn't just bump into each other in Switzerland, she knew my brother, Sebastian."

I decide to keep my personal knowledge of Seb Miller to myself. Mina doesn't know that it was me who identified Seb after Connor Ravenwood dumped his body in the Thames. Hell, Gav doesn't know that.

"I think they were pretty serious until she, along with the rest of UK, read about his death in the papers. Only Mary being Mary she tracked me down and in return for the use of my story she paid for my clinic stay."

"She must be rolling in it."

"*She* is," says another voice, throaty and laced with amusement. "Nikki, I'm Mary Maccallan, we spoke on the phone earlier."

"Hi, I'm a big fan of your family's Scotch," I joke.

"Ancient family tradition handed down over centuries. Ours is spelled with two c's, not one," Mary says, her Scottish accent becoming more pronounced, "If I didn't love the anonymity so much, I could set up my own publishing company and not even scratch the surface of our fortune. My father always said that you can't replace fine whiskey with pills or machines. So now you have not one but two massive pieces of information about me." She pulls her fair hair into a loose ponytail, removes her glasses, regarding me with the same green eyes I remember from the book launch party. At the time I thought they were so green they had to be contact lenses. No doubt this is Mary Snowfire. "I told you," she continues, "because Mina trusts you, and because you keep secrets for a living." Mary crosses to the bar in the corner, pulls out three glasses, "I'm having a tequila sunrise, join me?"

"Why not?" I say, watching as she cracks the seal on a bottle of grenadine, pours measures of the red syrup and tequila into a cocktail shaker, adds some ice screws the lid on and gives it a thorough shake.

"I understand your interest in Mina," I say, not quite ready to lower my guard, "but what do you need from me? If you know I keep secrets for a living you know I can't tell you anything about my clients, past or present."

Mary laughs, opens the shaker, pours a measure into each glass.

"Nikki, Nikki, Nikki," she admonishes, "Mina knows you. Her boyfriend Stark told me how you assisted him in a bell tower full of blood."

"It wasn't full of blood."

Mary shushes me with a hand, "It will be by the time I've finished writing it, hen.

"And to cap it all, one of the SAS types I had on my arm as extra security the night of the book launch says to his mate, 'Bugger me that's Nikki Doyle, haven't seen her since the Ravenwood fiasco.' They both agreed that they wouldn't want to get you angry. You might drop a gargoyle on their heads."

"Hmm," I say, "For the record I didn't drop the statue, it fell."

"Course it did, hen."

She brings our drinks over, then goes back for her own. She sits in between Mina and I, kicking off her shoes and raising her glass.

"Mina does a lot of the ground work for me, occasionally a little signpost might be useful. Who to talk to? Is a rumor true? I'm not asking you to spill the beans on your clients, I'm just looking for a little depth, a little clarity," Mary says. "I propose a toast, let's drink to clarity."

"To clarity."

"Were you a bartender in a former life?" I ask, after a careful taste. "This is great, the last time Gav tried to make one of these he used the tequila as a blunt instrument and the grenadine as food colouring."

Mary roars with laughter, then her expression turns serious.

"Mind if we talk business for a moment?"

"You talk, I'll listen."

"Very well, you know Mina has been in Antwerp?"

"Uh huh." We both look over at Mina who, after a couple of sips from her glass is curled up, blissfully asleep.

"I'm running the poor lass ragged but she's managed to make herself indispensable to a man I'm researching for my next book."

"How does that work? I know your stories are based on actual events but don't you run the risk of being sued?"

"Nikki, by the time I'm finished with them they wouldn't recognize themselves, different sex, different country, different name, mannerisms they don't even know they have. For instance the character in Dubai Deb, was a blend of my darling Seb and a man who makes pond scum look good. Mina generously allowed me to use her as a vessel for those two."

"*Pond* scum? Arthur Pond?"

"Ah, you've met him, hen. I shouldn't be surprised, after all you had lunch with Max Clausen yesterday, just before CeeCee Sullivan stroked out."

"God you have eyes everywhere don't you?"

"I was there, having lunch with a friend, it was a total coincidence which then snowballed when the other one turned up."

"CeeCee was the other one?"

"No, the Sheikh. His Royal Highness gave my dinner companion burnoose burn when his billowing robe ripped off the poor sod's specs. Interesting that Clausen can speak Arabic don't you think?"

Arabic! Of course, no wonder Yasser looked around at the other diners before starting in on Clausen, he was checking to see if anyone else could understand what he was saying.

"He didn't want mere mortals to overhear him."

Mary throws me an impish look, she hasn't twigged that I don't understand Arabic. I'm rather flattered that she has that high an opinion of my talents. My bluff could backfire if I'm not careful. I let her lead.

"Especially given what they were discussing," she says. "That gave me plenty more raw material I can tell you."

"Hmmm."

I sip a bit more of my drink, "What's so interesting about a lazy rich royal anyway?"

"HRH is putting together a portrait of his father, to his greatness. A mosaic. Rather unusual in the fact that instead of tesserae, the whole thing is made of precious stones and I plan on stealing it." My mouth drops open, "In my next book, of course."

"CeeCee said that HRH tends to exaggerate and she's known him for a long time so he's been doing that for a long time."

"Not with this, Nikki, it exists. I've seen it. I got his dad, the Supreme Highness, to show me the work in progress.

"You said you're a fan of my family's Scotch, so it turns out is the Supreme Highness. Last time I flew over we signed a deal that will keep him in Loch Maccallans until 2020. He's also a right royal show-off. The 'likeness' as he calls it, is protected by more high tech security than the english crown jewels. Lasers, pressure pads, codes, thumbprints, eye prints, he even had to breathe on a sensor. It's stunning now but when it is finished it will be even more incredible. All those diamonds supplied by Max Clausen. Why do you think Yasser and Max were having a wee spat yesterday?

That last piece of information, gives me an inkling of what Max and HRH, formerly known as Yasser, were arguing about.

"Max isn't HRH's supplier, he's head of a tech company. Where would he get hold of diamonds?"

Mary tuts her tongue against her teeth.

"Max is HRH's contact. He has friends in the diamond bizz, mostly in Antwerp. Max advises HRH on which stones to buy. The stones come across from Belgium or Holland by a route we haven't yet determined. When they reach the UK, they get funneled into the diplomatic pouch. I have a contact at the UAE's embassy who has personally placed the stones in there. If those diamonds came in legitimately they'd be subject to duty. Being rich HRH chooses not to pay the duty, their final destination is the UAE."

"They were arguing about a bloke called Kevin, they both mentioned him," I say.

Mary laughs so hard that she almost chokes, waking Mina, who starts yawning again.

"If you two don't mind, I think I'll crash upstairs for a bit, less noisy up there."

"Sorry hen," Mary says, waiting until Mina closes the door behind her.

"You know, you should look for this Kevin," she says, "Me, I'm more interested in the late Justin Sullivan. Did you ever meet him, Nikki?"

"No, closest I've been is ten feet away." I reach into my bag, "Damn, if my phone wasn't currently a paperweight, I'd show you the photo I took."

Mary takes the phone out of my hand, "I've got a charging station next to the bar, we'll juice it up in no time," she says, returning to the sofa.

"In the rough outline of my story one of the smugglers turns on his employer and steals the jewels. Justin was troubled, monied and a bit of an international man of mystery. I have a rough character sketch and a problem, he doesn't read sympathetically. He's not bad to the core, but in the draft I've written he's coming across as a bit of a reptile. I need another angle, something to warm his blood a little, a girlfriend, a close friend, someone he cares about who isn't a criminal? Right now I don't really care for him, and if I don't, what chance does a reader have?"

Mary bows out her bottom lip and puffs her fringe out of her eyes. I mentally compare this face-to-face encounter with Mary to the first time Mina and I met.

Mary is a completely different animal, I liked her from the moment we started talking. She has an agenda but I don't feel threatened by her. Mary doesn't set off my inner lie detector the way Mina did. I liked Mina from the start too, but I didn't trust her. At the time I dismissed it as a little residual jealousy, after all she was targeting Simon, my ex-boss, and he and I came close to being a thing.

"Cards on the table," Mary says, "I don't like being lied to and from what Mina has told me about you, you're not a fan of that either. Here's what I know.

"I think Justin had a girlfriend or maybe a boyfriend, I'm open minded. I was hoping you might have some input on that, having been in the Sullivan household."

Mary falls silent, now I have to choose. I can give her what I have and let her use the eyes and ears on her payroll to chase Justin's Aztec princess down. Justin wasn't my client and I have no duty to protect the girl, especially after that confrontation in the piazza.

"You know I may have something for you," I say, careful not to spill everything at once. I give Mary the context of Aztec girl, who I'm pretty sure was on the student roll at the University of Arizona and either was visiting Justin over here or traveled to the UK with him when he was kicked out of University.

"She may be just a friend, she may be a girlfriend, all I know is that the two of them were close."

"What are you basing that on?"

I tell her about Justin's screensaver.

"I find it interesting that Justin's friend, girlfriend whatever wasn't staying at the house," Mary opines.

"It does seem odd," I agree. "It would tend to suggest that she wasn't liked or even known about."

"Hmmm, it would, hen." Mary looks towards my charging phone,

"You didn't take a pic of that screensaver I suppose?"

"No, sorry. I didn't know I'd be running into her the next day. I should warn you she was pretty aggressive. She accused me of having her followed and offering her blood money, and I'd never even seen her in the flesh up until this morning."

Mary grabs a pad and scribbles down a bunch of notes.

"How old would you say this girl is?" she asks without looking up,

"Late teens? early twenties? This fell out of her pocket during our stand-off." I hand Mary the little purple stub I found earlier.

Mary gets up and walks down to the end of the room, she returns with a paper ordinance survey map of London, shakes it out and lays the map on the floor. With a marker pen she puts both my run-in with Aztec girl and the dry cleaners on the map with black crosses. She draws a line between them and in a bold hand draws a circle using the line as the radius.

"Odds are that she's somewhere in this area, we tend to stay close to home, especially when we feel vulnerable. Was she carrying any car keys?"

"Not that I saw."

"Which way did she go?"

"She ran into Covent Garden Market. From there she could've doubled back on herself or gone down James Street." Mary adds an arrow,

"So roughly north west?"

"If you say so."

Mary ponders the map for a little longer.

"This search area only works if she was on foot," she says, her finger circling the air above the map, "If she had a car parked on one of those streets."

"One of my old clients is a traffic warden," I interrupt her one-sided conversation, "They ticket and tow anything without a permit around those really narrow streets and permits are for residents only. So even if she has a car, and a permit, she's still somewhere inside that circle."

Mary snaps her fingers,

"I think I'll be having coffee in Covent Garden tomorrow, maybe mobilize some of my twitter followers to join us. Want to come along, hen?"

"Um, no. I managed to calm the Aztec princess down last time. If she sees me at Andronica's again there might be a lightning bolt with my name on it. Even their chocolate espresso is not worth that."

All this time, in the back of my mind, I've been turning over Mary's request for my help with her research. The way I see it, if I turn her down the offer won't be repeated. If I accept on my terms, I could end up with a valuable resource of my own, one that I won't be blabbing about to Beth or anyone else at Avalon.

"I've made a decision," I say, "You can ask me for information and as long as it doesn't compromise my clients, I'll point you in the right direction."

"That is super news, hen."

"Don't celebrate just yet," I warn her, "I have a couple of conditions. One: if my information lands you in trouble with police, government, corporations, there'll be no blowback, on me or the person I got it from.

"Two: this is a two-way street, you have access to contacts I can only dream about, so for every nugget I give you I have the chance to get information in return."

"What kind of information?" Mary isn't smiling now.

"Well for starters, let me know what you find out about Justin and his mystery girl. I'm going to be out of the country for a week, starting Friday but I'll keep my phone on."

"Sneaking out of the country with your clients in the middle of a murder investigation?" Mary raises an eyebrow, "The police might not read that as supportive behavior, hen."

"I don't need official permission from them and I'm not sneaking out of the country. Gav and I are flying to Vegas to get married. Mina doesn't even know that."

"Gosh, you kept that quiet, hen."

I feel a tiny sense of satisfaction that we did manage to keep things under the radar.

"No chance you could sneak me into the Sullivan house before you go, to have a look at Justin's computer?"

"The police have taken all of Justin's computers." I say. "In case you missed it, they're saying his death was 'suspicious.'"

"I'm sure you can pull a few strings, hen," Mary drains her glass, "and if you can I'll furnish you with a transcript of what Max and HRH actually argued about. How's that?

"Well then, that's enough business for now. The home cinema is upstairs. We've got a fridge full of ice cream, plenty of drinks and Ocean's 11, 12 and 13."

"What are we waiting for?"

CHAPTER 21

The following morning.

The movie marathon didn't finish until well after midnight and Mary wouldn't hear of me getting a cab. I wake with a start from a night spent in one of the cinema recliners. For a moment I thought I'd somehow landed in business class; what with the soft fuzzy blanket over me. Several gulps from the bottle of water sitting in the drinks holder help to dilute a self-induced Scotch hangover.

Oh well, not the first time I've slept in my clothes. The journey to the doorway takes a while, my watch says it is 8:30 a.m. and there's a radio playing somewhere downstairs.

"Mornin'." Mary, still in her dressing gown sends me a tired smile as I enter the kitchen. "Coffee's brewed, help yourself, hen."

"Thanks." I pour myself a half cup.

Mary pushes my fully charged phone towards me, "Your fella Gavin?' I nod. "He's been calling your phone every half hour."

"Arrgh. He said he was going out on the lash last night. He was supposed to crash at his mate's flat and go straight to work from there."

I finish my coffee and when the phone rings again.

"Hi Gav."

"Babe, where are you? I came back to shower before work and the bed hadn't been slept in, I was starting to worry."

"Gav I'm fine, I stayed over last night. It was safer than trying to flag down a cab on the street at two in the morning. We'll talk about it tonight. Okay?"

"Not okay, Nik. I've called you over ten times."

"Look, can we not do this now?"

He doesn't reply.

"See you tonight," I say and hang up, before turning the phone off altogether.

"Sorry," I say to Mary. "Apparently he has dibs on worrying about me."

"At least let me phone for a taxi," Mary says.

"Thanks." I go to the sink and rinse out the mug, "I had a really good time last night, thanks for inviting me."

"We'll do this again soon," Mary promises; she pours a slug of coffee into a travel mug and presses it into my hands. "Don't want you dozing off in the back of cab do we, hen?"

Despite Mary's attempts to help me ward off sleep, that's exactly what happens. I fell asleep somewhere just past Clapham Common, somehow managing to keep the mug upright; next thing I know the cabbie's calling through the partition.

"Oi luv, we're here!"

I fumble for my wallet, he shakes his head, "All paid up, luv." I give him a tip anyway.

The cab pulls away and I walk into our building, palming the doorman. The lift rises up to the third floor, I totter out, unlock the front door and consider lying down on the soft carpet, which looks pretty inviting right now. Instead, I kick off my shoes and force myself towards the shower, the day will be gone before I know it otherwise. I set the temperature as cold as I can stand and walk under the icy jets, the cold makes me gasp and squeak out several high pitched scales. When my entire body has numbed, I step out and wrap myself in a towel.

I intend to walk the hangover to death except, as the lift door opens out to the lobby, Gav is standing chatting with the doorman. He says something to the guy who retreats into his office, leaving us alone. Although I'm a little miffed I am determined not to let it show.

"Wow, the day just flew by."

"Nik, you had me worried."

"Evidently, you coming?" I point the way to the river exit, "'Cos I'm walking."

The towpath is deserted; wind juggles the litter, pushing my hair into my face. Gav stalks along beside me, hands stuffed into his pockets.

"You want to go first?" I ask, while pushing my hair clear of my face for the umpteenth time.

That throws him. I can see he's trying to pitch it right. He's angry at me for staying out all night and he's wondering how many times I've done it before.

"You don't have the monopoly on worrying you know."

"What's that supposed to mean?" he snaps.

I stop and face towards him so that my words won't get whipped away by the wind.

"You were worried. Knowing me, I get that. But get this. When *you* walk out of the door in the morning I have to trust that you'll come back in one piece at night."

That stops him cold.

"I was with Mary Maccallan, the Scotch heiress? She's a friend of Mina's and it was easier to stay the night at hers. I didn't intend to oversleep but I didn't think it would matter because you were staying at Matt's and I didn't think you'd be checking up on me."

"I wasn't checking up on you!" He rounds on me, "I came back to change my clothes. Some clumsy git slopped his pint all over my shirt last night. I couldn't go into work smelling like a brewery, could I?"

"No."

"And Mary Maccallan? You do know how to pick 'em Nik."

My turn to ask what he means,

"Mary is very well known to our industry, she hires for private functions, she pays well and she's our favourite open secret."

I'm not sure if we're talking about the same 'open secret' so I throw him my best confused Nikki look.

"Never mind," he says, "Forget I said that." He turns to lean on the barrier and look out over the water. "You really worry that much about me?"

"Yeah, of course I bloody worry. I just don't make a big deal of it."

He rests his head on his hands for a second, "Like me, you mean."

I put my hand against his back, "Like you."

"I'm an idiot, aren't I?"

"No, well maybe a little bit." He looks up to see me grinning at him, "Now we're done with trust-fest shouldn't you be on your way to work?"

"You going back to the flat?"

"Nope, I'm going to get this very expensive Scotch out of my system."

He hugs me, careful not to squeeze too hard. After a few paces he turns and comes back.

"Piece of advice Nik, you may think that Mary wants to be your friend. She might be more interested in what you know than she is in your sparkling personality. "Do you remember what you talked about?"

"I was drunk not insensible."

"Just tread carefully." Now he does walk away, leaving me in genuine confusion.

CHAPTER 22

May 29th

The trouble started with two words, 'That's odd'. Up until that point it was shaping up to be the best trip through Heathrow ever.

Thirty minutes ago.

Private jets have private terminals, our chauffeur driven limo (courtesy of Ravenwood) let us off outside the terminal. Gav and I made an unconscious decision to dress for the occasion. Gav in one of his beautifully cut pinstripe suits, me in black trousers and classic white shirt with my second favourite coat, the nipped in at the waist blue jacket over the top. So far we've seen five other people and two of those were staff.

"I could get used to this," I murmur in Gav's ear. As well as being all deep pile carpets and comfortable sofas and hot and cold running waiters; soft classical music plays in the background, *Pachelbel's Cannon*, I think. "We could *be* in an airline commercial."

"You've never flown by private jet before?"

"No, apparently there are levels of wealthy. We're pools winner wealthy, not private jet wealthy."

Our whispers are interrupted by the security check. A cheerful little chap, the reflection of his gold 'security' badge paints a small white dot on my jacket. He smiles, shakes Gav's hand and taking his passport, opens it to the back and runs a handheld scanner over the barcode.

"All clear sir." He hands back Gav's papers. "Miss?"

I fish out my passport.

"Thank you," he says, scanning the barcode. "Hmm." He runs the scanner over my passport again, "That's odd."

"Problem?" Gav asks.

"No, just a code I've never seen before. I will be right back, just have to look it up." He sashays towards a small corridor to our right.

"And there's Hawkes, our pilot." Gav raises a hand. Hawkes acknowledges with a similar gesture. He's dressed in the green and gold livery of Ravenwood, captain's hat held at stomach height. Matt mentioned him as small talk during our cab ride back to the hospital.

Hawkes is Jamaican born and grew up in Brixton. Matt told me how he was lured away by a rival firm with promises of big money and bonuses. When they didn't materialize after a year of working for them, he returned to the Ravenwood fold. His skin is ebony, his teeth dazzling and what little hair he has looks like it was drawn on with one of those fine-nibbed silver highlighter pens. Gav slaps palms with him.

"Gavin man, (with his accent it sounds like 'mon'.) Good to see you." After the two have had some manly back slaps, he turns to me, "You must be the missus, I hear good things. Always said my man has good taste."

"Pleased to meet you, Hawkes."

"Have you flown in anything this small before?" Hawkes asks, removing a blister pack of Dramamine from his jacket.

I wave them away,

"I've been in plenty of twin engine jobs," I say, "I usually jump out of them once we get to ten thousand feet."

"You two ever jump together?" Hawkes enquires, returning the anti-sickness pills to his pocket. "I hear the jumps over the Mohave are outta sight."

"We'll have to try that." Gav's hand squeezes mine. We haven't been able to skydive together yet. Our schedules keep conflicting.

"Are the happy couple ready to board?"

"We're just clearing security," Gav says.

"No rush, man. The first slot earmarked for us isn't for another half hour yet. I'll keep running through my pre-flight." As he goes through the door, the Ravenwood jet is visible through the opening. "See you two in a mo."

The other couples have left the lounge and still the security man hasn't returned.

"I'm going to see what's delaying our departure," Gav says, striding over to the corridor the guy vanished down and almost knocking him over as he emerges.

"Ah, sorry to keep you," he begins, I notice he's empty handed. "Your passport, Miss Doyle I'm afraid there's a hold on it."

"A what?"

"A temporary travel restriction. When I scanned your passport it automatically notified the police department who issued the hold that you were attempting to leave the country. They called, told me to stall you. I was hoping you wouldn't notice the delay."

"We noticed," Gav says and not kindly. "Was it Sussex police who issued the hold?" To me, "This has DI Randall's size nines all over it."

"No, it wasn't a Randall, it was..."

"DI Naylor, Metropolitan Police."

All three of us turn to look at the newcomers, Naylor in the center, accompanied by two uniformed officers. He is not a young man, everything about him, his pockmarked face, his wiry hair, his seen-it-all-before attitude can be described in one word, grizzled.

"Miss Doyle, before you skip the country, just a few questions, regarding Justin Sullivan's death."

"Can't this wait?" Gav gets in Naylor's face, "My fiancé didn't even know the kid."

"Oh? That's not what the browser history on her laptop says." Naylor looks at 'security', "Can we borrow your office?" He looks at me, "Unless you want to come down to the station?"

I am not falling for that one. We're airside and there is a distinct possibility that I can set Naylor straight on his 'couple of questions'.

"We have a plane to catch," I say, "so ask your questions."

Naylor insists that we use the office. 'Security' walks us down there, Gavin isn't included. I leave him fuming in the lounge. While 'security' fumbles with the keys I sneak a glance at Naylor. His words may sound sincere but he'd get killed at poker. If DI Naylor was a cat there would be bird feathers hanging out of the corners of his mouth. "Have a seat." Naylor takes the executive chair, leaving me with the employee side of the desk. "Oh and take your phone out and power it down." He waits until I show him the 'power down' screen and swipe it with my finger, then I drop it back into my pocket.

He empties a digital recorder onto the desk, fiddles about with it. Lays his phone down next to it, speed dials a number.

"Interview commenced with Veronica Doyle, May 29th 4 p.m. Present are DI's Naylor and Tate. "I should add that DI Tate isn't physically present, he's here on teleconference from our London HQ."

"Is Miss Doyle under caution?" Tate's rather adenoidal voice asks from the speaker.

"No," I say, "she is not. I've agreed to answer DI Naylor's questions, nothing more."

"Remember what we agreed Tate. We're just chatting, that's all."

"What are we chatting about?"

"We found your DNA on our victim, Justin Sullivan. How did it get there Miss Doyle?"

6 p.m.

"Let's go over this again." Naylor is relentless, he just keeps asking the same questions over and over as if at some point I'm going to change my answers. For my part, I'm running on fumes. Naylor hasn't offered me food or water and DI Tate hasn't suggested that he should.

"How did your DNA get on the victim?"

"How many times do I have to tell you, I DON'T KNOW!" My outburst silences Naylor's barrage of questions for a moment and in those moments of silence something occurs to me.

"Why are you so sure it's my DNA, because as far as I'm aware I've never been asked for my DNA."

That produces a reaction. Naylor slaps his notebook shut.

"Interview suspended at," he raises his wrist blinking a little as he checks the time and hides a yawn, "6.08 p.m." It occurs to me that he's as tired as I am. He can't keep going for much longer. Just after hitting the off button he says, "Tate, pit stop and refuel."

"Roger, signing off."

Naylor gathers up the phone. He stops at the door, looks back,

"Don't go anywhere," he says, then leaves, locking the door behind him.

Pit stop and refuel, sometimes it helps to be a girl, men use daft references thinking you won't understand their Formula One terminology. Naylor and Tate get to use the loo and eat food. I get to sit here with mild brain fog and no way to clear it. I get up and force myself to pace around the desk, passing the water dispenser several times. It sits in the corner, topped by an as yet unchanged empty plastic container. Taking one of the waxed paper cups I push the cold button; sometimes there's a little bit left in the reservoir, in this case a good half a cup. I gulp it down, hoping the grit I can taste is charcoal from the filtration unit.

The desk drawers aren't locked and in them, apart from lots of papers and a bunch of mini bar sized Johnnie Walkers is a Twix. Beggars can't be choosers, I think, helping myself to the snack. Naylor didn't make off with my wallet so several pound notes go into the drawer as payment.

Feeling a little more lucid, I wait for Naylor to return. I power up my phone.

Gav picks up immediately,

"Nik, I've called in some favours."

"Evans?" The former Detective Chief Superintendent would be a great name to pull on DI Naylor.

"No, better than that. I called the company lawyer, Badderly; the man is part Saville row, part Rottweiler. There's been a slight hitch in my plan 'cos Naylor's goons turned him away from the terminal."

"Oh."

"Don't worry, that just pissed him off, which is good for us, bad for Naylor and Co. Keep your chin up Nik, I just talked to Badderly. He's on his way to the Yard as we speak." Gav's voice changes to what Matt refers to as all business. "Yes, sir, they've been questioning Nikki for hours. They're just coming back from a break."

I take Gav's warning, kill the call and race through the settings, turning off every buzz, bing or ding the phone can make. I place the phone, set to airline mode, microphone uppermost and set to record on the desk in front of me. Naylor isn't playing by the rules so why should I? I've barely finished when Naylor unlocks the door, he looks refreshed; a passata or ketchup smudge decorating his shirt. I round my shoulders and keep pretending to yawn, mouthing rude words about Naylor while my mouth is covered.

He sets up the digital equipment and the teleconference again.

"Interview resumed at 6.30 p.m. DI's Tate and Naylor present."

"Everyone fed and watered?" Tate's stuffed-up voice holds a note of caution.

"No," I say, before Naylor can stop me, "I'm still starving and thirsty."

A new voice chips in from Tate's end.

"No food, no water, I'd say you need to remedy that situation to my satisfaction, gentlemen. Or do I need to remind you of the difference between a person of interest and an actual suspect. A simple trip across the hall to the Chief Superintendent's office will be enough to land the two of you in some very hot water."

"Who's that?" Naylor demands.

"Oh don't mind me, I'm not here in my official capacity, yet." I like the veiled threat in his words, "I'm Charles Badderly, legal council for the Ravenwood group. Mr. Lancaster called me and asked me to find out in his words, 'what the bloody hell is going on.'"

I could kiss Gav right now.

"Your colleague, Mr. Naylor, wouldn't give me access to his interview so I called in a favour from your Chief Super. I should've said I've been across the hall once already. Your DCS is also concerned about the welfare of Miss Doyle and he is most perplexed about the detention order that he doesn't seem to have paperwork filed for. I didn't mention the search warrant, yet. Now after you've ordered some food for Miss Doyle just continue your chat, don't mind me."

Naylor mutters something under his breath, which could've been 'halfwit,' or something else rhyming with 'wit'.

After I've demolished a small green salad, crackers and cheese, a Mars bar (there's a Twix too) and a small pot of tea, I sip some of the bottled water.

"Okay," I say. The food has sharpened my focus.

"Interview resumed at 7.20 p.m." Naylor flips his notebook open. "Let's try a different tack. My techs have been unbuttoning your computer. You researched Justin Sullivan pretty well for someone you'd never met and say you've never heard of."

"I didn't say I'd never heard of him, it would be difficult to be close to the Sullivan's and not know about Justin."

"Why the interest?" This from Tate.

"CeeCee didn't seem to like her nephew, I wondered why."

"Never heard of asking?"

"She'd had a few to drink when she let it slip, and I didn't want her to remember that she had told me."

"You looked at his University profile in America."

"I was curious to see what his mother looked like, I thought he might have family photos in his room. He didn't."

I can't not tell Naylor about the encounter I had with Justin. I pick up my phone, hit pause on the recording as I'm pretend powering it up, and show him the picture I took. "He followed me, and when I confronted him he just stood there so I took his picture and he went away. I didn't know who he was at the time. You can ask my therapist, Dr. Caroline Bradley. Checking I'd shaken him off almost made me late for my appointment."

Without Naylor asking, I pretend power down the phone and replace it on the desk.

Naylor seems satisfied, then he throws me a curveball.

"We got your DNA from your parents, from your school actually. They have a program where each child has their fingerprints and DNA taken in case they run away, or get abducted."

"Let's see what you have." Papers rustle at Tate's end. The lawyer reads a list; "Samples taken from the victim's clothing; one DNA sample, unknown female. One DNA sample attributed to Miss Doyle. Trace evidence hairs from C. Lanigera, whatever that is. Alum, Sodium Chloride, Potash, Sawdust, formaldehyde, strands of green thread, Sullivan's own blood." He tuts. "Most of this is circumstantial and the DNA could be a simple matter of contact between clothes."

"What, Sullivan's sweater had relations with Miss Doyle's clothing?"

"Do you have teenagers, Inspector Tate?" Badderly waits a beat then continues. "They leave things lying around all over the place, clothes, DVD's, iPads, skateboards. In my kitchen right now there is more outerwear on the backs of the chairs than there is in the hall cupboard. I'm sure my wife's and my own DNA is all over our kids clothes and its not from any recent personal contact I can tell you that."

Tate remains silent.

"Honestly, detectives, a first year legal student could shoot this lot down before the case even went to trial.

"Do you have any concrete evidence? Short of finding Justin Sullivan's blood on Nikki's clothes you have nothing here linking her to his murder. Do you?"

"Not yet," Naylor says, "but the manner of Justin's death was messy. Whoever killed him would have a substantial amount of blood on themselves and on the coat they were wearing when they committed the murder. Several people we talked to tell me that Miss Doyle owns a knee length dark green jacket, they called it a duster. She hasn't been wearing it recently and we both know, Mr. Badderly, that the first thing the defense will do is try and obfuscate the prosecution's case. They'll ask me why I didn't follow up every lead to rule out other suspects. Reasonable doubt is enough to poison the minds of a jury.

"Prove to me Miss Doyle didn't do it, Mr. Badderly. Get her to hand over that coat. If the fabric comes back negative for blood, she will drop down my list of suspects."

"I can't hand over the coat, it's missing." I say.

"How convenient," drawls Naylor.

I recount the circumstances. "As I'm sure you can understand I was more concerned with getting CeeCee to hospital than worrying about our coats. When I went back, CeeCee's was there, mine was gone."

"I have one last question before we wrap up for the night," Tate this time.

"Where were you between the hours of 2 and 5 p m on Tuesday the 19th of May."

I rack my brain, I haven't been in the office a lot recently. "I think I was working from home, that day."

"Anyone with you?" Tate asks.

"No."

"Did you make any phone calls?"

"No, I was translating the updated security protocols that Paul Eco and I drafted for the people at Delft University into Dutch."

"I see."

"Can I ask *you* a question, Mr. Tate?"

"Go ahead."

I'm skating on very thin ice here but it has to be said. These coppers may be trying to bend me to fit their theory but they don't seem to be trying to fit me up. Maybe I can introduce an element of reasonable doubt of my own. "You know what happened to Harold Eco?"

"It has been brought to our attention."

"Paul and I spent the last few weeks drafting those new security protocols for Eco Builders in order that what happened to Harold Eco could never happen to anyone else. So why would I dump a body in the very place where I knew it would be found?"

Tate pounces. "We didn't tell you where Justin's body was found."

"You didn't have to, Sully pretty much intimated it was in a house about to be foamed. Unless I'm wrong about the location."

Neither officer speaks. Tate yawns. So do I, for real this time.

"Gentlemen," Badderly's tone brooks no argument. "I propose that Nikki remains airside while you follow up on the leads she has provided.

"I don't think they let you sleep in the lounge area of this terminal." I yawn again.

"They do not but I have something more secure in mind. I'm about to arrange a transfer to terminal three."

Naylor lets slip a vicious grin.

"To the drafty and noisy airport custody suite?" he asks. "I'd be happy to go over there with her," his palms rub together. "Those airport coppers have cable and gaming chairs and real coffee."

"Feel free to tag along detective," Badderly says. "I'm sure they can find you a chair." The smile fades from Naylor's face.

***

A minibus is pulled up outside on the tarmac, engine idling. Naylor and I get in. I stare out of the window as the bus rockets along the network of roads and tunnels out of view of any travelers in the lounges above. A jumble of orange neon, fluorescent yellow vests and lots of dark shadowy oil soaked areas. The bus pulls up to terminal three, which is dead at this time of night. I'm so tired the marrow in my bones seems to have been ground to powder and Naylor has to pull me to my feet. Too quickly as it turns out. Sparks flare in front of my eyes and the last thing I hear is Naylor cursing me as my dead weight almost pulls him over.

My brain exercised its own form of tough love and shut down completely. When it boots up again, the first thing I hear is running water, not a slow steady drip, drip; it's a spray like a hose pipe or a shower. The sound is soothing and I must have drifted off to sleep again.

My eyelids snap up like a couple of errant roller blinds. The lights are dimmed, this is a very compact room, a larger version of those traveler's pods you can get in Japan but not by much. Above is another bed, I'm in the bottom bunk. I'm still wearing my clothes and watch. Twenty past one. The interview ended at 10 p.m.

"You're awake," Gav's voice. I push myself up on one elbow, he's sitting in the only chair in the room, his face in shadow. The robe he's wearing has a logo on the pocket.

"My eyes are open, not sure about the rest of me."

"Stop it." His voice rumbles when he's annoyed and it's rumbling now.

"Stop what?"

"Firing quips at me. I'm trying to help you and you're pulling the drawbridge up. Please don't shut me out. Talk to me, Nik."

"You want to discuss my feelings! Right now I feel like crap. I've got a gung-ho police officer who thinks I killed Justin Sullivan. I've answered more questions than a ruddy prime minister's question time, and I want to burn these clothes because they'll always remind me of the second worst day of my life."

"This doesn't count as the worst?"

"No, the worst is the day I thought you'd been killed."

He comes over and sits beside me on the bed, I look again at the logo on his robe.

"Where are we anyway?"

"We're in the Heathrow airside hotel. Badderly called in a favour from the hotel manager.

"Don't worry, all we have to do is find that coat and you're free as a bird."

"You sound so certain we'll find it."

"I am certain," he says, running his fingers through my hair, "Now get some sleep. There's still a chance they'll let us fly tomorrow."

"Sorry I mucked up our wedding."

"You haven't mucked it up, we're still getting married, maybe not in Vegas, but we'll get there."

CHAPTER 23

One week later

"Want to come and see a movie?" Mary Maccallan asks. She's not asking in person, the request comes from the speaker of a pay-as-you-go phone. She timed it perfectly. Appearing to stumble against me, and apologizing profusely, she dropped it into my pocket as we were getting off the train at Docklands several minutes ago. I just shrugged it off and walked back to the apartment, feeling the weight of the phone in my pocket.

Naylor and Co. had to let me go but the hold on my passport still stands. We had to cancel both the hotel and the ceremony in Vegas, and only the hotel gave us our deposit back. I donated the shirt and trousers worn during my interrogation to the nearest Oxfam. Gav's flying home from an assignment in Paris this afternoon. He's been running point on an EU partners technical conference and he and the lawyer, Badderly, are doing their best to get Naylor and Tate into hot water about their missteps in the investigation into Justin's death. The one piece of good news, the police haven't informed Avalon yet. My duster remains on the missing list.

I ignore the slightly tatty BMW containing Naylor's two-man surveillance team. They are the reason I'm reluctant to drag Mary into this.

"I don't think that's a good idea, with the wooden tops watching," I explain.

"I might have a lead on a certain green leather coat."

"How did you know about that?"

"Nikki, Charles Badderly isn't just Ravenwood's lawyer. He works with me too."

"Of course he does."

"Listen, they're running a sci-fi triple feature at the Odeon in Putney; Blade Runner, Forbidden Planet and Galaxy Quest. Get down there, buy a ticket and go in. I think your watchers are too cheap to follow you inside. Soon as you can, leave via the fire exit door on the side of the building. I'll be waiting."

Gav's Land Rover is currently in the long stay car park at Heathrow. So, time to be cheeky. I run over to the unmarked car and tap on the window.

"Hello chaps," I say, "Look, I'm heading over to Putney. Any chance you could give me a ride?" The officers trade looks, "Oh c'mon, I know you're old bill."

"Where in Putney?"

"The cinema, Time Out says Forbidden Planet is playing."

"I suppose."

I jump in the back of the car and spend the next twenty minutes boring the pants off the two poor officers with why they should see Forbidden Planet. I manage to bore the pants off myself in the process. I am far too over-enthusiastic which means they can't wait to let me out of the car. This Odeon is on

Putney's busy high street with, I'm happy to see, nowhere for them to park.

We cross Putney bridge and to let me out they have to swing into the bus lane, earning them the stink eye from the queue waiting for the next bus. I wave my watchers off and don't go into the cinema until they've vanished from view. I buy my ticket, hanging around just past the ticketed entry using a giant cardboard cutout of Robbie the Robot waving his arms around to keep an eye on the ticket booth, just in case one of the officers decides to keep tabs.

I move past the stream of people going into screen 3. There is only one fire exit here. I slip out, trying not to act as if I'm up to something. This is one of the few times I've wished for a packet of cigarettes. My old mentor, Fred used to use his fake cigarette habit to blend in; cadging lights off passers-by. I lean against the wall and pretend to be having a spirited conversation with the invisible person on the other end of my phone so that the couple with the baby, the two girls bunking off school and the rest of the daytime shoppers won't take any notice of me.

Mary arrives in the Fiat 500, I get in. Mary's driving style isn't as confident as I would expect. We drive a roundabout route back to her house.

"Drink?" she offers once we're inside her living room.

When I shake my head she fixes herself one; picking up the remote she pushes a button and the TV on the wall springs to life.

She checks her watch,

"This is footage from Cinquante the day we both dined there."

"Where did you get this?" Mary hits the pause button.

"None of your beeswax, hen."

"The maître d' lied to me. He said they didn't have security cameras covering reception."

"He doesn't know about these. They were installed by one of the owners."

"Why would they give this to you?"

"I convinced them that I was the lesser of two evils. Do you want to see this or not?"

"Please."

Mary un-pauses the action.

"This," she says, "confirms my belief that you treat everyone as you'd like to be treated.

"This woman," she points at the pouty brunette we can see strutting over to the reservations desk, "laid into the coat check girl. All the wee bairn did was catch the rich bitch's tennis bracelet on the lining as she was removing that beautiful fox fur coat."

On screen words are exchanged. We don't have any sound but it's clear that the work experience girl is getting a little more of the real world than she bargained for. She lowers her head and looks at her shoes. The maître d' puts himself between the customer and his employee. He sweeps the customer towards the lift.

As the lift doors close on rich bitch, Mary comes into shot. She not only removes her coat and hands it to the girl, she tries to engage the girl in conversation. All the while maître d' hovers close by. He and Mary both go out of shot, Mary to the lift, maître somewhere else, possibly to the loo or a break room?

The girl checks both ways, drops the fox fur on the ground and grinds her toe into it. Then she drags it back across the floor to the coat check and sticks in on a hanger. Mary's coat is treated with much more care. Mary fast-forwards until CeeCee and I arrive. It is really odd watching yourself just out in the world doing day-to-day stuff.

"The camera does add 10 pounds," I say. "And maître is quite protective of his employees."

"You noticed that too." Mary says, throwing another sly look at her watch. "I'm hungry, fancy a snack?"

"No thanks."

Mary gets up, opens a cupboard above the bar, and takes out a plastic pot of Pot Noodle. Once the kettle has boiled she drowns the contents. I keep watching the clip, which means I'm staring at not much for five minutes.

Mary is building up to something. I reign in my impatience and swallow a yawn. It's her party and I sense she won't be rushed.

"Now I can say I know someone who actually likes Pot Noodle," I say, as Mary sits down beside me and unsheathes a pair of disposable chopsticks.

"Don't knock it 'till you've tried it, hen."

"I prefer my noodles fresh."

"CeeCee Sullivan's coat is gorge," Mary says, pausing to swallow a mouthful of noodles. "But we both know there are no foxes that colour."

"Not fox, its chinchilla."

"Are there purple chinchillas?"

"Not anymore." I let the idea sit for a beat, then grin to let Mary know she's been had.

"Don't be daft, it was grey, originally. CeeCee told me that changing the colour cost more than the coat did."

"You two close?"

"We're friends, right now. Once the project is finished," I shrug. "You know how some friendships just stick and some don't."

"Aye." Mary picks up the remote, using one hand to fast-forward the action, her other still occupied with Pot noodling.

"I wanted to give you some context before I showed you the gold." she says. "This is shift change." Coat check girl comes out carrying two coats, she slips my green duster inside the other, puts both over her arm and walks out.

"The thieving little cow!"

"I'm glad you feel that way." Mary freezes the frame. "Because I sent the other copy of this to your would-be nemesis, Naylor. And I followed that up with an anonymous tip to Crime stoppers."

"You never said exactly how you got hold of this footage."

"I didn't did I" Mary picks up her keys. "Time we got you back to your movie, hen."

In the car she drops a bombshell.

"I'm still looking for Justin's girlfriend, if that's what she is. I'm getting closer, talked to the admissions people at Arizona State yesterday. Justin was kicked out for gross misuse of University property."

"Knew that," I say.

"Do you know what that gross misuse consisted of?"

"No."

"He was using their media lab after hours. They're not sure how long he'd been doing that. His professor suspects that he was using the equipment for at least a year, maybe longer than that."

"What caught him out?"

"The caretaker. The professor blew a bulb during one of his demonstrations and asked maintenance to fix it before the start of class the next day. Maintenance went into a supposedly empty lab and found Justin. He tried to bribe the caretaker to not report him. The caretaker wasn't having any of it and Justin was suspended and booted days later."

"He could've argued that it was for a project, maybe taken a suspension and still been alive today."

"I have a wild theory, want to hear it?"

"Go on."

"Justin is the one behind 'Finger on the Pulse,' Mary says. I mean have you looked at it recently?"

"No, I've been a little busy."

"The quality has been a little rough the last few weeks. It is definitely headed off a cliff. I really want to get my hands on Justin's computers now."

Mary lets me out at the same place she picked me up; we appear to be BMW free. "Did you ask about female students that are no-shows this term?" I ask.

"Way ahead of you, hen. They're going through their records and compiling a list for me. Keep in touch."

Putney bridge station is an easy walk from here. Once I get past the church next to the cinema, Putney high street gives straight onto Putney bridge for traffic and pedestrians. The railway-only bridge is several hundred feet to my right. Walking past the ornate streetlights that remind me of lampshades, I stop for a moment. This part of the river sports the usual cammo green and standing on the bridge, even with the cars speeding by feet away from me, there is a feeling of space between the river beneath and the clouds scudding past in the sky above. But I wouldn't advise getting carried away and taking a lungful of air. It'll be 70% exhaust.

After the bridge, little tube signs start to appear every few lampposts along. I cut to my right past a building site. On my left The Royal Yeomanry and some lightly occupied tables outside the Eight Bells pub. Down below is one of the old brick railway bridges. Next to it, Putney Bridge tube. While I've been walking I've been thinking about what Mary said about her being 'the lesser of two evils' and my conclusion makes me call her while I'm standing on the district line platform.

"You forget something, hen?"

"Tell me honestly, did you use," I check to make sure I can't be overheard, "*blackmail* to get hold of that footage?"

"Of course," she seems surprised, "how else was I going to get it? Don't worry, I was careful, nothing can tie me to the method I used. I'm not a blackmail virgin you know."

"That's not something to be proud of," I hiss. The burner phone goes silent and doesn't start ringing again until I'm stuck in the melee of Earls Court. It's my actual phone. I take one look at the elbowing and shoving going on just to get into the carriages and move away from the train towards a scarred wooden bench close to the tunnel entrance.

The number shows up as 'unknown caller', which could be anything from a cold call to a friend with a new number. Sometimes it is useful to be a secretary, your own.

"Nikki Doyle's phone."

"Is Miss Doyle available?" A cultured and German sounding voice enquires. Oh god, somehow Max von creepy has gotten hold of my number.

"She has stepped away for a few moments, may I take a message?"

"Surely, I am Dieter Brug. I work for Bleeding Edge magazine; I got this number from an English colleague." Another train clatters into the station.

"Herr Brug, forgive me, I *am* Nikki Doyle. I thought you were someone else. My almost, I mean my stepson subscribes to the online version of your magazine. What can I do for you?"

"I'd like to pick your brain, about Max Clausen."

"Er, I only met him the other day and it's not an experience I am keen to repeat."

"I understand," Dieter blows on his hands, or at least that's what it sounds like from here. "Sorry for the heavy breath. I wasn't expecting to find myself out in the cold, but some idiot tripped the fire alarm in the cafe I normally hang out in. Anyway, a brisk walk never hurt anyone.

"Can we meet? I'm stuck here on a story but I could fly you out, everything on me."

"That's not possible, right now. I'm kind of not allowed to fly."

"Pneumonia?"

"Government." I say, getting to my feet. The next tube train is arriving, belching diesel smoke and brakes screeching like banshees. "But, I think I have an idea, do you have Skype on your computer?"

Brug snorts, "Skype is full of bloat ware, you don't have a Mac?"

"I do not."

"Well, I suppose I can re-download the application."

I give him my Skype ID.

"I'll be home in about an hour, let's talk then."

For a change it only takes another 45 minutes to reach the apartment. Paddy's jacket drapes over the back of the sofa and the PlayStation is in full battle cry.

"Hi Paddy." I call out to the slumped figure sitting in semi darkness.

"Afternoon Nik. Can't stop, got an airstrike to call up."

"Do you want to stay for dinner tonight? I'm doing lamb with the chili, garlic, rosemary rub, its Gav's favourite."

"I saw the stuff in the fridge. Yeah, I'm in. Extra chilis for me. I am hot stuff after all!"

Shaking my head and wondering if the kid will ever experience real combat like his dad, I set up the computer on the kitchen counter. I even have time to brew myself a coffee before Brug calls.

The screen starts pulsing, and I flip the speakers on in time to hear the cheerful burping bubbles of the incoming Skype call.

I click the green button and Dieter Brug's face appears in front of me.

"You!" I say, not bothering to hide my surprise. Dieter was Mary's dinner companion in Cinquante, the one who lost his glasses. I wonder if Mary knows she had lunch with an investigative journalist.

"Hello again."

I get right to the point. "Max Clausen—what do you want to know?"

"What did the two of you talk about?"

"Mostly about where he went to school. I was just trying to be sociable. I hate sitting in awkward silence."

"What did you think of him?"

"Old fashioned, a bit creepy, doted on CeeCee, Mrs. Sullivan."

"What about that fight, and all the shouting, heh?"

"It got pretty heated, but I didn't understand a word of it."

"The Arab, he has serious brass balls. I wouldn't go up against Clausen on his home ground."

I'm flummoxed and it shows. Brug can tell he has to enlighten me.

"Max Clausen is a co-owner, of Cinquante, that's why I was there. He's almost always wheeling and dealing or wining and dining in there."

"Co-owner?"

"Ja, he runs it with the Arab."

"You're writing a piece on him for Bleeding Edge?"

Brug's eyes narrow and his smile vanishes. At the same time the two small fragments of information flitting just out of reach in my brain come crashing together. Mary used blackmail on either the Sheik or Clausen to get hold of that tape.

"Are you alright? Either my colour balance is malfunctioning or you've gone a little pale."

"Colour balance," I lie, "Usually turns me red. You were saying, about Clausen."

"I wasn't, and yes, I am doing a piece on him and it's not flattering. Under that civil exterior the man is a ruthless predator. Several of our competitors have approached him for an interview; he won't even agree to a fluff piece. He doesn't like anyone getting anything over on him, that's why you can't tell anyone what we discussed. I want to keep walking around. You cross Clausen, you get hurt. I have a week before this story goes live and I want everything ready to throw up on the web as soon as my editor gives me the green light. On that day I'm booked on all the major news shows, ostensibly to talk about net neutrality. Once I go public, I'm safe and I have no family that he can threaten."

"Can we go hypothetical for a moment?"

"Sure."

"A friend of mine may have coerced some information from Max Clausen. How would that go down?"

"Hypothetically, I'd check if your friend has their life insurance up to date. Clausen's hands won't get bloody, he has a professional for that. Are we still talking hypothetically?"

"Yes."

"Because if we are not, I would tell your friend to get out of London for a while. Clausen will strike hard and fast at whoever he thinks is responsible."

"I'll pass that along. Stay safe."

"You too."

Brug signs off and as soon as the screen goes blank the burner phone is in my hand, Mary picks up before the second ring.

"Hello, hen."

"Mary, I've just been talking to Dieter Brug."

"How on earth did you track him down?"

"I didn't, it was the other way around."

"And what did the oh so serious journalist want?"

"He wanted to know what Clausen and I discussed and I couldn't give him much but he told me something disturbing. Clausen plays hardball and from what you and Dieter have told me, I'm putting two and two together and saying you blackmailed that footage out of Clausen."

"Yes, I blackmailed Clausen but there is no way that he can trace it back to me. And I thought Dieter wanted to have lunch at Cinquante so we could discuss the technical innovations going in at Maccallan's new distillery. Seems I wasn't the only one with an ulterior motive."

In the background I hear a creak.

"What was that?"

"The front door I expect. Mina's been out running around town for me all afternoon.

"Hello Mina," she calls out.

There's no answer,

"Please go and check its Mina."

"Worrywort!" Mary grouses. "All right I'll check.

"Mina's not here but her handbag's on the floor by the door, she's probably popped to the loo.

"Honestly hen, though I appreciate your concern for my wellbeing, I took every precaution to keep my identity a secret.

"The post office box I had Clausen send the footage to is rented. If he asks, the listing shows as Jones and Son accountants and yes I paid cash to rent the box, back in January of this year. I have PO boxes all over the place."

"Y' know I never said thanks, Mary. I owe you for getting Naylor off my back."

"Oh stop it, all I did was provide him with the means to recover the evidence that will rule you out of the investigation. The end justified the means, hen. And now I have to go and put my editing hat on. We'll talk soon."

As Mary hangs up it occurs to me that I didn't ask how long she'd been in possession of the footage or when she sent it to Naylor and Co. Did Mary's clever idea backfire? Naylor got the footage but he thinks I'm the anonymous sender; that somehow I succeeded where he failed? (I'm sure he would not see the funny side of that). I'd rather be suspected of blackmail than murder. Actually I'd rather not be suspected of anything at all.

If Mary is so convinced I've been ruled out of the investigation, why is the surveillance still on? In my haste to get back to the apartment, I didn't pay attention to the cars parked along the street.

I walk over to the side window. From here there is a very limited view of the road and I can't see the aftermarket BMW containing the two police officers. Doesn't mean they aren't there though.

CHAPTER 24

A shout of triumph comes from Paddy, "Winner!"

"Paddy?" I call out, "Now you've taken down the baddies, d'you want to go and pick up some wine for tonight. We've only got white and that doesn't go with lamb."

"Who says?" Paddy gathers his jacket and wallet.

"I do," I grin at him. "Oh and while you're out there, let me know if you see a dark blue Beemer parked across the street from the entrance. It's a bit tatty looking."

"I know what your watchers look like. Yous think they'd be out catching real baddies, not pulling a cushy surveillance."

"As someone who has suffered surveillance, it's anything but cushy." I start removing lamb and veggies from the fridge. "By the way, how are your extra choral activities?"

A smile spreads across his face. "We've made it into the quarter finals, which for an amateur choir is pretty great."

With the PlayStation on pause, the silence is distracting. I put iTunes on shuffle. When Gav cooks it looks like a bomb has gone off in the kitchen, I tend to wash up as I go for a big meal like this, so the sink is full of hot soapy water. I've just finished lining the roasting tin with foil, ready for the lamb, and started to chop veggies when the buzzer goes. After a minute or so of running my hands under the tap, I stab the intercom.

"Yes?"

"Package for your apartment Miss Doyle, the chappie needs a signature."

Gavin didn't say anything was coming but then he never does.

"I'll be right down."

I'm about to take the stairs but just in case I push the lift call button and the doors slide open,

"Bonus," I say and take the lazy way down.

The doors open and sure enough, there is the doorman and a courier, head bent over his phone; carrying one of those stiff cardboard envelopes under his arm. He holds out a signature pad, I sign, take the envelope and carry it back upstairs, locking the door behind me. I set the package down on the coffee table, restart iTunes, put the oven on and score the lamb, rubbing the freshly cut herbs and spices into the score lines. I'm careful to keep washing my hands in the other portion of the double sink.

Sometimes I have trouble assigning a ring tone to a particular person, with Stark it was easy, *Who are You?* by the Who. When I told him what I'd done he was most annoyed. He hates that show which was kind of the idea. I press 'pause',and put his call on speaker.

"Hey Stark." I chop up some more habaneros and bash the remaining garlic cloves with the flat of my knife.

"Good afternoon to you too," Stark sounds buoyant. "I've just come back from an expensive but useful lunch. I thought you'd like a little heads up on the trace report for your coat.

They tested some suspicious stains on the sleeve, which turned out to be, wait for it, Cadburys flake. The only thing you're guilty of is being a messy eater."

My mind is only half working on a comeback, the rest of it is making a mental note to get an electrician to look at the kitchen lights, the bulb above my head just gave up, again. I reach to my left to flip the under cupboard lighting on and my phone explodes. Shocked, I see a hand the size of a ham hock is responsible.

I try to spin around, an intense and crippling shot to the back of my legs would've made me fall to the floor except a hand grabs the waistband of my jeans, the other the back of my shirt, and slams me headfirst into the backsplash. An entire constellation erupts in front of my eyes as my face heads for the water. Splaying both hands against the sink I pull my knees up to my chest and kick out as hard as I can. The grip relaxes for a few seconds, but the pain winds me. It feels like I just kicked a brick wall. I struggle to get some purchase before my assailant tries drowning me in soapy washing up water. The roasting tin crashes to the floor. My head should be fuzzy from the blow, but my fight reflex along with the pain focuses my senses with pin sharp clarity. My hand squishes the just chopped veggies sending me off balance. Spittle lands on my hand. The bastard just spat at me. Then he cracks his knuckles and moves in for, well I don't want to think about that. Instead I do the unexpected, I take the fight to him, launching myself with my other hand straight into his face. I can see every whisker of stubble, the gout of blood coming from his nose courtesy of my flailing feet.

I'm still in the air when I realize that this is going to be akin to head butting a tree. My hands reach him first, masking his eyes, pushing the lids closed. I squeeze my knees under each of my attacker's armpits, turning myself into the human equivalent of a Bjorn, minus mewling baby. Unable to see, he tries shaking me off. One hand mashes my arm. It hurts but the alternative of letting go would be much worse. He lets out a wounded roar and with me still clinging to him, runs full tilt across the room, heading straight towards the windows and miniscule balcony beyond. Not wanting to be mashed I let go, tucking and rolling on the carpeted floor. He keeps on running, sledgehammering into the floor to ceiling window. He would've shattered a normal pane but a selling point of these apartments is their impact resistant glass and it resists him beautifully. I catch a glimpse of an open-mouthed Paddy in the doorway before watching the man bounce upright and keel over backwards, his body hitting the floor like a downed California redwood.

Paddy helps me onto the sofa but before he can call the police suddenly there they are; plus Gav, Stark and the outraged neighbour from downstairs who keeps telling everyone that he came to complain about the 'dreadful racket coming from the floor above'. My internal clock is skewed, throwing flashes of the fight at me before, slowing down the actions going on around me to a crawl. I can't take my eyes off the body on the floor. The blows he inflicted spark in sequence until they blur into one big sea of pain. An officer rolls the body into the recovery position, cuffing the man's hands behind his back and throwing a blanket over his prone figure. The sofa is soft and welcoming, and it's tempting to check out until the pain dies down. I start to close my eyes. Two quick slaps to either cheek and I open them, only to have a Penlite shone into them.

"Ow." I shove the light off to one side, It returns to shine in the other eye. "Keep that thing away from me," I warn the person holding it, a paramedic who looks to be about twelve years old.

"I'll save you the trouble, my name is Nikki Doyle. You're not holding up any fingers. Today's date is, June 5th happy? Look my skull's made of granite. I think I broke my toe though."

He ignores me and continues his inspection, Gav joins me on the sofa, holding a tot of brandy.

"Stark just took off, DI Naylor is on his way up, thought you might need this." The spirit hits my throat before the paramedic can complain. He pens me again.

"Do that once more and that thing'll be backlighting your tonsils!"

"Nik, he's trying to help," says Gav, inadvertently squeezing my bad arm and nearly making me pass out.

"We meet again." Naylor's nose would do Rudolph the Reindeer proud. He looks at the lump under the blanket, ambles over, toes it up and looks underneath. "Strewth!" He lets the blanket drop. "Has anyone gone through his pockets?"

Naylor uses the same 'test it to destruction' method of questioning that I remember from the airport. He constantly picks up details like dropped stitches as I try and walk him through what I can remember, which is surprisingly difficult.

"Here's what makes no sense," Naylor says. "One moment this hulking great oaf is trying to dunk you in washing up water and the next he runs over and nuts the window."

"He had a fit of some kind?" Gav interjects.

"Quiet you," Naylor snaps.

"The kid?"

"My son," Gav says with a mixture of pride in Paddy and warning to Naylor. "His name is Paddy."

A wave of tiredness sweeps over me.

"So Paddy says that you were riding the suspect," Naylor says.

"You jumped on his back?"

"No Gav, I went straight at him, I went for the eyes, like you taught me."

"The eyes you say." Naylor makes his way over to the sink, pokes around on the counter. "You, young lady have the luck of old nick. Bunch of squashed veg here, garlic and chilis."

"Habaneros," I correct him.

"I'm not a betting man but 10 to 1 the juices on your hands ended up in his eyes."

Naylor fires another question.

"How did he get in?"

Another wave of tiredness rises over me, I point at the package on the table and allow the wave to carry me out to sea.

When I come around they're still at it.

"My fiancé was attacked and you don't seem to care."

"She brought this on herself. Don't expect any sympathy from me, Mr. Lancaster."

I can feel Gav simmering from here.

"Couple of days ago we received some interesting footage, the note attached said it came from the security feed at Cinquante the day your girl lost her coat. It was sent in by a 'concerned taxpayer'. The footage did indeed lead us to the coat and establish your girl's innocence as a result. But I kept asking myself, where did it come from and why did it drop so conveniently into my lap?"

"Lucky break?" Gav doesn't exactly sound convincing.

"The maître d' was only too happy to help in return for a caution for his daughter."

Daughter! No wonder he was being so protective of the girl.

Naylor continues, "For the low price of no black marks coming to the attention of the headmaster at St Paul's, the maître d' provided us with a list of regular patrons. I called on a few of them. The ones who saw CeeCee Sullivan's collapse all said the same thing, that before it happened the co-owners had a shouting match that nobody understood, which culminated in one knocking the other to the floor. Your girl had a ringside seat. I think she used something she heard to put pressure on one of them."

"You're really out to get Nik aren't you?" Gav says, disgusted. "You can't get her for murder so you're trying for blackmail. Any one of the security staff could've sent you that footage."

"That had occurred to me, however the security staff only knew about the cameras covering the exterior entrances and exits. They swear blind that there are no other cameras on the premises. These came from a private security feed.

"We searched rent-a-thug and you know what we found? A list. Several of the names on it are people I questioned. The first two names have been crossed off, they're going be eating lunch through a hospital straw for the foreseeable future. I think your girl was careful, covered her tracks. So well in fact that the blackmailer had no one to lash out against, so he did the unthinkable and punished everyone present, or was going to if contestant number three hadn't stopped him. Like I said, brought it on herself.

"Here's what is going to happen, starting Tuesday of next week, your girl Nikki is going to report to the lobby of St. Ermin's Hotel at midday. It's a stone's throw from the Yard. If she has uncovered anything pertaining to the case, she tells me. If she has nothing to tell me she still comes, I may have more questions for her. Short of placing her under house arrest, I can't stop her poking around but you tell her that if I catch her in the act of doing anything illegal or talking to anyone even loosely connected to my case, I'll throw the book at her. Obstruction, perjury, evidence tampering, disturbing the peace and anything else I can think of. She's been lucky twice Mr. Lancaster. The third time it might be her luck that runs out or that of someone close to her. Because of her actions I have to circulate extra patrols, that costs money, blows my overtime budget for this quarter and makes the bean counters very, very pissed off with me."

By the time Gav returns from showing Naylor out I've pulled myself into a sitting position with my back propped against the sloped arm of the sofa. Gav sits down close to my knees.

"You're grounded," he says.

"Yeah, I heard. He really doesn't like me does he?"

"You've put him into an impossible position. Oh I know you didn't do it. This has Domino's fingerprints all over it. I told you that woman was trouble and now look what she's landed you in."

"Mina wasn't at the restaurant, and the people who were are going to be stunned when they hear what happened. They'll act on their own, given time. No one could've predicted this."

"You knew about the blackmail and you didn't tell me?"

I nod a yes, which sets him pacing, scrubbing at his temples.

"Gav, I wasn't happy about it, they swore to me that every precaution had been taken. And I knew you'd worry if I told you the whole story. Without her taking action I'd still be a suspect." I slipped, I said 'her' but I think he's too worked up to notice.

He comes to a dead stop in front of me,

"This blackmailer, it's Mary Maccallan isn't it?"

I pause for a fraction of a second to consider lying.

"It all makes sense, she was in the restaurant the same time as you were. Oh god, it is. Bloody Mary Snowfire's behind this!"

"How do you know she's Mary Snowfire?" I throw the question out, trying to divert his attention.

Gav's look is a mixture of pity and sarcasm.

"It's one of the biggest open secrets in the UK security industry. Like which MP snorts coke in the back of the limo on the way home from the house of commons, and the identity of Top Gear's Stig."

For a second I'm the one who's sidetracked, "You know who the Stig is?"

"I've had driving lessons from him." Gav glares at me. "Stop trying to change the subject, the only reason that these secrets don't see the light of day is that these people treat everyone they come into contact with respectfully. There are lines we draw in the sand. If their little habit isn't hurting anybody else, i.e. they're not corrupting or hurting anyone but themselves, we turn a blind eye.

"As I said before Mary pays very well, almost triple what other people offer, and she makes sure the security team doesn't starve. But this, this is a whole new level. I have no idea how she'll react.

"You knew about the blackmail Nik. That makes you an accessory. How close a friend is she?" he demands, "Because if she panics and throws you under the bus, we'll have to be ready to throw her under a bigger one."

"She won't, I haven't known her very long but she won't."

"And you're basing this on what, blind faith?"

"I'm a pretty good judge of character!" I shoot back.

"Nik, blackmail is a crime. If the victim decides to press charges, it's at least ten years in prison."

"Gav, Max Clausen isn't going to air his dirty laundry in public. He'd never press charges."

"That was before the police got involved. He could choose to leave the thug he hired twisting in the wind and go the legal route. Don't you see, this is serious. I know you have a certain disregard for the law, Nik, but cops like Naylor will take any result they can get and your loyalty in protecting Mary may be misplaced.

"If she doesn't come forward by this time next week. You, me, and Ravenwood's lawyer will be meeting with DI Naylor to work out some kind of deal. Agreed?"

"Agreed," I cover a yawn, "I'm too tired to fight with you."

CHAPTER 25

The next morning.

I wait for Gav to leave, having solemnly promised to keep resting my badges of honour from the fight. The paramedic told me to stay off my feet today and tomorrow. An ice pack rests across both ankles. Both feet are up on the coffee table. They ache all the way up to hip level and my left foot is swathed in a compression bandage to keep the swelling down. When my foot met rent-a-thug's face yesterday, his nose dislocated my big toe. The arm he gouged is stiff as a board and my forehead is a ghastly shade of purple. I am alone up here, but, despite Naylor's conviction that this is my fault; there's a panda car parked across the road from the main apartment entrance and Gav assured me that the regular doorman is taking a few days off.

Matt will be keeping an eye on the comings and goings at our main entrance (a role he has filled before) until Gav or Mr. Evans say otherwise.

Hobbling into our bedroom I retrieve the pay-as-you-go phone from my knicker drawer, careful to stuff it into the pocket of my tracksuit bottoms so that I can use the furniture and walls to hop between there and the sofa. When my legs are elevated again, I settle back onto the cushions and call Mary. I knew from Gav's reaction the day before, that if I revealed the existence of this phone he would've talked me into calling her there and then and I needed some time to think about what I was going to say to her.

"The mobile device you are calling is not in service at this time, please hang up and try again later," the phone informs me. While waiting to call back I use the time to construct a makeshift coffee station. Each item is carried over from the kitchen one piece at a time; instant coffee, electric kettle, mug, water jug. I exchange the plug for the DVD with the kettle's. My toe starts to throb. I stick my heel back on the coffee table until the pain subsides, stretching my arm to try and ease a little of the stiffness. I call Mary back and get the same message. Mina isn't answering her phone either, and her mailbox is full so I can't leave a message.

I make the mistake of turning on the television. After twenty minutes of watching feral chavs throw chairs at each other, which is horrifyingly addictive and stupor inducing, (or is that stupid inducing) all at the same time, I kill the TV and call Mina again.

"I can't talk to you, right now." She is brusque and hangs up on me before I can say anything else. Is Gavin right? I don't want to entertain the thought I've been cast off.

The Mary I know wouldn't do that, except I may not know Mary at all. The thought of sitting here for another day and a half rattles around in my head. I make another cup of coffee, put the TV back on, but switch to The Science Channel. They're having a 'How Do They Do That?" all-day marathon. I drift in and out of topics including; how to get a ship up the Panama canal, how they cope with power at peak times, like during the cup final, how they make swords to be used as props in film and TV shows, the finer points of building a Lamborghini Gallardo, and how to give furs a new lease on life. They're into a piece on how they turn cocoa beans into chocolate when I doze off; waking up several hours later with an intense need to pee. Crawling around toddler style isn't elegant but it gets me where I need to go, fast. My appetite is flat, and when Gav comes home from work and suggests a takeaway, I barely touch it.

The following morning Gav leaves me in bed. As soon as he's out the door I force myself to get up and eat some toast. Carrying the handset from the landline and my laptop over to the sofa, I start to make some calls. First to Beth, who is in a meeting and her assistant promises to have her call me back. Then Sully to see how CeeCee is doing,

"Not much change, I've got my best people with her and now we've got a police car at the end of the drive."

I'm about to say that's down to me when a thought occurs. Naylor may be conducting his investigation by seeing what spills from each visit he makes and who talks to whom. That may be his m.o.

"Yeah, I've got one too." I say and leave it at that.

"Bloke asked CeeCee if there was anything unusual about the lunch you had with her, apart from the fight. She didn't give any dirt on Max Clausen so while I was showing the Detective Inspector out, I pointed him at Clausen. He seemed very interested."

I'll bet he did.

"Your lot sent flowers, very thoughtful," Sully says. That'll be Beth's doing.

"Have you been into the office recently?" I ask.

"No, I've moved most of my operations to the house. I'm having Justin's old room turned into an office for my P.A. I've got my chauffeur running around picking up heaps of magazines for CeeCee to flip through. He dotes on her and he can tune into her vocals a lot better than her nurse can. He's my translator. He's a human version of a Springer Spaniel."

The buzzer goes.

"Are you at home?"

"Yeah, feeling a bit under the weather."

"Get back on your feet. I'm going to need you when we ramp up again."

"Give CeeCee my best."

After he hangs up, the buzzer goes again; for longer this time. I'm getting more creative with furniture as props and by using the kitchen stool as a makeshift walker it only takes me a few minutes to get to the intercom.

"Hello?"

"Ah Nik," Matt's voice, "I was beginning to think you'd had another prang."

"I'm not exactly Speedy Gonzales at the moment, Matt."

"There's someone here to see you."

"Can you send them away? Company's the last thing I need right now."

"Trust me Nik, we need to see you," her voice butts in.

"Mina?"

"Of course, Mina. Stark's with me, Mary thought you'd need a bit of a boost."

"Come on up."

I remain leaning by the door ready to let them in. As soon as the lift dings I check the peephole. Stark has his back to me, he and Mina are carrying a large plastic box between them.

"What's in there?" I ask from the now open door.

"A projector. Don't worry, we haven't come to bore you with home movies."

Mina turns around and manages to cover her shock. Despite a liberal dose of arnica cream, my facial bruises are jaundiced green this morning. She pumps a bit more bounce into every movement to compensate. "Stark took me on a field trip yesterday. I was his official crime scene videographer."

"*The* crime scene?"

"The same," Stark says having deposited the projector on the cluttered coffee table, "I called in some heavy-duty markers to gain access. You shouldn't be putting any weight on that foot." He and Mina let me lock the front door then I drape an arm around each of their shoulders and they support me as far as the sofa.

"Okay, I'm good," I say. My foot was starting to send warning signals. I'm grateful that the pair don't coddle me. Mina walks into the kitchen, cupboards open and close, she runs the water into something, china clinks.

"What are you doing back there?"

"Brewing some real coffee, not that muck that you've been drinking."

Once she has finished making coffee, Mina joins me on the sofa, handing me a steaming mug.

Stark is on his knees about to reach behind the wall mounted flat screen TV.

"By the way Stark, thanks for calling the police and Gav the other day," I say. A tiny frown line appears on Stark's face. "Oops, sorry! Didn't mean to steal your thunder, tell it your way."

Stark's story is slightly muffled as his top half has vanished behind the wall mount.

"First of all I thought we'd just been cut off. Except the more I thought about it, the more that didn't seem like an ordinary dropped call to me and I would've been happy to be wrong. I dialed the 999 operator, told them that I'd heard signs of a struggle and backed it up with my name and ID badge number.

"Although internal affairs think they have me in limbo, I'm still quite active as a consultant and my details are still in the police system. Gavin was my second call and we both arrived here at the same time.

"Gavin covered for me, said I was the closest thing he knew to a Doctor that he could call. The copper at the door taking names seemed to accept that and I could see you were in good hands so I made myself scarce."

"He came straight to Mary and me," Mina takes over. "And last night a Detective Inspector Tate came to the house. Stark and I stayed upstairs.

Mary answered Tate's questions and he went away after Mary told him she'd make her own security arrangements. I could see she was gutted by what happened. I didn't realize how gutted.

"Yesterday morning she called her lawyers and together they descended on Tate and the other investigating officer, Naylor. She left us a note to that effect. She is co-operating with the investigation and that's all she could tell us when she returned yesterday. She has ditched the disposable phone and suggests you do the same.

"Oh," Mina reaches into her bag and pulls out an iPhone, "That reminds me, Mary said to give you this. She can't live without hers and I assured her you are the same way. It's all charged up, you just need to put your Apple ID in to pull all your info off the cloud."

"Thanks."

Although the landline still works, we rarely use it and the only people who know the number seem to be trying to sell us double-glazing or timeshares so most of the time it feeds messages to the answering machine. The very first thing on my to-do list was to get a replacement iPhone.

Stark has placed the digital projector onto another of the kitchen stools, "All wired up and ready to go." He picks up the remote. We all turn at the sound of a key in the lock. Gav shoves the door open, he scans the room, on alert, sees all is well and the muscle in his jaw relaxes.

"I didn't know you had visitors," he says, "I came in through the underground car park."

"Gav, Stark you know, and this is Mina."

Stark acknowledges Gavin but stays put. Mina gets up. She walks over with her hand out, "Gavin, good to finally meet you. I've heard some pretty impressive things."

Gav shakes her hand but doesn't reciprocate. Mina keeps on going.

"You're just in time, we were about to show Nikki what we found at the crime scene, yesterday. An extra pair of eyes might pick up something we've missed." She's laying it on with a trowel and Gav is either swallowing it, which is unlikely, or being polite for my sake, far more likely.

"I'm surprised you got past Matt," I say, not quite willing to let him off the hook. Matt must've been on the phone to Gav seconds after Stark and Mina got into the lift, and Gav must've either been close by or he broke several speed limits getting here so fast. I'm both touched by his concern and narked by the fact that he still doesn't fully trust Mina.

Gav sits down next to me, Mina on the other side, no room for Stark, it's a three-seat sofa. Stark stands beside the screen using a chopstick, leftover from last night's takeaway, as a pointer.

"We managed to determine that there were *two* crimes not one." Stark begins, as Mina's rather jerky tracking shot shows a muddle of tyre treads at the main gate. "The night before Justin's body was discovered, Eco builders suffered a break-in. The original theory was that whoever killed Justin came in the front gate at Eco, dumped his body and made off with one of the lorries on the site.

"Now that theory never sat right with me because if they came in a vehicle, why steal another one? All you're doing is drawing attention to yourself. The team who worked the scene were thorough, except they only worked the area from the front gate to the spot where Justin's body was later found."

The images on the screen become a lot smoother,

"I'd finally got the hang of the camera by this point," Mina chips in. "You can see the exact time when I found the image stabilizer button."

I'm glad she found that button too, I was beginning to feel a little queasy from her 'Blair Witch' style footage.

"According to my colleagues," Stark continues, "they pinpointed Justin's TOD as over a day later than the break in. Lucky for us Essex is in the middle of a drought, so our evidence was pretty much uncompromised.

"Mina and I started from the murder scene and worked a circular pattern outwards." The camera pans around. "As you can see, the fence and walls to north, south and west don't have any gates and I found nothing to suggest anyone throwing the body over the fence and coming down after it."

The chopstick resonates as Stark sneezes.

"To the east there is a thick hedgerow which looks unbroken. As you can see, when Mina pans down, the ground shows signs of human traffic so we followed the footprints." The Stark on-screen can be heard muttering to himself that 'there must be a gap in the hedge.' And he is right. One hedgerow turns out to be two, planted to overlap. A narrow twitten allowing those in the know access. 'Mina, get a shot of these fibres.'

She zooms in on first a colourful chrysalis lodged low among the twigs then after a curt instruction from Stark moves the lens up to focus on two sets of fibres, one light, one darker, snagged on the exterior twigs.

"This is where I got the local boys involved," the Stark standing in our living room says. "They came back out and collected samples."

Gavin speaks for the first time since he sat down, "Where does the path lead?" he asks.

Stark is explaining that it took them to an unmade road at the back of the industrial estate. Meanwhile I'm looking at the green strands waving from a stray twig. An idea is flying around in my head like a fly bouncing off a windowpane.

"Are these fibres from Justin?"

"The green ones are, they came from the cashmere jumper he was wearing. The black ones definitely are not."

"I think I know how my DNA got onto Justin's clothes. The day you got sent to Antwerp, Mina, I had breakfast at the Sullivan's. There was a green cashmere sweater over the back of my chair, I draped my coat over it."

"He was wearing jeans, cowboy boots and the green sweater when he was found, no scarf, no coat." Stark recites the list from memory even though he has a file on the table in front of him.

"Did you find a car?" Gavin again.

"No," says Stark, "which I think is significant. Either Justin and whoever killed him traveled together or Justin had someone drop him off."

"Justin seems to be a lot of a loner," I say, "the only person who seemed to care about him is the girlfriend. Has Mary had any luck finding her?"

Mina sighs, "No, and it's not for want of trying. I've had people on my trail before and when that happens you just hunker down and wait for them to lose interest. I think that's what this girl is doing. She may never surface. For all we know she hopped on a plane back to South America or wherever she comes from. It's what I would do."

Stark looks over. I've seen that look of loving frustration from Gavin many times, "You don't have to run any more, Mina," Stark says.

"Can I look at the footage again?" I ask, "Unless you made me a copy."

"I'm afraid that was verboten." Stark says.

I watch the footage several more times and while nothing jumps out at me, every detail is etched into my brain. In the meantime we order takeout, which Mina insists is her treat and I'm pleased to find that my taste for twice-cooked pork has returned with a vengeance. Gav works in a different way to me; he keeps lobbing questions at Stark as things occur to him.

"If the road isn't used the only tracks would've been from the vehicle or vehicles that the killer and Justin arrived in. Why didn't you get any footage of those?"

"There were some tyre tracks," Stark replies, "but I couldn't get near enough to see how many. Once we gave them another avenue to investigate the local boys didn't want to be seen sharing. I'll find out soon.

"All I can tell you is that there were dark fibres at both ends of the twitten so there was definitely another person who used that pathway and they were wearing a dark coat."

"My theory is that Justin was wearing the dark coat," Mina interrupts; her words rather distorted by the mouthful of food she's chewing. "And there was something on it that incriminated his killer so they took it with them. That would mean at least two sets of tyre tracks."

"As I said in the car on the way back to town, that is an interesting theory, but, it is just a theory." Stark lets Mina down gently. I imagine that if she was one of his lab techs the dismissal might carry a little more bite.

"What about the unknown female, have they tracked her down yet?" I ask.

"No, no sign of her. Whoever she is, she may have rubbed off on Justin, the same way you think you did and I can't get back onto the site now. I'd be in danger of contaminating evidence and I'd blow my mate Allen's goodwill. This is all we're going to get." Stark and Mina pack the projector away.

Mina slaps her forehead,

"I nearly forgot, though we haven't located Justin's girlfriend, we may be close to identifying her. Arizona State simply asked the students if they had their full compliment of roommates and hers came forward. The description matches the one you gave us, dark hair, dark eyes, South American."

"Has anyone interviewed this roommate yet?"

"Well," Mina thinks for a minute, "I was going to. They've got the student coming in after she's finished her classes tomorrow, but you might get more out of her. Got something I can write a number on?"

"Here." Gavin scoops our notepad and a pen off the table, Mina takes it and prints a number, area code and extension details, plus a couple of names. "That's the guidance councilor's office. They're expecting a call at 10 a.m. our time."

Friday

I get up when Gav does and while balanced against the breakfast bar put some tentative weight on the damaged foot. It throbs a warning, which is miles better than two days ago when it felt like someone had lanced my sole with a plasma torch. I've always healed fast, I'm lucky that way.

"Gav, I'm dying for some fresh air. I don't need to walk very far, just to get outside would be heaven."

"Open a window, get some of that Thames air in your lungs," Gav says, giving me a hug and going out the front door. He reopens it seconds later, "And no going up to the roof."

After several cups of coffee and at the exact time Mina specified, I put in a call to Arizona.

The student health councillor (Mina underlined the words and wrote 'no kidding' next to them) answers with that happy, clappy optimism that makes my toes curl.

"Good afternoon!"

"Hi, could I speak to Cindy please?"

"This is she."

"Cindy, I'm Nikki Doyle. You talked to my colleague Miss St Clare yesterday?"

"Why I surely did, Kelly-Lou's running a little (it comes out as 'liddle') late.

Mina's neat handwriting identifies Kelly-Lou as Kelly Louise Sampson, roommate of one Inez Ramirez, who is possibly hiding out in London.

"That isn't a problem," It occurs to me that Cindy may have had contact with Inez and she confirms that the young woman has been to see her on several occasions.

"Inez is a bright student, she sought my advice about suspending her studies. She was here on a student visa and I told her she might get sucked into family matters if she returned to her native country and find herself unable to return."

"And when was this?"

"Oh, about a year ago." Somewhere in the background a door bangs open.

"Sorry I'm late, our T.A. doesn't know the meaning of exact time."

"That's okay Kelly-Lou, Nikki and I have been chatting. Want me to stay in here?"

"Naw," there are sounds of Cindy retreating, "Inez isn't in any trouble, is she?"

Interesting question.

"Not as far as I know, it's just that Justin's been in an accident and no one seems to know where Inez is. She may not know what's happened to him."

This may be where the conversation ends. I have my fingers crossed it doesn't or we're back to square one. What I get from Kelly-Lou is a sharp intake of breath and, "Justin's hurt?

Oh my lord, poor Inez'll be going out of mind when she finds out."

The key to unlocking Kelly-Lou is three little words,

"They are close?"

Kelly-Lou spills how Inez 'practically moved in with Justin,' that she was 'crazy about him.'

"They met at Arizona State?" I ask.

"Naw, Inez said his parents were rich, that as kids Justin had looked out for her. She said he made her feel safe."

"Her parents were friends of Justin's mum and dad?"

"Naw, she told me his momma and daddy died, it was sooo romantic." Kelly-Lou claps her palms together, "Inez said she wished for a playmate and the next day Justin appeared. Um not that I think his parents dying is romantic, it sucks," she adds.

"Inez was *living* with the Sullivans?"

"I suppose. Hey, Justin's last name is Sullivan, they must be related."

"They must," I try and think of anything else to say, "Kelly-Lou, did Inez talk to you about suspending her studies?"

"Oh yeah, last year when her momma passed and Inez's Uncle wanted her to come back for the funeral." Kelly-Lou's gum makes a sound like a mousetrap being sprung, over and over.

"Y'know, Inez never talked much about her folks. I got the impression they didn't really get along. Her Uncle phoned when her momma died and I walked in to hear her yelling at him in Portuguese, it's my major. Anyhow she was screaming

'You're not my father, they don' have phone boxes in hell!' She hung up on him and when she saw me she accused me of listening to the whole conversation, not just the iddy biddy snippet I did hear. I finally managed to calm her down. She's a beautiful soul 'cept when she's mad and then you feel like she could zap you right out of existence if she wanted to."

I nod even though Kelly-Lou can't see me down the phone. I felt the same way when Inez reached into her jacket pocket during our confrontation in Covent Garden. I've no doubt we've got the right girl. "Kelly-Lou, can you ask Cindy to email me a copy of Inez's picture."

"Sure thing, what's y'all's email address?"

I give it to her and after a few more pleasantries ring off. I'm racking my brain to work out how Inez and Justin knew each other as kids. Maybe the Ramirez family were neighbours. If I wasn't restricted by this damn foot I'd walk the towpath until an answer popped into my head. I have to get mobile again and soon. Conventional wisdom used to say don't move whatever you've hurt, broken, whatever, it will heal better. Now it is more like 'move it or lose it'.

I don't have any parallel bars to practice on so the gap between the back of the sofa and the dining room table, which are the same height, will have to do. Only one problem, the dining table is too heavy to move by myself even when I'm standing on my own two feet.

"Nikki, I was just about to call you." Matt says, "The chap one floor below you just called down to complain, he says it sounds like you're moving furniture up there."

"Well I am, I need your help moving the kitchen table."

"You're supposed to be staying off that foot, is what I heard."

"Matt, I've been sat on my backside for over two days and I'm going to go stir crazy up here if I don't get outside soon."

"All right," he grumbles, "I can only be a few minutes."

He arrives at the door, I let him in. He moves the table like it was made out of tissue paper.

As he's leaving he looks at me. "Gav's going out with the lads tonight, he'll sleep in tomorrow morning, he always does after a good night out. You really want to get some fresh air?"

"Yes please."

"Alright," he says, "Gav will have my guts for garters if he finds out, but it'll be our little secret, okay? He's trying to protect you and all he's doing is exposing you to daytime TV, which will rot your brain or send you stark staring bonkers.

"I don't work weekends so I'll be out here at 4.30 tomorrow morning, I always start the day with a jog. We'll get you some park time and you'll be back in bed long before he wakes up."

"Okay."

My makeshift rehab gym is perfect, I start with five laps back and forth every half hour. I keep working up and by lunchtime I have one hundred laps under my belt, and I'm starving. I walk slowly over to the kitchen without the help of any furniture. Gav calls just after I've heated and eaten a bowl of minestrone soup.

"Nik, I've been roped into a boys night out, tonight. You okay with that?"

"Sure," I say, "have a good time, I'll see you tomorrow morning."

"Can't wait," Gav says, signing off.

The rest of the day goes smoothly, I watch a couple of movies, going to bed around eleven. Gav rolls in sometime after one, he crawls into bed and is breathing deeply moments later.

CHAPTER 26

I can't sleep. I can't wait to be outside again. Forced inactivity like this is not my style. Time crawls and by 3.30 I ease myself out of bed and start stretching my calf muscles before getting dressed. Good job Gav is pretty much out cold because I knock the alarm clock over, which starts a chain reaction ending up with my favourite necklace skittering across the floor and me having to go down on hands and knees to find it. Track suited, I turn my attention to footwear. There's no way I can put trainers on. I settle for my calf length side-zip boots. It is almost 4.30 and Matt won't be late. The first jacket I grab out of the cupboard is Gav's heavy pea coat. Until sunrise it will be pretty cold out.

"I am not getting in that thing!" I say, motioning at the wheelchair parked next to Matt.

"Keep your voice down!" Matt shushes me. "I can move you faster in a wheelchair, Nikki. It's this or we're not going."

"Fine." I say, lowering myself in.

Once out of the lift, Matt wheels me outside to one of Ravenwood's company vans, lifts me out of the chair and into the front seat. I shrug him off when he tries to buckle me in, "I can do that."

He folds up the wheelchair, lays it in the back and off we go. This early we pretty much have the road to ourselves. We leave Docklands, bypassing central London.

"Hampstead?" I ask.

Matt nods, his eyes fixed on the road.

The last time I came out this way it was to the Sullivan residence, in a taxi. The only things working in Hampstead right now are streets lights and traffic lights. Matt appears deep in thought. He parks the van. I know where we're going, Parliament Hill.

From here London is laid out below us like a giant 3D model. Matt offers to carry me. I decide on the wheelchair option instead. He takes me over to the bench where Colonel Ravenwood and I met that fateful last time. Nothing much has changed, except the last time I was here you couldn't move for joggers and people walking their dogs and I'm pretty sure there wasn't a gazebo parked at the top of the hill, glowing fluorescent white.

"Your sunrise will be along in a mo. Fancy some coffee to warm you up? I've got a flask in the van." He doesn't wait for an answer, just trots back up the path. The tiniest blush is pushing up into the dark sky. I stand slowly ready to greet the sunrise and promise myself that before long I'll be running up and down the hill that drops away a few feet in front of me. Matt comes back with the flask, his footsteps stop behind me.

"Would you believe I've never seen the sunrise from here?" I turn around and nearly lose my balance. *Gav* is standing behind me, not Matt. He's wearing jogging gear similar to mine and looking remarkably fresh for someone who went out and supposedly got drunk last night. He walks around in front of me,

"Will you marry me?" he says.

Flustered I counter, "I've already said yes, of course I'll marry you."

"No Nik, I mean will you marry me, now." He points over at the gazebo.

Suddenly I understand, there was me thinking how clever I'd been and I had no idea that I was the one being tricked.

"I'll carry you over," Gav says, "or the sun'll be up by the time we get there."

"Aren't you supposed to do this afterwards?" I joke, "and where on earth did you rustle up a gazebo?"

"Compliments of James Farmer, he and Cass offered to let us use Cluedo manor, but I thought this would work better. However, I did invite a couple of people." Matt's holding an iPad, Mum and Dad are waving at me from inside it.

Moving towards the gazebo is what looks like a floating broken halo. It resolves into a compact little man with a dog collar around his neck.

"Nik, meet Father Michael, he's our former army chaplain and a very early riser."

"Hello Father." I shake his hand and we all hop inside the gazebo, which I would normally feel like a complete twit doing but I have this curious warm feeling spreading throughout my body.

"Don't we need another witness?"

"Yous mean me?" Paddy steps out of the shadows, also carrying an iPad.

As golden light begins to bounce around the steel and glass of London's skyscrapers, the chaplain clears his throat to begin.

"Before you are joined in matrimony it is my duty to remind you of the solemn and binding character of the vows you are about to make. Marriage in this country is the union of two people voluntarily entered into for life to the exclusion of all others."

Father Michael looks at us with a serious expression,

"Repeat after me," he says and first Gav and then I state that that we know no legal reason, the chaplain calls it a lawful impediment (which sounds really painful to me) why we can't marry each other.

The ceremony is taking longer than I expected and with the rising sun come the dog walkers and joggers, who, so far are keeping their distance. A woman carrying a yoga mat comes up the hill, lays it down and starts performing sun salutations. Below us the London skyline is ablaze with light as we exchange rings and follow the prompts of Father Michael.

"I, Gavin take you, Nikki to be my lawful wedded wife. To have and to hold, from this day forward. For better for worse, for richer for poorer. In sickness and in health, to love and to cherish, till death do us part, and this is my solemn promise according to the law."

I say my piece also following the same prompts.

"I believe the two of you have prepared some words of your own?" says Father Michael.

Gav speaks first, leaning in so that our foreheads touch.

"Nik, I promise to be your co-pilot, side-kick, champion, lover and friend. I plan to spend the rest of my life with you my little trouble magnet."

Now the sun's rays wash over the gherkin shape of 30 St Mary Axe and it's my turn. Before our aborted wedding attempt, what seems like years ago now, I wrote down and memorized what I wanted to say to Gav and although it comes out in slightly the wrong order I mean every word I say.

"Gav, you protect me, sometimes that's not an easy task, but you never hold me back. I choose to be with you for as long as we both have breath in our bodies. I love you and I always will."

The dome of St Paul's is flashing semaphore at the Shard and Father Michael puts our hands together and pronounces us, 'husband and wife.'

"You may kiss the bride," he says and just before Gav does, he leans over and whispers in my ear.

"Shall we go back to bed Mrs. Lancaster?"

"Uh huh." I murmur.

"There are a few formalities you have to take care of, papers to sign and such, to make this union legal," Father Michael interjects. I turn to the iPad containing my parents.

"Mum, Dad, thanks for attending, sorry you couldn't be here in person."

"Beautiful ceremony, Petal," says my dad. Mum is silent but not dry-eyed.

"Operation stealth wedding almost complete." Gav says to me, as we exit the gazebo. Matt and Paddy are standing either side of the doorway, there's a pop and I taste confetti on my tongue, the pair let off another couple of confetti poppers. I see a few phone screens pointed our way, the locals are getting curious.

"C'mon," Gav says. "Before we end up on YouTube."

The paperwork that we have to sign to make things legal is in Father Michael's car. Paddy sidles up as the chaplain arranges the documents on the passenger seat and pats his pockets for a pen.

"I just checked the video I took, in case there was any Photoshop I'd have to do. Yous bruises just look like a golden glow."

Christ, that hadn't even occurred to me!

We're on our way back home when Gav pulls another surprise.

"One more present from James and Cass." We detour to Stansted heliport. "They wanted to give us a decent honeymoon."

We board the helicopter, which takes us to a country hotel.

All I'm going to say is that, flying back on Sunday night, I was happy and exhausted and totally relaxed. I don't know how couples can go away for two whole weeks, they must have a lot more stamina than I do.

CHAPTER 27

Monday

The beginning of the week and I'm due to meet Naylor the next day. Beth called me back first thing this morning which is why I'm in a taxi on the way to Covent Garden. The driver drops me as close as he can without driving onto the piazza.

The cafes are only just starting to put out chairs Beth is already seated and watches me approach. My steps are confident, if slow. My legs no longer feel like jelly but the attack has had a strange side effect I would never have expected. I know they say a sixth sense is bollocks, and pre attack I would've agreed with them, except now each person that passes me has a feature emphasized, bright colours in some, darks in others. A guy who gives me a wide grin has darkness in his eyes that makes me grip the mini can of pepper spray I always keep in my pocket. Beth has a worried look on her face and the red flowers on her scarf are almost pulsating.

"What on earth happened to you?" she asks before I've even pulled the chair out.

"There have been some developments, professional and personal," I say, carefully lowering myself onto the seat. "Some good, some fantastically bad. Good news first." I flash the ring.

"Oh my god!" Beth has known me a long time. Before she poached me away from Archimedes, she and I worked pretty well together. She's out of her chair, enfolding me in a very unboss-like hug.

"Congratulations! It's about time Gavin made an honest woman of you."

"Ow! Thanks."

Beth releases me, "I take it your condition is related to this case?"

She orders for both of us, and I fill her in on *almost* everything. Mary's alter ego is off the table. Talking to Beth is always useful because she doesn't tolerate waffle. Everything has to be concise.

"You should've come to me sooner," Beth says, her expression troubled as I finish up.

"And that would've led to me being taken off this project," I counter, "because you would've been duty bound to inform the board."

Our drinks arrive without incident. I'm telling her about the crime scene and what Stark and Mina uncovered.

"I got a text from Stark on my way over here; there was only one set of tyre tracks at the scene. I won't bore you with the make and model."

"You know I'm tyre stupid," Beth replies, "What else did they find?"

I casually scan the area for any sign of Inez while telling Beth about the fibres Stark photographed. "and there was this purplish lump at the bottom of the hedgerow, that Stark thinks might be a chrysalis. He's got a call in to some forensic butterfly expert to see if they can identify the species from the photo or if he needs to put the expert and his mate Allen together."

Beth mulls over what I've just told her, checks her watch,

"I have to go in a few minutes, I'm not going to tell the board however; I think it can wait until next week's meeting. Things should be cleared up by then, yes?"

"If they're not, I'll take full responsibility."

"These are on me," Beth says, "And I presume that there will be a party to celebrate the wedding?"

"Oh there will. We're still compiling a list. Don't worry, you're on it."

"Good," she pushes her chair back, "and your friend Stark has one thing wrong, that thing couldn't be a chrysalis for a couple of reasons."

I give her a *huh?* look.

"Tony's father collects butterflies. Remember last year Tony and I were invited to go with him on one of his trips?"

"Vaguely," I say, taking another sip of my chocolate espresso and looking up at her, "I thought that trip didn't go very well."

"That's a mild understatement. It was lots of walking, lumpy beds, cowpats, Latin names and butterfly murder. Frankly I was bored rigid and I ruined a decent pair of walking boots. I did pick up a few things though. Caterpillars are around now, they don't start to cocoon themselves for at least another month and in the unlikely event that this was a cocoon it would be camouflaged to blend in with the leaves around it, anything bright would be too attractive to the birds."

"Huh," I say.

"Take care of yourself, Nikki." Beth gives me a gentler hug. "and for heaven's sake don't do anything else daft."

She walks across the square, vanishing into the market place with smooth self-assured steps. I linger over my coffee, turning over our conversation.

The new phone plays the opening notes of 'Who are You?',

"Hi Stark."

"Did you get my text?"

"Yes and I have a question. Did they take samples of everything in that hedgerow?"

"I'm not sure, I can ask. Why am I asking?"

I pass on Beth's butterfly knowledge.

"I'll check and get back to you," he says.

When he does finally call me, it's a welcome interruption from the constant chat from my cab driver. I paid a Big Issue seller to flag one down for me as I was having no luck.

Sitting on the back seat I hold my hand up, "Sorry but I have to take this."

Stark doesn't have good news.

"I checked with my mate Allen. He says there were only the two sets of fibres, nothing else. He documented before he collected. I'm sending you a still he took."

He rings off and I check my inbox. Sure enough, the curled-up mass of whatever it was; lodged in the lower part of the hedge is missing. Another picture arrives, a still from Stark's video presentation at our flat. He's calling back.

"Check your inbox."

"I'm looking at the pictures now."

"Nikki, whatever that was, it must've just blown away. No one else came near those bushes until Allen and his merry band of techs arrived. And Allen's as straight an arrow as you can get. If he says he didn't see it, he didn't see it."

He rings off when I don't comment. I look at the thing again. Now I that know what it isn't, I try looking at it with fresh eyes, until the phone turns itself off.

The taxi driver feels he has to fill the silence with chatter as he heads towards Docklands.

Matt is on the phone when I pass the main desk. He gives me a tiny salute and then goes back to trying to placate whoever is on the other end of the call.

It's been a busy morning and most of the afternoon. As soon as my eyes close, I'm out.

"Nik?" A hand is shaking my shoulder.

"Uh," I shake my head to clear it. Gav is standing in front of me holding a package.

"Hello sleepy wife," he bends down and plants a kiss on my lips, the package ends up in my lap. "This was couriered over for you. Matt says he checked it and it's not ticking."

"Funny, Gav." I yawn, "Anyway I'll get to it later."

CHAPTER 28

Tuesday, noon

Naylor is late, not that I'm complaining. He chose St. Ermin's for our meeting because it's convenient for Scotland Yard. What he doesn't know is this is where mum and I used to stay if we were too knackered to come home after a London shopping spree. Even though it's in the middle of central London, the place has a four-star rating. Once past those gates and onto the tree-lined courtyard that stretches around a hundred feet back from Caxton street, it becomes an oasis of calm. The lobby is immaculate with staircases going off every which way. The very first time we came here, I had just finished reading 'And Then There Were None' by Agatha Christie and I thought the place looked very Christie-esque.

The lobby bar is being monopolized by two braying hoorays, so I wander into the Caxton bar. I prefer the Terrace bar but it is no place for a private conversation, plus I don't want to risk those stairs. I'm wearing a business suit and carrying a briefcase full of papers. The barman takes my order of Loch Maccallans and a small Cornish pasty, and compliments me on my choice of Scotch. I take my tray over to the fireplace and take the comfy chair. Naylor will have to find his own. His running late could be police business though I suspect he's just trying to show me who's boss.

The envelope that Gav dropped in my lap last night is in the stack of papers I brought along. I grabbed it just as I was going out the door. Beth knows my penchant for deleting company-wide emails without reading them so she has her PA print out the two or three really important ones and every couple of months they arrive in one of these plain cardboard envelopes with the 'DO NOT BEND' warning across the front. Reading all that mind numbing jargon should put me in the right frame of mind for a light grilling by Naylor.

I slit the top with the St. Ermin's knife next to my plate and shake out five printed sheets, plus pages torn from a yellow legal pad. These are not policy directives from Avalon. There is a monogrammed Post-it note stuck to the front of the first sheet, written in a flourishing hand.

Nikki, here's an angle for you. I gave this information to DIs Naylor and Tate.

Tate translated it and Naylor informs me – not their case not their problem. To keep you honest the attached transcript is mine, not his. See what you can do with it. I promised it to you anyway.

M

I take a forkful of pasty. It's hot. As well as the normal lamb, potato and swede, there's onion relish on the side of the plate and a good dose of HP sauce mixed in with the main ingredients. I'm in the process of picking up the Scotch when I start reading. My hand pauses then slowly sets the glass back down.

I'm not a code breaker as such; my skills extend to completing the codeword in the coffee break section of the Daily Mail, but I know an information key when I see one. Several random pieces of data that have been quietly floating around in the tidal pools of my mind suddenly make a lot more sense.

"Excuse me," I call to the barman, "any chance you've got some paper lying around?"

He rummages under the bar, comes up empty. Without waiting for me to say anything he trots out to the lobby, returning with a couple of notepads.

"A4 or A5?" he asks.

"A4 and you are a star."

He beams and hands me a pen.

For the next few minutes I write down everything I think is relevant and I start to arrange it and link it together.

As I underline one word, the hairs on the back of my neck prickle. I cover the notes and twist carefully around.

"You got back on your feet fast." Naylor's world-weary voice makes my recovery sound like a crime. "I was expecting you to play the sympathy card, crutches, bruising all that malarkey."

"I won't be competing in the hundred metres sprint any time soon," I say, keeping it businesslike, "but in my family if someone knocks you down you get back up and keep going." I keep the 'so screw you, Inspector' in my head.

"What've you got for me?"

I uncover my notes and he takes a quick look, zeroing in on the underlined word.

"Fake?" says Naylor, "What's all this scribble?"

Mary's note is stuck to the front of the printed version. I'll have to ask her where she got a program that prints Arabic. And I'll take the lead she's offered me. While Naylor stalks up to the bar I detach the sticky note and place it into my briefcase.

I get my opening argument ready, if I can steamroller the Inspector with as many facts as possible he might let me get to the point without threatening me with anything.

Naylor plonks his pint down on the table next to my now-cold food.

"Oh you're one of those," he says. "One bite wonders."

"No, I'm one of those, 'I let it go cold, I'll get the barman to microwave it,' types."

"Why waste it?" Naylor says, digging in.

"Please help yourself."

If he's a gentleman he won't try and talk with his mouth full.

"You told me not to go near your case, so I'm working another angle. Mary furnished me with the transcript of the fight between the Sheik and Max Clausen, which she assures me you didn't want to know about. I have some additional perspective that might be pertinent to your case and a possible motive for Justin's murder."

Naylor's eyes are sending lightning bolts my way but he isn't indicating that I stop. He gulps down his next mouthful of my Cornish pasty.

"I did have a ringside seat for the fight between Clausen and the Sheik." Naylor acknowledges my recent eavesdropping admission with a downwards lip-curl. "However my Arabic is non-existent. I did latch onto one word though. At the time I thought it was a name, 'Kevin', which Mary thought was hilarious and now I can see why because it actually translates as 'fakes'.

"Big deal," Naylor replies, "I read the translation of that whole altercation between Clausen and his nibs, the Arab and the transcript just says, 'they're fakes,' to which Clausen replies 'I assure you they aren't fakes,' after he knocked the Sheik to the floor. He could be talking about his girlfriend's boobs or stock certificates, or paintings."

"Or he could have been talking about diamonds."

Naylor locks gazes with me.

"You have ten minutes of my undivided attention. Starting now."

When I worked for Archimedes my speciality, with a success rate of around seventy percent, was the hook. The trick is to hit the client with a juicy bit of information and then fill in the blanks with what they respond to; my own version of cold reading. Naylor's pupils just got bigger and he motions with his finger for me to carry on.

"Remember Harold Eco?"

"Co-owner of Eco builders, recently deceased, found in similar circumstances to Justin Sullivan, except Eco's head wasn't bashed in. Death ruled an accident, so why am I wasting my breath rehashing this, again?"

"Because of what he had in his shirt pocket, a small package of cubic zirconia, and this may have been a deliberate mistake to stir up Eco's conspirators, or it may just've been a flub." I rush on before Naylor can interject some sarcastic comment about 'murder by flub'.

"Cubic zirconia are often substituted for diamonds. You could say they're 'fake' diamonds."

"My patience is wearing thin."

"Harry knew Max and the Sheik, they all went to the same posh school. CeeCee told me. She and Sully went there too. Point is, the Sheik is under daddy's thumb and he's sucking up by making this tribute to his father's greatness, a mosaic made of precious stones, specifically diamonds and," I save the best for last, "Max has been advising him on his purchases."

"Hmmm." Naylor attacks his pint and I drop the scenario that Mary outlined for me at our first meeting into his lap.

"You and Mary Maccallan really are thick as thieves, aren't you?"

"I haven't known her long but yes, she's a good friend."

"It's almost credible," Naylor says, "A diamond smuggling ring. Max the buyer, Harry the smuggler, and the Sheik spirits the lot out of the country in the diplomatic pouch."

"And this little arrangement runs for years like clockwork, until,"

"Harry dies." Naylor falls silent while he finishes my lunch and most of his pint.

"And the details listed in the coroner's verdict stirs up the Sheik so much that he drives to the restaurant and confronts Clausen. Why not just have the diamonds he already has assayed?"

"He'd have to get daddy's permission?" I shrug. "CeeCee gave me the impression he's not exactly a go-getter and his robe did more damage to the diners than he managed to do to Clausen."

"Interesting story, with a distinct lack of proof."

It's my turn to fall to silence. Recalling what happened to Harry has tripped another memory. I open my abused Facebook page. "What's your email address?"

He gives me a dusty old .msn address.

"I'm sending you the picture I took of Harry the day I found him walled-up. The long and short of it, he was on the phone when he died and as far as I know no one ever admitted to being on the line with him when he croaked."

"They would've pulled his phone history with his carrier," Naylor signals the barman for the bill. "Standard procedure in a suspicious death."

"It quickly went from 'suspicious' to 'accident'. I'm guessing they didn't try too hard after the first attempt."

"And what, if anything, does this have to do with Justin's death?" Naylor pulls us back on topic.

"With Harry gone, Max needed another mule. He could've approached Justin as a possible replacement."

Yeah, it's a shot in the dark, because from the picture I'm building up of Justin he wouldn't have batted an eyelid about smuggling diamonds. His only obstacle would be how to ingratiate himself with CeeCee, or more likely Sully.

Naylor doesn't seem to be buying it either.

"So you think that the black sheep of the Sullivan clan had a fit of conscience and threatened to blow the whole operation? I can't see that myself. Still you have provided some rather interesting lines of enquiry. See what else you can uncover, but stay away from my case."

Naylor swallows the dregs of his pint, looks up at the approaching barman and says, "This goes on my bar tab." He turns back to me, totally missing the death stare from the barman. "Ta for the pasty. This time next week. Don't be late."

I nurse the Scotch for another half hour, while the bar fills up with suits. Then I walk out of the hotel to the end of the courtyard and flag down a black cab. Something I said to Naylor is bothering me,

"How did it go?" the cabbie asks without turning around, he winks at me in the rearview mirror. Gavin.

I recognize the cab now, it's a Ravenwood special; possibly the same one Matt was driving the day of CeeCee's collapse.

"How long have you been hanging around?"

"I haven't been 'hanging around'" Gav says, trying and failing to sound insulted, "I've been taking fares. You wouldn't believe who I've had in the back of this cab in the last hour or so." He brakes to avoid mowing down a pedestrian who wanders into the road, oblivious to the roughly 4000lbs of metal bearing down on him. I know this because it was a question on 'Million Pound Drop' the other night. I'm a fount of useless information.

The pedestrian wanders up the middle of Gav's lane, phone still clamped to his ear. Gav leans hard on the horn and the chap nearly tosses the phone over his head in shock. He manages to catch it and then, wheeling around, his anger carries him towards the still stationary cab. Gav puts on his best stony face. He also revs the engine but it's electric and therefore silent. The pedestrian thinks better of what he was about to do, pockets the phone, and walks away at just under a trot.

"There goes another statistic," Gav eyes meet mine in the mirror as we start moving again. "Something's bothering you, I know that look, what is it?"

"I'm going back over what I told Naylor. Can you just drive around for a bit?"

Everything seems to check out except I keep coming back to the smuggling ring theory, the members. I don't think I have their roles wrong, I think I'm one short.

"Scotland Yard."

"Inspector Naylor's line please."

A brief snatch of Greensleeves.

"Naylor."

"Naylor this is Nikki, I think there are four people in the smuggling ring, not three."

"Why does that matter?"

"Harry hated London, both CeeCee and Max joked about it. I'm missing a link."

"Well get on and find it and stop bothering me." Naylor hangs up.

"Nik, I'm borrowing this cab, they need it for a job at two," Gav calls back.

"You did this on your lunch hour?"

"Of course, don't worry I have a packet of sarnies up front with me."

He drops me outside Victoria.

"We'll talk later," he says, as I come level with his window. I lean in and give him a long slow kiss. I pull back and he's licking his lips a little. "Keep the change," I tell him, and enter the station, a satisfied smile playing across my lips.

Out of his sight I sit down for a few minutes to regroup. Even though I'm on the mend the walk into the station winded me.

Twenty minutes later

One train change and soon the towers of Docklands loom in front of me. The swaying of the train and the chat, chat, chat, CHA song of the rails, allows my brain to free associate. In the background, despite all of the things going on around me, I've been worrying that weird piece of information imparted by Kelly-Lou Sampson. It started at Victoria, when a little girl and her mum got on carrying a bag of fresh-baked cookies from Millie's on the station concourse. The little girl promptly offered the cookies to everyone in our carriage with the mother frantically shaking her head when the little one wasn't looking. As they got off I heard the little girl complaining, "Nobody wanted the cookies, Lucy."

The mother replied with a slight Australian accent, "Good job too, your mother would be upset if she didn't get her chocolate chips."

So the 'mother' was either the nanny or au pair. Their colouring might be similar but their relationship wasn't what I, or most of us in the carriage had assumed. From there my brain leap frogs to the Sullivan's cook, and then back to mine and Matt's run in with the police at the Sullivan's front gate. We had quite an audience of gardeners, chauffeurs and maids who came out to watch. And there was the answer, staring me in the face. Inez's parents weren't neighbours of the Sullivans, they were their *employees*.

I compose a short message in my head to put on the personals section of Craigslist when I get back to the flat. It goes something like this.

Seeking information on couple surname Ramirez, maid/cook and chauffeur/gardener working in the Hampstead area, late 1990s. Everything private, £££s paid for the right information.

I use my iCloud address, excalND@icloud.com

Seconds later a message pings into my inbox.

Dear excal, you want maidslist. Can I have some money?

Cheeky bugger.

I Google it and sure enough there is a 'maidslist' page. Back inside the flat I boot up my laptop and visit the site.

Scrolling through the posts it becomes clear that 'maidslist' is not a well moderated web site. The staff of the great and the good use it as a kind of safety valve. Sounding off about their employers, networking to get new better paid positions and most interesting to me, tipping off society columnists for money over their employer's shenanigans.

Wonder boy, one of the reporters trawling the site used to work the entertainment beat during my time at Archimedes. He has tipster requests all over the public part of the site. These days he's graduated to covering polo matches, charity galas and royal playdates but I've seen his byline marching across the middle pages of one of our tabloids. He gets his fair share of scoops and I wonder if this site is his secret weapon. Before posting my message I tag him.

Wotcha, wonder boy.

Who's this?

Nik from Archimedes

Wth are you doing on here?

That's a tricky question, too much info and he's going to want to pry; not enough and he'll be suspicious and start to dig.

Oh you know, clients.

In the background I'm completing the registration process because I can't post anything until my registration is 'in process' according to the site guidelines. I also can't access the private chat rooms until I'm granted access. The irony isn't lost on me that once you're approved you can do whatever you like. The request I've made is allowed to post 'subject to approval by the website's operators' and it warns me that any replies can't come through until my approval is complete and that 'all communication with other maidslist members is exclusively via this list serve. Members are forbidden to contact each other off-list.'

Wonder boy and I chat for another few minutes, then he jumps off the site to chase a 'hot tip'. I read a few more of the posts, then log myself off leaving the computer open on the coffee table.

The next day I've had no replies and Gavin is at home because he is down with food poisoning, which makes him über cranky. The flat is suddenly very small, and I want to get out for a couple of hours.

I start out with the intention of going down the towpath but my feet disagree with my choice. They take me in the direction of the station as if I'm going to Sullivan's HQ. I've been wanting to contact the contingent in Delft and the office does seem like a better place to do it. I'd like to go and see them in person but the no-fly thing is still in place. Apparently it takes at least six months to get off the list once you are put on it.

The people who know me well know that I really don't like going in the front door. Give me a back door or a side entrance every time. I have my reasons for this. The main one at Avalon being that I don't want to run into Simon. He still blames me for Domino now Mina and probably for the disintegration of their relationship too, who knows, I haven't been close enough for him to tackle me on that one.

At Sully's the loading dock is my entry point of choice, and arriving armed with two trays of coffee, (3 lattes no sugar, 1 double espresso, 4 black coffees, 1 heavily sugared) means I don't have to sign in. These big toughs are a bunch of pussy-cats if you treat them right.

Sullivan's outer office door isn't locked. He keeps all the paperwork in his inner office and that is protected by a silent alarm. I sit down at my desk, and prepare to contact the Dutch. Just have to take this call first.

"Where are you, hen?"

"Mary, I'm at Sullivan's offices, why?"

"Blast, I'm at a coffee shop in Hampstead, waiting for your Aztec princess. She agreed to meet with me."

"Inez Ramirez?"

"The same, she was staying with some friends in Covent Garden, that's why we couldn't find her; we were canvassing hotels and hostels. I just happened to catch her at that café you both like so much. Oooh, she's walking past the window, want to listen in?"

"Yes!"

"I don't want her to know she's on speaker it might spook her, hen. No matter what tone my questions take, you stay silent, got it?"

"Got it."

"Thank you for meeting with me," Mary's voice comes from the speaker.

For the next forty minutes I sit, rapt, as the story unfolds. Inez talks about Justin with deep affection. I'm struck by the 180-degree difference in her view of him compared to CeeCee's. Mary doesn't rush into her questions. She chats in general about the facts we have on her, her major, her roommate, Justin—the University of Arizona boy, not her childhood playmate. They're on their second cups of coffee before she starts to zero in.

I have never had to take a lie detector test, and I hope I never do. But I've seen enough depictions on TV and in the movies, and being curious about such things I've done my own research. It seems to me that Mary is establishing a baseline; she's asking questions and observing Inez's responses voice and otherwise. When we lie our bodies give us away, we sweat; the fancy name for this is *galvanic skin response*. Our pupils flicker down and to the left even if only for a fraction of a second, and our heart rate goes up. There are some people that can master these responses but a skilled reader can interpret all the peaks and troughs. And it's clear to me that Inez is skirting around two major issues. The day Justin died and her parents.

"Inez, did you see Justin the day he died?"

"No," Inez responds, way too quickly.

"Inez, you said you saw him every day so how come you didn't meet on the day he died?"

Inez is defensive and Mary gently wears her down.

After asking the same question several different ways, Inez admits, "I met him in the morning, the day he died. He wanted a ride down to Essex, he said he had to meet somebody."

"You gave him a ride? Where did you let him out of the car?"

It strikes me that Mary would be a great detective, she doesn't let on that she has technically placed Inez close to the scene of Justin's death. Instead she turns her attention to something seemingly insignificant.

"Did Justin have a coat with him? Did you?"

"Why you ask?"

"He wasn't wearing a coat when he was found just the sweater and jeans."

"He had his road mender coat on, thick, black, it was cold, I gave him my scarf."

Mary moves on to where Inez dropped Justin off. Inez admits that Justin programmed the GPS and she just followed its directions, the junction had an 'A' after it and it brought them around onto 'a muddy road'.

"Did you see anyone else?"

"No, he walked away from me, up the hill and that was the last time I saw him."

There's a break for tissues. Once Inez has herself together again, "Why didn't you wait for him?"

"He me no to wait, he said his friend would drive him back. Some friend," her tone is bitter.

Mary talks fluff for a few minutes and then, "Tell me about your parents."

"What do they have to do with anything? Parental influence, what the fuck does that have to do with anything?" Inez's voice turns sarcastic, "They no longer walk this earth. They have nothing to do with this."

Mary backs off, over the speaker I hear scribbling noises.

"Inez, this is the number for Detective Inspector Naylor. He and Inspector Tate are the officers working Justin's case. I'm pretty sure that some of the information you've given me will help them. At least take the number. You want Justin's killer caught don't you?"

"Of course." Silence, then Inez speaks again, "I no trust the police, in my country you go to the po-lice and sometimes you don't come back. Or you get back home and then they come for you in the dark of night."

"This is my business card, Inez. You can call my number any time. You don't have to go to Scotland Yard. Call me, Inez. I can arrange a meeting close by. Our police work for the people, not the state."

"I think about it."

Sounds of a chair being pushed back.

"Well that was enlightening," Mary says a few minutes later. "What did you think, Nik?"

"Honestly, the only time she hedged was the parents thing. I think she's had some kind of therapy."

"Explain."

"Terms like parental influence don't really come up in South America, she had some kind of therapy in England or in Europe at least. I was looking at the parents already."

"Why?"

"Because I think Inez's parents worked for the Sullivans in some capacity."

"Arrrgh, why didn't I think of that?"

"Don't beat yourself up over it. I dated our gardener's son for a while; it didn't end well." While I'm talking, my mind replays, loving and losing while my eyes roam the room, settling on CeeCee's collection of furs. Now Mary's talking and the sliver of an idea that was close to surfacing melts away. If it was important it will come back.

The week continues. My internet enquiry is producing nothing. Mary on the other hand has been working on Inez, meeting with her almost every day. The major stumbling block is getting her into a police station, *any* police station. Our solution requires a bit of trickery however if it means Inez getting face time with Naylor, I'm willing to risk it, and my part in it. Mary is going to go to Naylor with a 'material witness' and suggest the bar at St Ermin's as neutral ground. All I have to do is arrive at the hotel one hour later than I did this week. Simple.

Monday night

"He's going for it, hen," Mary tells me over the phone.

I'm standing on the Aberdeen Angus' terrace, recently extended to enforce their newly opened restaurant's *take it outside* mobile phone policy. Gav and Paddy are attacking their steaks in the sparsely populated interior. Hopefully Paddy will use my departure as a chance to break the news to his dad that his extra choral activities have landed him and the other choir members in the semi-finals, a ticketed event at the Albert Hall.

"Naylor's not happy with you," Mary says.

"That seems to be a permanent condition with him," I say. "I'll get there at one, but I'll poke my head in first, to make sure Inez has gone. If the meeting runs long I'll be up at the terrace bar."

"Aye," Mary rings off. I slide the terrace door open and return to our booth. Gav is sitting facing the door as usual, which means he has his back to the terrace and that masks the sound of my footsteps. I catch the end of his last sentence,

"There are other ways to meet girls, Pad."

"I'm not doing it just for Alex, I enjoy singing. Lucky me, I get my pipes from me mammy."

"You sure as hell didn't get them from me."

"Are we going to meet Alex?" I ask, Gav slides himself and his plate over one place to let me sit back down.

"Yup, but as choir director. I haven't asked her out yet."

"Why not?"

"I'm waiting until we win."

"Ask her out," Gav says, "Before one of your mates does."

CHAPTER 29

Tuesday morning

Something's happened, I went down to take Matt a coffee and he wasn't there. The regular chatty desk guy is back. It takes a while to extricate myself from his recap of the last month and by the time I do, I'm running late and it's gone midday. I return to the desk, to get him to call a cab for me. As soon as the cab pulls in front of the doors, I disengage with "Got to go, late already."

Matt is driving the cab, with Gav in the back.

"Don't you two ever do any work?" I half joke as we pull away.

"Our client is currently getting stuck into a long liquid lunch."

"And you just happened to be hanging around out here."

"No, I'm taking a better safe than sorry approach. Max Clausen has disappeared. Got in his private jet a couple of days ago and legged it. He was heading for the US according to the itinerary he filed. He never arrived."

"And you tell me this now?"

"I wanted to poke around a bit, see if I could get a bit more info and I have. Clausen's in Dubai, my contact said the jet landed there and the lone passenger was in his words 'removed from the plane'.

"With the immediate threat neutralized I couldn't justify having Matt baby-sitting you, but, as I said, our client is putting away so much alcohol he won't be going anywhere for the rest of the day. We've got a man in the restaurant, he'll signal us when we're needed."

Matt guides the cab through worsening lunchtime traffic. With his expertise it is quarter to one as we approach the driveway leading to St Ermin's. Matt pulls up in front and hops out to open the door and let me out.

"That's Inez," I say, watching her approaching over Matt's right shoulder, a determined set to her face, she sees the cab and shouts,

"Taxi!"

Beside me Gav stiffens,

He leans across me, blocking Inez's view. "Matt, take the lady where she wants to go, I'll cover it with Evans." We slide out of the other side as Inez gets in. Matt puts the right indicator on and vanishes into the flow of traffic.

"Why did you do that?"

"She's most likely going home. You and Mary never did find out where she's been staying. You go in. I'll sort things with Evans."

Mary comes running out of the hotel entrance,

"Nik, did Inez come this way?"

"Yeah, she just left in a taxi, something wrong?"

"Naylor went all bad cop on her and she freaked out. She threw her coke all over him. The barman took Naylor into the back room to clean up, and I went to the desk to get housekeeping to come and take care of the mess. When I came back she'd gone."

Naylor is sitting fuming when we get to the bar. He's wiped the coke off his face. His hair however is sticky with it at the front and the barman's attempts at clean-up have given him an exclamation mark over his forehead.

"What did you say to her?" Mary demands.

"I simply asked for her alibi," he looks at the files on the table, shoves them aside. "She's taken my evidence folder."

Mary goes a little pale, "Are you sure?"

"Of course I'm bloody sure. That's the whole reason for her being here, to look at the stills I got from the traffic cameras. That was the tidbit I dangled in front of her when she called in. The little bitch covered me in coke on purpose and now she's god knows where and she can sift through that evidence at her leisure."

"She's in the back of one of Ravenwood's special taxis," I say and for a second Naylor actually looks grateful, then annoyed.

"Didn't I tell you to stay out of this?"

I feel a hand on my back and Gav's voice, while low, is so precise that Naylor doesn't miss the anger it is laced with.

"If you want to know exactly where she is, you'll let my wife off for trying to help you. I saw Inez carrying a black leather folder, not exactly standard issue for evidence, unless you're smuggling it out of the building." Now Naylor is the one to lose colour.

"That was the only set of stills, I didn't think I'd need copies."

Gav shakes his head.

"Let's see if I can raise Matt."

"Be careful not to tip her off," Naylor warns.

"Relax Naylor," Gav takes out his phone and shushes us, "He's got one of those Motorola walkie talkies with him. I'll just pretend to be the dispatcher."

"Cab 419 do you copy, over?"

There is a few moments of silence and then,

"Copy."

"Status?"

"Just dropping off my fare, you got something for me?" Matt sounds bored. A moment later he's back on and a lot more animated.

"OK," he says, "I've just dropped Inez at a house on Valiant way."

"Did she have a folder with her?"

"She did, she spent most of the journey flipping through it.

"Want me to report her next destination?" Matt sounds extremely smug. "She asked me to wait for her. She's just picking something up and I told her I can be here for two minutes before I risk getting a ticket."

"Yes, stand by."

Gav addresses Naylor, "Inspector, I'm playing a hunch here. Inez is a Latina and they're big on that whole revenge thing. I think she's planning on avenging herself on Justin's killer. No offence Mary, she's been playing you. I think she knows a lot more than she's been letting on."

"What do you propose?" Naylor is all business now, more of the career detective than the riding it down to retirement version I've seen so far.

"Flag down a cab and be ready to go when Matt tells us where to head to."

We make an unlikely group, Mary and I, Gav and Naylor fanned out side by side. At the road Naylor steps out in front of the first cab that cruises past, his police folder extended in front of him. The cabbie burns a lot of rubber off his tires as they bite into the asphalt. Anyone within earshot stops and looks over. Gav piles into the front passenger side leaving the rest of us to squeeze together in the back.

"Bad news," Matt's voice fills the cab, Gav has him on speaker. "Some officious sod of a policeman waved me on and I had to go around the block. I got back here just in time to see Inez climbing into a mini cab. I'm a couple of cars behind them they're staying south of the river."

"Description?" Naylor demands.

"Mankey old Toyota Celica, faded racing green, can't see a number plate, it might've fallen off.

"There's a lot of pointing going on. I think she's as clueless as he is." Over the speaker we can't fail to miss the clash of horns. "Holy crackers," Matt says, "that was the mini cab cutting three lanes of fast-moving traffic, nearly took the nose off a Range Rover."

"Any ideas on final destination?" Gav's gone into full operational mode, almost barking the question at Matt.

"Nope, we've gone past Buckingham Palace, now we're turning onto Park Lane, I think he's trying to give her the tourist tour."

"That isn't likely to go down well," I raise my voice so Matt can hear me. "Where were you headed before all the pointing started?"

"We were on the A400, and if we stay on this road we should intersect with that road again. Yep, we're taking Marylebone, back towards the City, Euston and King's Cross."

"You," Naylor addresses the cabbie, "Where are they going?"

"Do I look like mystic flaming Meg?" the cabbie retorts, sawing the wheel to avoid a trundling bus. "You commandeer my cab, and expect me to be Johnny the physic taxi driver!"

"Where are you Matt?"

"Camden, I've just passed a sign for Swiss Cottage, Kilburn, Hampstead and Chalk Farm, there's also a left turn coming up for Regents Park and Primrose Hill but they're in the wrong lane for that."

In the back the three of us are getting thrown around and I nearly end up in Naylor's lap when the cab's back wheel mounts a kerb.

Gav twists around to us. "We have to work out where she's going! And get there before she does."

Being bounced up and down and sliding all over the place coupled with Gav's sense of urgency means we start throwing out what we know about Inez.

"Inez and Justin were friends when her family worked for the Sullivans and *they* live in Hampstead," Mary volunteers.

"They still headed for Hampstead?" Gav yells to Matt.

"No, they just took a turn for Primrose sodding Hill."

"So not Hampstead, we're back to square bloody one. Stop!" Naylor yells. The cabbie slows down, he can't stop because we are crawling through Camden threading our way through a narrow corridor of cars and buses. A wall of Chelsea tractors blocks any view of the street beside us.

"Ewww," Mary brushes several of Naylor's grey hairs off her jacket. Meanwhile Naylor pulls an off white display handkerchief from his suit jacket pocket and dabs his forehead with it. Several pieces of lint come out too, and a creased piece of paper. Naylor and Gav consult with Matt who thinks Inez has spotted him and is doing this on purpose. The cabbie's eyes follow the paper, I reach down and scoop it up so that we don't get a complaint for littering. He has every right to throw us out of his cab and we need to be mobile.

"Naylor, you dropped this."

Naylor waves my hand away and I start to worry the corner of the paper, one of Gav's bad habits that I've picked up,

"They've turned around again," Matt's frustration comes out loud and clear. "The traffic's thinning out, I'm getting more obvious by the minute. Hang on, I'm going to overtake them."

"Matt, we're on the same road as you, if you keep coming this way we're going to pass you."

"That had occurred to me, look they're still behind me, we could slow them down the old-fashioned way."

"Stand by," Gav almost climbs into the back with Naylor.

He and Naylor have a heated but whispered discussion. "Have you lost your mind man?" Naylor hisses. "Doing that would bring traffic to a standstill. You want to be responsible for that, I know I don't."

Matt cuts into the conversation,

"Are we a go?"

For a brief moment I think Gav's going to reach for the steering wheel. Ravenwood did a defensive driving course last year, strictly for spouses and significant others because they reasoned that we should have a little knowledge of the black arts our other halves dabble in. If I had to I could now perform both a J turn and a Y turn. The manoeuvre I think that he's considering is to tap the back wheel of the Celica as it passes us. If we're moving fast enough it will spin the car around, blocking the road. He could also ram the Celica in the same place disabling it and the result would be the same. This works well on a test track with both drivers knowing what's coming. Here, people could get hurt.

I will him not to.

"Negative, too many variables."

Moments later Matt passes us, the Celica is roughly five cars behind tucked in behind a Securicor truck.

Naylor gets on the phone, trying to get security cameras onto the Celica before Matt loses it completely.

"I've lost them," Matt reports, "They turned off on one of the side streets. My view was blocked, I'm doubling back to try and reacquire the Celica."

"I'm on with the traffic cam people now, and they can't see any sign. We're dead in the water." Naylor reports.

"Ow!" I look down at my hand, a thin smear of blood trickles from my index finger. The damn list has given me a paper cut. I spread it out on my lap, fully intending to fold the thing into a paper dart and fling it out of the window.

Instead I start reading.

What fell out of Naylor's pocket is a more detailed version of the forensic report for Justin Sullivan. It identifies the trace found on his body. With the conclusions of the tech who processed the evidence and some handwritten notes. There is a detailed note next to C. lanigera.

Indication that subject spent time with breeder or owner s?

Breeders or owners of what?

Scribbled next to it is a note to *check breeders and cross-reference with known associates and pet shops in and around the Hampstead area.* The result in a different hand,

No breeders or pet shops in that area. Mr. Sullivan did not keep them as pets.

"What's C. lanigera?" I ask Naylor, who helpfully presents me with the palm of his hand.

I try Googling it. Seems the entire population of Camden are on Wi-Fi right now and the page takes an age to load.

"You lot don't have a clue where you want to go, and the meter is still running!" the cabbie complains.

Mary reaches into her pocket, she pulls out a £50 note and dangles it in front of the cab driver.

"That's yours if you stay on this road, regardless of how much we rack up on the meter," she says. We watch the note vanish into the driver's pocket.

I check my download, half the page has loaded, C. lanigera is the long tailed, oh crap, the *long tailed chinchilla!*

"Gav, give me your phone," he thrusts it towards me, "Matt, you still there?"

"Yeah."

"You were going the right way, it is Hampstead." Three pairs of eyes swivel my way.

"You sure, Nik?" he queries.

"Ninety eight percent sure."

"On my way, I know a shortcut."

"Hampstead," I say to our cabbie, "I'll explain on the way."

I hand the list to Naylor, who splutters, when he sees what it is.

"It fell out of your pocket. You said you didn't care what happened to it. Show it to Mary,"

Mary looks at the list and I tell her what Google just told me. "Nikki's right, Inspector, Justin didn't come into contact with a chinchilla he was with someone wearing a chinchilla fur coat."

"Well I'll be damned," Naylor mutters.

"CeeCee Sullivan owns a purple fur coat, its chinchilla."

"Hampstead and step on it!" Naylor yells at the cabbie as if he just thought of it.

"Where in Hampstead?"

"Millionaires row." I give him the local's name for Bishops Avenue.

I toss Mary my phone,

"Call Sully. We need to warn him."

"He's not answering, it just went to voicemail."

The speaker crackles in Gav's hand,

"I'm at the gate," Matt reports, "No sign of the Celica or Inez, I might've made it here first."

For a second I'm seized with indecision, did I just stick two unrelated facts together?

"Inez won't use the main gate," Mary says, "She told me that as bairns she and Justin used to sneak out of the house to go to the closest sweet shop, they never got caught by the adults."

"Nik, can you remember the gate code?" Matt cuts in.

"Hang on Matt." I try and call up the image of the keypad, I punched the code in twice once for the gate, once for the house. The first six digits I can remember but the last two? Was it zero one, or one zero?

"Zero one." I tell him, with more confidence than I feel.

Naylor is also on the phone, "Blue and twos, all of them. If she's going after Mrs. Sullivan the sirens might spook her."

"I'm in," Matt reports, "on my way up to the house."

All of us look at the phone, willing words to come out of it. Mary's bribe has loosened the cabbie's morals. He breaks numerous traffic laws and damn the speed limit.

"Sullivan's on the floor in the hall," Matt reports. "Nasty cut on the back of his head. I think she beaned him with an umbrella, he's out cold. Where's Mrs. Sullivan's room?"

"Up one flight, to the end of the hall. There should be a nurse on duty."

"Going up now."

We screech through an underground car park, exiting through the in lane and going down several linked but horrifyingly narrow back alleys, emerging close to Hampstead High Street where we tack onto the end of a blues and twos procession.

"We're five minutes away from Bishops Ave," the cabbie announces, "We overtaking this lot?"

"Stay behind them," Naylor orders.

"I can see the nurse, she's outside the room, in a bit of a state but seems unharmed," Matt says. "Miss, are you okay?"

"She ordered me out, she's got, a gun, she's got a gun."

"Police are on their way. What I want you to do is go and help Mr. Sullivan. He's in the hall. Look after him for me, okay?"

"Okay."

The police car we're following stops in the middle of the street so suddenly that we nearly plough into it.

The passenger gets out and as he approaches the window, Naylor hops out of the back and badges the officer.

"I'm the one who called this in. DI Naylor. We're wasting time," he tells the officer. The procession continues, stopping just down the road from the Sullivans' gate.

"Now what's holding us up?" Naylor mutters.

Gav opens his door and stands on the doorsill to get a better view, "The gate's closed." He gets back in, turns to me.

"Nik, you're up."

We're at the back of a line of police cars all with their sirens blaring thanks to Naylor. I'll be half deaf by the time I get to the gate! I'm wearing a suit so I don't have my headphones on me and they wouldn't block much noise anyway.

Help comes from an unexpected source. The cabbie presents me with a small plastic bag,

"The wife drags me to a lot of concerts," he yells over the din. "These things keep her happy and me sane." I tell myself that his earwax won't kill me and stuff the orange foam pellets into each ear. Instantly the noise level drops away.

"Thanks," I say, or most likely yell. I get out and walk briskly up to the front gate. The officers are staying in their patrol cars. Two senior officers stand in front of the gate, one of them moves to block me. There's too much noise to try and explain so I stab the air a couple of times with my finger and point at the keypad next to the gate and they fall back. I rub my hands on my trousers, key in the sequence, the gates start to swing open. Patrol cars go streaming up the drive. The taxi comes level with me and I get back in; just as we come up to the gate it begins to close, courtesy of the officer pushing the button. The cabbie slams the cab in reverse and backs away from the gates, I pull the earplugs out.

"What are you doing man, these things are built like tanks!" Naylor howls.

"You're sitting in my livelihood, mate," the cabbie snaps, "and po-lice or no, I'll thank you to get the hell out of my cab!"

Naylor obliges.

"Oi," we can hear him yelling at the hapless officer, "Move your car, sonny!"

"Sorry sir, I have my orders, uniforms only."

"I'm a senior officer!" Naylor waves his badge around. This time it has no effect.

"All due respect but you're not *my* senior officer, sir."

The younger officer manoeuvres his car sideways across the drive, with Naylor still raining down threats of sending him to a deserted island in the North Sea. Satisfied with his work the copper turns in the direction of the house.

"We'll have this gate open the moment you're out of sight sonny, and then you and I are going to have a little chat!"

"Shut up, Naylor," Gav begs from his front seat position. "Just stop talking right now."

The young officer goes to the rear of his car, takes out a sturdy bike lock, gets back into the panda car and powers down the windows, that done he hooks the bike lock through the bars of the gate (avoiding Naylor's flailing hands), extends the lock to full length and calmly attaches it to the metal support between the driver's side front and back windows. He doesn't bother looking back, just turns and sprints up towards the house.

The cabbie is almost bent double over the steering wheel, wisely keeping his laughter silent. Naylor kicks the gate hard, and then hobbles back in our direction.

"Matt!" Gav is yelling into the phone, "Armed police on their way to you, stand down. I repeat, stand down."

"I can't," Matt sounds more determined than I've ever heard him. "The cops are stuck outside and unless they have the code they're not getting in."

"Matt, the plod have locked us out. We can't back you up."

"Look mate," Matt says, "Inez and Mrs. Sullivan are calm right now, just two women talking. I don't have a sight line. I do have the equipment to get one. And you know how fast a situation can turn to crap, especially if the heavy boot of the law gets introduced. Wait a minute. I'll call you back. I think the maid had a phone."

"Matt knows what he's doing," I put my hand on Gav's arm.

Gav nods, "You're right. But someone should have his back and that someone should be me." He breaks off to stare at the bars. "I could probably scale that gate, hotwire the police car and get us up to the house."

"And then what?" Mary asks. "Nikki would have to let them in and your friend may get hurt as a result."

"No Mary, the code that got them through the gate is the same for the back door and they don't know that. Neither does Naylor. The only person the alarm company would give the number to is unconscious in his own hallway. Yelling at the alarm company over the phone will get Naylor's colleagues nowhere."

Gav is out of the car before I've finished. He scales the wrought iron gate in his usual economic style places one hand on the points at the top and yanks it back, sucking his finger.

"I could use some of your floor mats." he yells to the cabbie.

"And I could use a Caribbean holiday," the cabbie grouses. "Both of those things ain't gonna happen."

"It's Al, isn't it?" Mary injects a bit more Scots purr into her voice, "Al Murray, like the comedian?"

"Yes Miss that's me."

"Al, we are lucky that you were the taxi the Inspector managed to flag down. You've done everything asked of you. Like it or not you're in the middle of something big. When this is over, whichever way it goes, you'll be hailed as a hero. Media will want to talk to you, TV, magazines. You have what we in the trade call insider access."

"I do?"

Mary stays silent as the dapper little Al, thinks it over. Gav, fed up with waiting is coming to get what he needs but before he gets to the cab, Al the cabbie has his door open handing Gav the solid rubber front and rear floor mats.

Gav's phone shows up 'unknown number'.

"Matt?"

"Where's Gav?"

Gav is in the process of draping the floor mats over the top of the gate, he jackknifes his body up and over. Only one body part hits the protected spikes, so instead of impaling himself by the forearm he drops to the tarmac, unharmed. I heave a sigh of relief.

"He's over the gate and about to hot-wire a police car."

"Good, I could use some extra help. Look I'm going back up. Tell Gav I'm using the stethoscope app."

Gav has the car started now, proving he hasn't lost his touch. He backs the police car out of the way and opens the gate. Once our cabbie drives through, Gav shuts them again and he and Naylor pile into the taxi, the house is in sight in moments.

"Matt said he was using the stethoscope app," I tell Gav.

"How is a stethoscope going to help us?" Naylor enquires.

"It's an add-on we're testing. Coupled with the iPhone's camera it enables us to assess a situation without being seen. It uses fibre optics. He can poke it under the door and see what's going on in there."

"Like one of those cameras they stick down your throat?"

"Smaller, but yes."

Naylor gets out and starts waving his badge around while he explains our inside man to the other senior officers; Matt comes back on the line.

"Gav! Matt's on again."

He comes running over, "Two people in the room, Mrs. Sullivan in bed, Inez is standing in the middle of the room. She has a gun trained on Mrs. Sullivan, safety catch is still engaged. No one is getting shot right now."

Mary is staring hard past Naylor, "Nikki, they have a battering ram."

"Naylor, what are they doing?"

"I would've thought that was obvious, we need to get in there."

"Wait, I can get you in, I have the security code for the door how do you think Matt got in?"

Naylor raises his voice, the battering ram is already in motion, and the noise drowns him out.

"Matt," Gav shouts into his phone, "the plod has a battering ram, they'll be coming your way," the door gives way in a splintering of wood, "any minute."

"Understood."

There's a crash and Matt commands,

"Drop the gun Inez, drop it now!"

The double 'bang' from inside the house and a fraction of a second later from the speaker on Gav's phone sends an icicle rocketing up my spine. The next few seconds Gav, Mary and I stare at each other, numb, confused and then as scores of police issue boots pound up the stairs, we race towards the front door.

CHAPTER 30

The interview with Inez takes place in the Sullivan kitchen. CeeCee's nurse already patched up Sully; he's in the dining room being grilled by another detective. Inez, her hand bandaged, sits at the table, her other hand cuffed to the officer beside her. Her defiance gone she looks smaller, more fragile. The gun she was carrying (bullets now removed) is on the far side of the table, along with her purse and the folder of photographs that she lifted from Naylor.

Matt struggled with her, getting his hands on the gun just as Inez took the safety off. The bullet from the shot we heard buried itself harmlessly in the side wall.

Matt had the safety back on and was in the middle of taking the bullets out of the weapon when four officers burst through the door of CeeCee's room, saw the gun in his hand and piled on top of him, leaving Inez free to attack Mrs. Sullivan. Lucky for us she wasn't armed with anything else. Matt was knocked out during the struggle. Gav, who is outside with him, assures me the concussion Matt suffered is going to be a drop in the ocean compared to Matt's wounded pride when he wakes up.

Mary, without being asked, made a massive pot of tea and she's handing mugs full to anyone within reach. The recipients slurp away, gratefully. Mary, clever girl, gets to stay and listen in to the interrogation. She drifts across to look over my shoulder. I'm working my way through the traffic cam stills, Naylor's carrot to Inez. Naylor spoke the truth. All the cars that got off the motorway at the same junction as the industrial park where Inez dropped Justin off were recorded. Each hour is marked with a tab. There are a surprising number but only one for the time frame she gave us. Inez and Justin can be seen through the windscreen, a greased thumbprint covers his face. I'm guessing Inez's. I start flipping backwards.

Naylor, having stamped his authority on the investigation, is starting his questioning by offering Inez tea. Inez puts her head down. I've been standing out of her eye line. Now I move towards the espresso machine on the counter and fire it up, pulling levers and expelling a fair amount of steam. I pour Inez a cup; place it in front of her.

"There isn't any chocolate in it," I say, "Sorry about that, Inez."

"You!" she skewers me with a glare. "You *are* working with the police."

"She most definitely is not!" Naylor's denial makes Inez pause, she tries the espresso, registers approval, drinks some more.

"We know why you came here today, armed." Naylor tempers his words, well attempts to. It still sounds like an accusation to me, and apparently to Inez too as she demands that he explain it to her, "In case there's something you've missed mister policeman."

Now would be a good time to distance myself from Naylor. The thing about us English is we are mostly law-abiding citizens. Inez's culture has a distrust of police and therefore scant respect for their authority.

Mary and I both move out of earshot.

"Naylor's well on his way to being jiggered, hen."

"What-ered?"

"Screwed," Mary translates, still carrying the book. She lays it flat and continues turning the pages, "The Sullivan's won't want this kind of publicity. Unless Naylor cracks Inez before Sullivan can bring his lawyers in, his case is going to melt away before his eyes and I think he knows it."

"How, no, why would Sully do that? Inez came here armed."

"Ooch, hen," Mary shakes her head, "Your naïveté is adorable. Those with money manipulate. They rig the game to their advantage. You should see my arrest sheet."

"You don't have one."

"No, because my da wanted me to get into University so he made my wild child phase, short and intense as it was, go byebye. He wanted to keep the firm in the family so he didn't have a choice in who took over the company. Imagine what Sully would do for his beloved wife," she turns the page. I grab her wrist.

"Go back. That car." The time stamp on the picture shows 11 a.m. "I've been driven around in that car. Chauffeur driven."

"We should tell Naylor."

We find him out in the hallway conferring with another officer,

"These questions only," Naylor is saying. "I'm particularly interested in the answer to Q3.

"Mr. Sullivan!" he calls up through the banisters. Halfway up, Sully freezes in his tracks. "My officer is going to take your wife's statement. Please come back down here." Sully tramps down the stairs, passing the officer on her way up.

Mary distracts Sully, leading him away from the kitchen. I keep pace with Naylor.

"I presume you found something?" Naylor goes to the counter and pours himself a massive mug of tea. Inez still has her police escort. I don't see any sign of her cuffs though.

"Sully's chauffeur driven Mercedes." I keep one eye on Inez, tapping the photo with my finger. "Arrives on the industrial estate at eleven in the morning." I flip to the last few pictures. "Here's the car getting back onto the motorway around five.

"The next time CeeCee used it was the day she collapsed at lunch, when I heard her tell the chauffeur to valet the Merc inside and out."

His expression unreadable, Naylor shares a look with Inez. *What did I miss?* I wonder. *He's treating her more like a colleague than a suspect.*

"Wonderful." His remarks aren't really addressed at me, more to the room in general. "All evidence of Justin being in the car removed."

"Justin was never in the car," Inez interrupts. "He told me someone was waiting for him, I never saw who."

Mary enters the kitchen at a trot,

"I think Sullivan knows," she says. "He was just incredibly rude to me, hurtful even. Didn't give me a chance to defend myself so I went steaming after him, he's locked himself in his office. I can hear a shredder going full blast."

"Of course he knows." I could kick myself for being so stupid. "The forensic summary. Mr. Sullivan wasn't Justin, it was Sully. They asked him if he kept chinchillas. He's probably shredding CeeCee's appointments diary."

"Who's shredding things?" For someone who looks so old and creaky Naylor can move like a cat sometimes. Mary repeats what she just told me, adding, "The chauffeur! He'd know who he drove and where he drove them to."

From the hallway we hear the front door open.

"We need to get to him before Sullivan does," I add as the three of us bundle through the front door, "or your evidence could just..." I break off at the sight of the Mercedes trundling off down the drive. "...drive away."

Sully is standing at the choke point of the drive. Even with the Inspector haranguing them into their cars the officers can't go after the Merc without mowing down Sully.

"What the hell are you doing, Sully?"

"Oh, just sent our man to pick up one of my clients at the airport. I'd forgotten he was coming in today."

"No you're not. You're making evidence disappear."

Mary warned me they'd change the game, and here is Sully doing just that. He'll have a hard time explaining the chauffeur on camera but how easy will it be to coerce Phillip Eco into going along with them. Evidence altered, missing altogether, the word of upstanding businessman Topher 'Sully' Sullivan against Inez.

Sully plasters on a puzzled expression,

"Don't know what you're talking about Nikki." He calls over my shoulder, "Inspector, tell me you're not buying into this nonsense. Ramirez's parents extorted money from us, clearly the apple doesn't fall far from the tree."

All the respect I had for Sully just evaporated.

"Mr. Sullivan, blackmail is a very serious allegation. I take it you have the evidence to back it up."

There is a momentary flash of panic, before Sully gets himself under control. Naylor, by accident or design has steered Sully onto some very shaky ground indeed.

"We, I mean *I* didn't meet her here. . ." Sully isn't allowed to finish his waffling.

"We just have a few more statements to take, Mr. Sullivan. Once we're satisfied that your wife is in no danger, we'll be on our way. I will need to talk to your man when he returns from his airport errand." Naylor turns away from Sully and as he does so he winks at me. Sully ambles back into the house.

Naylor's good mood is short-lived, the Merc has vanished into thin air. "It's a hulking great Mercedes, how can you mislay one of those?" he demands.

I feel sorry for the traffic camera people.

"I dunno sir. The Merc doesn't register on any of our cameras. It would've hit the airport road by now. Chances are it is still somewhere in Hampstead."

"I hate cases like this, it's like playing Find the Lady. The game is rigged and there's always a ringer waiting to surprise you."

"How could Sullivan light a fire under the chauffeur that easily?" one of the braver young officers ventures to ask.

"It could be something as simple as a keyword," Naylor snaps. "Or he's so loyal to the family that he's an accessory to the murder. Or Sullivan could've just said 'lose the car and yourself,' no questions asked.

"My only hope is that the statements that Inez and Mrs. Sullivan give don't match," he says on the way back to the Sullivan kitchen.

***

"So we can't prove that CeeCee killed him." Inez curls her slender fingers into fists.

"I'll send one of my constables to search upstairs but if she'd any sense the clothes she wore that day would be incinerated the minute she returned from her business meetings."

"What about her purse?"

Inez throws in the comment, which sets me thinking. In all the times I saw her she always carried a purse, never let the thing out of her sight.

"The woman has literally hundreds of purses."

I push Inez's words aside. "The inspector would need a search warrant. We're only here because of, well because of you.

"Oh you idiot!" I speed dial, stick the phone to my ear, "Stark? It's Nikki, is Mina there?"

"Hold on," Stark puts his hand over the speaker. "Mina!"

While I wait I fill Naylor and Inez in on my 'idiot' comment. "Your lab boys found traces of CeeCee's coat on Justin." Naylor nods. "CeeCee would destroy the clothes she was wearing without a second thought. That coat however would be whisked off to the dry cleaners."

"Then our evidence is already gone."

"No. It was never sent. Hang on a sec. Mina?"

She comes across as a little breathless, one part of my brain is listening to Naylor conferring with Inez.

"Mina, can you and Stark drive over to Sullivan Inc's HQ? Tell Stark to bring his kit." I tell her where to find the coat. "It's wrapped in plastic."

"Sully hasn't been to the office since CeeCee's collapse. The coat is hanging in plain sight but no one's been in there to see it."

"You two." Naylor points at two constables drinking tea over in the corner. "Get over to Sullivan Inc. Secure that coat."

"What do you need Stark to do?" Mina asks me.

"Test for blood. There are two coppers coming too. They'll meet you outside. Don't go into the office without them. Tell Stark to treat the coat like he would a body."

"Document everything, got it."

I hang up and then we wait.

When the constable returns from taking CeeCee's statement, Naylor sends everyone out of the kitchen. The last view I get of him is sitting at the table with the two statements side by side and a pen in his hand. Inez, while being polite, refuses to discuss her statement.

I walk outside to where they're treating Matt. Before I get there several police radios crackle. Naylor's voice announces, "We've done all we can here. We will proceed back to the Yard. Clear everyone out." I increase my pace a little. "That includes all unauthorized civilians." I swear under my breath but keep moving.

"Miss?" a policeman's hand is on my arm. "Come with me please."

He gently, but firmly puts me in the back of the police car. Mary joins me a moment later.

"I'll let you off at Hampstead tube," The officer says. I can see Inez being put into the car in front of me, and in the car behind, Naylor, sitting in the passenger seat.

At the gates the convoy splits, or rather one car splits from the pack, ours. The policeman drops us outside Hampstead tube as he promised. Mary and I are left by the side of the road, scratching our heads as he drives away. She tries calling Mina while I try calling Stark, both our calls go to voicemail. Mary hangs up, calling Naylor a 'rat bastard'.

"Well hen, I guess we're shut out."

"I gave him CeeCee's coat. He could've at least let us know the results."

"You will have to do what the rest of the UK does, read it in the papers." Mary says, turning towards the tube. "You coming? Let's go and drown our sorrows."

CHAPTER 31

Later that week

The day after Mary and I were left like orphans outside Hampstead tube, as promised, Naylor dumped me out of the investigation. All the newspapers called this a police operation. Even the taxi driver (with Mary's fifty quid burning a hole in his pocket) developed a sudden case of blindness over his other passengers. According to him, Naylor alone 'flagged him down' and 'directed him from the backseat.'

The tabloids all carried pictures of the Inspector standing next to a wheelchair containing CeeCee. Handcuffing her to it was a bit unnecessary, I thought.

I'm sitting on the floor in our flat, my back resting against the sofa, a fresh coat of just applied polish drying on my toenails.

"Can you pass me the remote?" I call towards the kitchen where Gav is making bacon sandwiches. "I left it on the breakfast bar, next to my laptop."

"Here," Gav walks over, carrying a plate of bacon sarnies in one hand, the remote control in the other. He looks at my newly painted toes, "Wow Nik, I didn't know Tango did nail polish."

The neon orange didn't look that bright in the bottle.

"It's called 'desert sunrise'," I say as Gav cannonballs onto the sofa behind me, grabs a sandwich and munches on it.

"Radioactive desert sunrise." The insides of his knees lightly touch my shoulders.

"It's cheerful." I argue, reaching forward to snag the next sandwich on the pile. As usual he's made enough to feed a family of four. "I'm in need of cheerful right now. I've taken myself off Sully's project and Beth 'wants to meet' outside of the office. That's never a good sign, and to cap it all off Naylor's lot still haven't released my coat from evidence."

Gav polishes off his food, reaches past me to grab a tissue. Once his fingers are grease free they come to rest on my shoulder blades and he begins to knead.

At the push of a button the satellite box blinks to life and I flick to the news.

"You know this is the scaremonger channel?" Gav enquires.

"Can't be helped, they're going to be interviewing Inez Ramirez during the show. Of course they're not going to say when."

Inez, as far as I know hasn't been charged with anything, she has declined interview after interview. Since CeeCee's arrest, her silence has been total.

"Odd that she picked this lot for an exclusive."

"Hmmm." I sigh.

Despite trying to pay attention to two so-called 'experts' arguing over the fate of a missing commuter jet, the combination of having to watch the channel in question and his fingers working their magic on my scapula, I was almost asleep.

Gav taps my back.

"We now take you to our live and exclusive interview with the woman at the center of the media circus that surrounds the upcoming murder trial of business mogul CeeCee Sullivan.

"Correspondents from both sides of the pond have been vying to quiz Miss Ramirez. Our colleague, Sam Coburn, beat all of them to the punch. In case you haven't heard of Sam over here, I can assure you, you're in for a treat."

There then follows a five-minute promotional video. Sam is Samantha Coburn, a snub nosed frosted blonde with a complexion sculpted from pink marble. Her startling blue eyes almost overpower her face.

"What is this," Gav wants to know, "An interview or a boxing match?"

According to the video, Sam is a 'media heavyweight' in her native USA known for (metaphorically) burning her interviewees' houses down to the ground. You don't get interviewed by her, you get 'burned'.

Coburn has a camera facing her and one facing Inez, she favours the split-screen format because, as the promo stated, 'the viewer misses nothing from either side and then gets to make up their own mind.'

Inez and Coburn sit on stools, just feet apart. Inez is still casually dressed. Coburn's power suit looks like it came from the Barbie business range, although the steely glint in her eye is there to remind you, the viewer, that beneath that blonde hair and perfect makeup beats the heart of a king (or should that be queen?) cobra.

"I'm surprised you aren't a little more dressed up, Mizz Ramirez," Coburn drawls.

Inez's eyes flash.

"I'm a student, I don't (it comes out as 'don') have a wardrobe of fancy fancy. This is who I am."

Coburn regains her poise, throwing out some warmup questions, leading up to several about Inez's childhood. A carelessly lobbed supposition about Inez being jealous of the family her parents were serving is smashed back with studied politeness. This cobra just met a mongoose.

Inez initiates the next part,

"You wanna know about *that night* right? This is why I'm here. Mrs. Sullivan is going on trial soon and you want to make her out to be a cold blood (sic) killer, I will tell you it's not that black and white."

Coburn's mouth forms a tiny pout. She's not used to being up against the likes of the Latin beauty in front of her. Inez is intelligent, articulate and 'doesn't suffer fools gladly,' as my mum is fond of saying.

"That night," Inez begins, "Justin and I were playing in the garage. My father, he drove the big Rolls Royce that chauffeured the Sullivans around.

"We finish playing and my father comes in, tells Justin tea is ready and his step mama is looking for him. He go and my father, he lock the door and say it is playtime for us too."

"Play time?" Coburn has her steely-eyed look back, "What kind of play time?"

"The kind you are thinking of. My papa, he likes the little girls, he play how you say, doctor? with me?"

"Jesus!" Gav's appalled comment floats over my shoulder.

"He abused you?" On screen, a calculating expression crosses Coburn's face while fake sincerity pours out of her mouth. At this point I would normally turn off the TV and fling the remote away in disgust except she's reached the crux of the whole interview as far as I'm concerned. I can't stop watching yet.

Gav stirs behind me. "I'm getting a beer, you want one?"

"No thanks."

Gav takes his hands off my shoulders but makes no move towards the fridge.

"He abused you didn't he, Mizz Ramirez?" Coburn's prompt sounds a little too sharp to her own ears and she winces. At the first question Inez bowed her head, on the second she looks up at Coburn, her eyes brimming, fingers clenched into fists.

"For how long?" Coburn demands.

"Since I was five years old." Inez's voice drops to a whisper.

"And your mother didn't stop him?" Coburn's voice now bears a distinct resemblance to Minnie Mouse.

Inez again shakes her head,

"Mama, she knew, she also know that he want another baby. Another couple of years and I would be too old, you know what I mean?"

Coburn gapes. I wait for the makeup to crack, showering Inez with shrapnel, it doesn't happen.

"I am totally alone until Justin come to live with the Sullivans. He was like a brother to me. He defended me when people would be rude to me on our walks. I trusted him, enough that I told him what was going on.

"He wanted to go to tell mama. I stopped him from doing that. I have to tell him why and he got really angry. He wanted to go tell his parents. I stop him again. No good could come of that. We would be sent back home. I can endure, this, this, because of him."

"Let me," Coburn clears her throat, then continues at normal pitch. "Let me take you back to that night. Justin went to get help?"

"No. I told you my papa sent him to the house for his tea. But he came back. I don't know if he ever left." Coburn suddenly finds herself a bystander at her own interview. Although Inez is sitting in front of her, her mind is somewhere else, somewhere bad.

"I shut my eyes, try to no cry. Worse for me if I make a sound. Then noise, a lot of it. My papa yelling and Justin is standing over him with a plank of wood. He whack him on the bare ass hard, over and over. My papa shove me away. He stand up and Justin grabs the can of petrol for the mower, takes the cap off and he throw petrol into papa's eyes. While papa is blinded and screaming, Justin drag me out of the garage and he yell at my papa, 'you leave her alone or next time I will burn you.'

"To prove his point he pulls a lighter out of his pocket, lights it and waves it around. We didn't know about petrol fumes, and they ignite. Whoof!"

Coburn rears back in her seat.

"We were blown backwards across the gravel, we land on the grass. Justin has burns on his hand, no eyebrows, my clothes are ripped and for a moment we just sat there looking at the fire."

"And then?" Coburn's words break the spell. Inez is back in the room. Her eyes bore into the camera lens.

"I run to the house, to the kitchen. I get mama. She and Mrs. Sullivan they run outside, see the flames. Mrs. Sullivan tells my mama to dial 999 and mama does, although she mess up a couple of times. The police come. They don't talk to mama and me. I want to see Justin but mama won't let me. Telling me that 'he'll never hurt you again' and 'we go home', she and I leave very late at night by taxi with all our belongings straight to the airport. Tickets are waiting. We fly home. Mama has a lot of money now."

Coburn breaks into Inez's narrative.

"You think she blackmailed the Sullivans?"

"I know she did," Inez replies.

"Tell me how you know that."

"She told me, the day I left to go to college. When she knew she'd never have to look me in the eye again."

"You never knew what happened to Justin?"

Inez shakes her head.

"I was young. I didn't know the way the world worked. We had a good life back home. My mama spent more on herself than on me, but I saved what little she gave me and guilted her into letting me go and study in America as long as I no come back. Ever."

The interview is briefly interrupted while Coburn downs a glass of water.

"Now you cross paths with Justin again at the University of Arizona?" Coburn is on safer ground here.

"Yes," Inez's eyes light up. She looks a little younger and you can see that she cared about Justin a lot. "We met freshman week, I couldn't believe it was him. For two years we were really happy and then he got kicked out of U of A and everything started to unravel.

"We never discussed the night my papa died. Justin didn't want to revisit it and neither did I. The first time we talked about it was on the flight to England.

"When I found out the truth, that my mama had heaped all the blame on Justin, I was ashamed. She told the Sullivans that *he* had attacked me, even painted my father as the tragic hero who died saving me. She killed two birds with one stone, got rid of papa and made herself a ton of money to keep quiet. All those places Justin got sent away to, because he was protecting me."

"Why didn't you come forward?"

"I told you. When it happened I was young and stupid and it seemed to be normal behavior to me. I had never known anything different. Had I known the truth I would've come forward.

"This is why things are not clear with Mrs. Sullivan. She believed the lies my mother told her."

"Why come to England at all?"

"Justin needed money, and I needed a British passport. He had an internet business. All the money went from his PayPal account into his English bank account. He had to be present to withdraw all of it and to close the account. We used the money to fast track my passport. One more day and we would've been away from here."

Inez unconsciously rubs the plain gold ring on her left hand; Coburn totally misses or misinterprets the gesture and plows on.

"Justin married Inez," I say half to myself. "She'd never have qualified for a British passport otherwise."

Back in the studio, Coburn turns the page on her notes.

"Tell me why you went back to the Sullivan house."

"I learned from a source I will not name that Mrs. Sullivan was Justin's killer."

"Inspector Naylor?"

"No comment."

"How did she find out about you and Justin?"

"I guess she had him followed." For the first time in the interview Inez gets fidgety. "He told me she was always doing that." She rubs her eye and sits up straighter again.

"My sources tell me that you went to the Sullivan's house carrying a loaded gun."

"No comment."

"Would you have killed her, Mizz Ramirez?"

"In my culture, we take an eye for an eye," Inez says. After a few moments, "My personal opinion, her physical condition is punishment enough. She's trapped in her own body with the truth of what she did."

"So you believe that the stroke she had was a direct result of conscience?"

"Yes, Mizz Coburn, I do."

"Mrs. Sullivan was making a slow, steady recovery which has now gone into total reverse."

"The truth hurts," Inez shrugs. "And because she's locked into her body, she's too expensive to jail. I think we're done here." Inez stands, removes her clip-on microphone and places it neatly on the stool leaving Coburn alone in the studio.

"Y'know," Gav reaches down and wrestles the remote away from me, turning the screen to black, "this is why I'm glad we're not super rich."

"Oh yeah?" I twist around to face him. "I like the way you added 'super' in there and not just rich."

"We don't have to worry about being blackmailed by the maid," Gav points out. "I know I shouldn't but I feel for CeeCee Sullivan. She killed her stepson over a lie."

"Yeah, I did not see that coming. To be honest I thought Justin had done something to Inez and she had either blanked it out or developed some twisted attachment to him because of it. I disagree with Inez on one count though, I don't think it was conscience that gave CeeCee a stroke, I think it was guilt. The stress of covering up one death by calling it an accident, the psychological damage she and Sully did to Justin, and then she finds out about Inez. And in, I dunno, some warped attempt to save her from Justin once again she kills him." I stand up and stretch, "I'd love to know what CeeCee and Inez talked about before Matt burst in. It makes me realize that I'm not comfortable being spoon-fed someone else's interpretation of the facts."

"Nik, the only reason it doesn't sit well with you is that you know what really happened, well some of it. The truth is dirty and jagged and so can't be packaged up and tied with a neat little bow to be trotted out on the evening news."

"True." I stretch again, "Look I'm going to get an early night. I've got that morning meeting with Beth tomorrow. You coming?"

"No, I think I'll go for a run, and Nik, don't worry, Beth's your friend."

"She's my boss." Saying those words I do not feel reassured.

CHAPTER 32

To try and combat the butterflies in my stomach I get off the tube two stops early and walk the rest of the way to Covent Garden. London is stirring, outside the shops displays are going up, awnings being hoisted. A motorized sweeper scours the pavements of takeaway containers, dropped food and worse, gathering an army of foot commuters in its wake. Coming onto the slight slope of the street that leads down to the back of the plaza, the group goes straight on. I peel off, my boot steps going left, between the parallel rows of shops, careful not to bump any of the street performers who are busy setting up their pitch for the day. I am always careful around this area at this time of day. Delivery trucks are everywhere and some of them don't beep when they back up.

Beth is easy to spot; she's wearing her knee length peacock blue cashmere coat, a present from husband Tony. She has her back to me, one hand resting on the metal table, index finger hooked around the little white espresso cup. They've only just set up for the day. There are another couple of businessmen having a pre-work coffee under the heat lamp close to the café entrance. Beth is sitting as far out as you can get; totally out of their earshot.

"This is a great place to people-watch," I say, so as not to startle her.

"Morning Nikki, sit down," she says without turning around. "I ordered you a coffee." Another espresso cup sat masked behind the other one, contents gently steaming. No small talk, straight to business, not a good sign.

"How bad is it?"

"Bad, but salvageable. We've exercised our right to take over the project. Sully isn't in a position to push back too hard and he needs all of his energy to defend his wife."

"Phillip Eco might be able to help, I could call him for you."

"That won't be necessary, I've already spoken to Mr. Eco and made arrangements to go down to meet him and his staff."

I want to ask, *what about me?* Difficult to do without coming off as whiney. Instead I shut up and drink my coffee.

"You should know that I stuck my neck out for you. Everything that you and I discussed did not make it into my report."

Beth puts down her espresso and signals the waiter. When she has his attention she draws two fingers back and forth across her palm, sign language for the bill.

"I had a call from DI Naylor," she continues. "He suggested that it would not be in Avalon's best interests to divulge any involvement in the case by either my employees or this agency.

"He also told me that they think they found Max Clausen. He came in by private jet a couple of days ago. No ID but he matches the description they have and he's been placed in a clinic out in the black forest."

"So not dead then?"

"Naylor said it might be better if he was. He didn't go into detail. He just said Clausen's punishment was 'fitting'."

The waiter returns with the bill and we both sit quietly, her people watching, me finishing my coffee.

"You know," Beth breaks the silence, "stuff like this makes me wonder if we're all kidding ourselves somehow. All the scheming and secrets and the lies those people told each other."

"C'mon Beth. Gav and I talked about this last night, after the interview. We all lie to each other to some degree, fibs oil the wheels of polite society."

"One of my mother's favourite sayings was, 'oh what a tangled web we weave when first we practice to deceive'." Beth waves off a marauding pigeon, "I used to think it was just a saying that she trotted out. It's not. There are two key words in there, 'practice' and 'deceive'. Fibs may be a way of making life move a little more smoothly, deceit is another matter. It is lying to mislead, to hurt, to trick, to destroy."

I can't argue with that.

"Now Nikki, you and I are going to get this project in on time and under budget. Aren't we?"

"Yes, yes we are."

"The board are both impressed and a little concerned about the number and scale of the projects Excalibur is tackling," Beth says. "They think more oversight is needed and short of finding a way to clone myself I cannot run the day-to-day operations and carry out site visits. They proposed that Simon takes on those responsibilities, which I think is the worst of both worlds. I counter proposed. Rather than take on another project, what do you think of being my roving ambassador, couple of days onsite, report back to me, move on to the next one?"

"That's a lot of traveling, especially for someone still stuck on the no-fly list."

"Naylor has promised to expedite your no-fly status. You could visit all the UK sites first, and once you're cleared to fly again, where possible you'd be using the jet. The board fly all over Europe so it wouldn't be a problem sharing, and let's face it, even you can't get into trouble in two days."

I am sure Gav would disagree on that point, I decide to keep this observation to myself.

"Strictly Monday to Friday?"

"That shouldn't be a sticking point."

"Let me think about it."

"I'll give you a week." Beth pushes her chair back, "I'm hoping it won't take you that long to say yes."

"You'll know my decision as soon as I've talked to Gav about it."

"Fair enough."

Beth walks away passing someone familiar to me but not to her. Stark drops into the empty chair.

"Mary's ordering coffees and some food, so we don't have much time. I wanted you to know, we found those purple fibres, the ones from CeeCee's coat. You won't believe where they ended up."

"I won't?"

"They were less than ten feet from the hedgerow, some sparrow took them for nesting material.

"Oh and Naylor's pressing charges against Sully for trying to tamper with evidence. We don't know if he talked to CeeCee or worked it out on his own. He sent one of his secretaries up to snatch the coat. Of course he didn't tell her why, so when we turned up she handed it over. Without your quick thinking that coat would've gone the way of Sullivan's car. We still haven't found that."

"There was blood on the coat?"

"Yes, there were a few tense moments when we couldn't detect blood spatter on the front. I reasoned she hadn't buttoned it and low and behold, there it was, blood, splattered across the lining. Allen's lab matched it to Justin. Credit where it's due I say." He mimes a salute. "Naylor will have my head on a pike if he knows we've talked."

He changes the subject as Mary approaches. "Mina says 'Hi'."

Mary sits down. "How you doing hen? What about that interview eh?"

"I'm good, and the interview helped clear a few more things up."

"We can't discuss the case," Mary says. I make sure not to look at Stark.

"Are you going to be able to use any of this as material for another book?"

"Ooch, I'd like to, but too soon, as they say."

"Did we ever find out if Justin was behind 'Finger on the Pulse'?" I ask.

"They don't have definitive proof," Mary takes a bite of the Panini she ordered. "The website hasn't been updated since his death. If I was a betting girl, which I'm not, I'd lay odds that Justin used 'Finger' to mock the Sullivans."

"It's a shame." I wait while the server refills my water glass. Any more coffee and I'm going to be in pinball mode for the rest of the day. "'Finger' or not, he was clearly talented and he and Inez would've just dropped off the radar. Married, happy and never to bother the Sullivan's again."

Mary toasts me with her coffee cup, "Mizz Coburn totally missed that nugget and they've shipped her back to the States now, so she'll never know." she raises her coffee cup to her lips, "What's next for you, hen?"

"A lot of hours getting Sully's project up and running and then," I tell Mary about Beth's offer.

"She thinks two days is enough time to survey and report and not enough time for me to get myself into trouble."

Mary's full-bodied laugh carries clear across Covent Garden,

"We know better," she chortles, "Don't we, hen?"

THE END

ABOUT THE AUTHOR

Paula Longhurst was born in Sussex, England. She read her first thriller at ten years old (Ian Fleming's Casino Royale) and hasn't looked back since. After a varied career, Paula currently works at The King's English Bookstore in Salt Lake City, Utah where she will be happy to sell you a good twisty mystery.

Author of six published novels including ROLLOVER, THUNDERBALL and MS.SCARLETT, Paula is based in Salt Lake City sharing a home with husband Chris and Daisy Pattmore the cat.

Paula is always happy to chat with book groups about her books and always includes the books she is currently reading/loving (usually mysteries, but she may surprise you.) She can be reached at the following social media links

Instagram : @paulajlong

Blog: englishrosesloverain.blogspot.com

Email: paulalonghurstwriter@gmail.com

CPSIA information can be obtained
at www.ICGtesting.com
Printed in the USA
BVHW071251130423
662286BV00008B/615